"You're g[...]

Jay continued, "Otherwise, you can't ride on the same bike I'm on."

It took almost a full minute, but Ellen managed to mount without coming into contact with his body. He gave her some brief instructions about moving with him, leaning and not leaning, general principles of keeping the bike balanced.

"Where do I put my hands?"

"On me," he said, staring straight ahead. "That's the point of this exercise."

"I know that. Where on you?" It sounded as though she was gritting her teeth.

"Your choice. You're the boss. For this exercise, my body represents your safety. It is fully at your disposal—like a tornado shelter in a storm, or a fort during battle. Trust it."

Her touch wasn't much, a light resting of her fingers on the top of his shoulders, but as soon as he felt it, he started the bike and put it in gear.

"Hold on." With a twist of his wrist he upped the throttle a notch. And received slightly more pressure on his shoulders.

"Faster," she said, five more minutes down the road.

He increased the speed once more and she laughed out loud.

And that's when the whole damn thing went bad. The laugh, the touch of her hands...whatever... generated heat in Jay that he had no right to feel.

Dear Reader,

Ever wonder why true love lands on some people but not on others? Or how you can come across real and lasting happiness?

Ellen Moore might have wondered those things. She certainly had reason to wonder. But Ellen doesn't allow herself to ask why. She presses forward. Makes things happen. And she's so busy raising her five-year-old son and working and helping other people that she doesn't have time to wonder about much of anything.

Jay Billingsley is a black-leather-vested biker dude on a mission. He's also a renowned medical massage therapist, able to help victims of violence overcome aversion to physical touch.

Ellen and Jay seemed like a perfect fit to me when I first sat down to write this book. But, not surprisingly, the two of them had different ideas. This is their story. Told by them. And it's a much better version than mine....

Welcome to Shelter Valley! I hope you enjoy the visit enough to want to come back and stay a while.

I love to hear from readers. You can reach me at staff@tarataylorquinn.com. Or visit me at www.tarataylorquinn.com. I'm also on Facebook and Twitter.

Tara Taylor Quinn

Full Contact
Tara Taylor Quinn

TORONTO NEW YORK LONDON
AMSTERDAM PARIS SYDNEY HAMBURG
STOCKHOLM ATHENS TOKYO MILAN MADRID
PRAGUE WARSAW BUDAPEST AUCKLAND

Recycling programs
for this product may
not exist in your area.

ISBN-13: 978-0-373-71726-2

FULL CONTACT

www.Harlequin.com

Printed in U.S.A.

ABOUT THE AUTHOR

The author of more than fifty-four original novels in twenty languages, Tara Taylor Quinn is a *USA TODAY* bestseller with over six million copies sold. She is known for delivering deeply emotional and psychologically astute novels of suspense and romance. Tara won the 2008 Reader's Choice Award, is a four-time finalist for the Romance Writers of America RITA® Award, a multiple finalist for the Reviewer's Choice Award, the Booksellers' Best Award, the Holt Medallion and appears regularly on the Waldenbooks bestsellers list. She has appeared on national and local TV across the country, including *CBS Sunday Morning.* Tara is the author of the successful Chapman Files series and, with her husband, recently wrote and saw the release of her own true love story, *It Happened on Maple Street,* from HCI books. When she's not writing, fulfilling speaking engagements or tending to the needs of her two very spoiled and adored four-legged family members, Tara loves to travel with her husband, stopping wherever the spirit takes them. They've been spotted in casinos and quaint little small-town antiques shops all across the country.

Books by Tara Taylor Quinn

HARLEQUIN SUPERROMANCE

1309—THE PROMISE OF CHRISTMAS
1350—A CHILD'S WISH
1381—MERRY CHRISTMAS, BABIES
1428—SARA'S SON
1446—THE BABY GAMBLE
1465—THE VALENTINE GIFT
    "Valentine's Daughters"
1500—TRUSTING RYAN
1527—THE HOLIDAY VISITOR
1550—SOPHIE'S SECRET*
1584—A DAUGHTER'S TRUST
1656—THE FIRST WIFE#

HARLEQUIN SINGLE TITLE

SHELTERED IN HIS ARMS*

MIRA BOOKS

WHERE THE ROAD ENDS
STREET SMART
HIDDEN
IN PLAIN SIGHT
BEHIND CLOSED DOORS
AT CLOSE RANGE
THE SECOND LIE#
THE THIRD SECRET#
THE FOURTH VICTIM#

*Shelter Valley Stories
#Chapman Files

For Courtney VanGarderen.
May you always have the strength to reach
for your happiness and never,
ever settle for less than that.

CHAPTER ONE

"YOU SURE YOU DON'T want me to come in with you?" Shelley asked.

"I'm sure." Ellen Moore's voice, infused with confidence and cheer for the sake of five-year-old Josh climbing out of the backseat of her sister's car, sounded strong and healthy to her.

Because she was strong and healthy. She could do this. No big deal. Thousands of women all over the country shared parenting with divorced spouses.

Though maybe not all of them had their younger sisters driving them to the airport for the month-long parental switch.

Martha Moore Marks, the girls' mother, had been adamant about Ellen not making the trip alone. That was fine with Ellen. Her sister Shelley wanted Ellen's opinion on an outfit she was considering for an upcoming vocal performance with the Phoenix Symphony, so they could take care of that while they were in the city. Then the sisters were treating themselves to lunch at their favorite Mexican restaurant in Fountain Hills—a quaint Phoenix suburb—before heading home to Shelter Valley.

"I want to wear my backpack." The solemn voice of her son grabbed Ellen's attention. And heart. "I don't want Daddy to think I'm a baby or something."

"He's not going to think that, bud," she said, resisting the urge to run her fingers through her little guy's dark, silky hair. At home, especially when he was sleepy, he'd let her get away with it, but not here. Not now.

Instead, she helped him secure the straps of the new full-size backpack he'd specifically requested for the trip. The canvas bag—loaded down with his electronic handheld game console; extra discs; dried fruit snacks; animal cookies; cheese crackers; his Cars insulated water bottle filled with juice; two of his favorite nighttime storybooks, both starring Cars characters; and the stuffed Woody doll she'd bought him for Christmas the year before—replaced the smaller plastic one that had been suitable when he'd been going to preschool and day care.

He was starting kindergarten a couple of days after he returned from visiting his father.

"Remember, put Woody under the covers with you at night," she told him as Shelley popped the trunk on her Chevy sedan. Ellen hauled out the first of two big suitcases, pulling up the roller bar.

"No one will know he's there," she said, dropping the second bag next to her and closing the trunk while her sister picked Josh right up off the ground with the force of her goodbye hug.

"You be a good boy and have fun, okay?" Shelley said, nose to nose with Josh.

Josh, arms wrapped tightly around Shelley's neck, rubbed noses with his aunt. "I get to go fishing in the Colorado River," the little boy said.

"I know, pal. And you better call me if you catch anything." Shelley let Josh's thin body slide to the ground.

"I will."

"I love you."

"I love you, too."

Shelley nodded at Ellen, climbed behind the wheel and drove off to the call lot where she could wait until Ellen was ready to be picked up.

With a roller bar in each hand, and Josh's hand next to hers on one handle, Ellen pulled the bags to the curbside check-in station. Josh didn't need a special-needs tag because, while he was checking in alone, he wouldn't be flying alone.

Then they were in the terminal, Josh's hand in hers whether he liked it or not, and Ellen swore to herself that the smile would stay pasted on her lips if it killed her.

It wouldn't kill her. She was a survivor.

The squeeze of her son's fingers around her own made her own angst seem selfish and petty.

"You're going to have a blast," she promised him.

"Why can't Daddy and I have a blast right here?"

"Because he doesn't live here. His job is in Colorado. And he has a room all ready for you in his new house and you're going to love it."

The terminal was bustling, with as many families as businesspeople hurrying around them in spite of the fact that it was a Monday morning.

"Then why can't you come?"

"Because my job is here. Besides, Jaime is there and is looking forward to hanging out with you. You like Jaime, remember?" The beautiful model her ex-husband Aaron had chosen as a replacement for his damaged wife loved Josh and had taken off the entire month of August to care for him.

As far as Ellen was concerned, Josh was all that mattered.

"Yeah."

She couldn't really blame Aaron for choosing someone who oozed feminine perfection and sexuality. He'd been far too young to handle the emotional and physical backlash that had consumed Ellen after her attack. Too young to handle her physical rejection of him.

She would have opted out, too, if she'd had that choice.

Aaron had needed to get out of Shelter Valley, to start a new life away from the tragedy, and Ellen couldn't imagine ever leaving Shelter Valley. There was no future in that kind of standoff.

Josh's grasp did not loosen even a little bit as they approached the bustling rotunda where they'd arranged to meet Aaron. There was less than an hour's turnaround between his arriving flight and his departing one with Josh. Aaron and Ellen had both decided whisking Josh off quickly was the best plan.

She was searching the crowd for the familiar dark hair of her ex when Josh stopped suddenly.

"What's up?" she asked, gazing into his solemn face.

"I don't want to go."

"But you miss your daddy, Josh. You say so a lot."

"I know."

"You're going to have such a great time with him. You always do."

"But he always comed here."

"*Came* here. You're older now, bud. And Daddy wants to have time with you in his house, too. He bought you your own bed and it has Cars sheets and everything."

Josh stared at her then his lower lip started to tremble.

Kneeling in front of her son, Ellen held him by the shoulders and looked him straight in the eye. "Josh? What's going on?"

His eyes filled with tears. "I don't want to leave you here by yourself. You'll be sad."

"Ah, buddy, I'm going to miss you for sure. Remember the list we went over last night? The one on the refrigerator?"

He nodded.

"Those are all the things I'm going to be doing after work while you're gone. And that list is so big, I won't have a chance to get too sad."

He didn't look convinced.

"Name some of them for me," Ellen said. "What am I going to be doing today after work?"

"Going running. Every day."

"And then what?"

"You're going to help Sophie make the nursery in their new house."

He'd paid attention—and hopefully had pictures in his head of her busy and happy.

"What else was on the list?"

"Babysitting for Aunt Caro and Uncle John when they're in Kentucky at their farm. Do I ever get to go to their farm like you said?"

"I'm house-sitting," Ellen corrected him. "They're taking the kids with them." Caroline had moved to Shelter Valley, alone and pregnant, at a time when Ellen had been lost as well, and the two, though more than ten years apart in age, had formed a bond that Ellen cherished. "And yes, we'll go to Kentucky. Maybe next summer."

Which gave her another year to work up the desire to leave Shelter Valley for a few weeks.

Ellen took a seat on a bench with a clear view of the entrances to the A boarding gates, pulling Josh, backpack and all, in between her legs, keeping her arms linked loosely around him.

"And you're going to put junk in jars," he said.

"Canning tomatoes and peaches and corn and green beans to send to the food pantry in Phoenix," she said, knowing he probably wouldn't remember that part. A group of older ladies from the three churches in Shelter Valley met every year for the service project. They had lost a couple of members of their group during the past year and needed extra hands. Ellen was good in the kitchen—and eager to learn how to can.

Aaron still hadn't appeared. Josh was shifting weight from one foot to the other and picking at a thread from the flowered embroidery on the front of Ellen's T-shirt.

"What else?" she asked. "What am I going to be doing for you?"

"Painting my room."

"Painting what in your room?"

He grinned. "Trains."

"That's right. What colors?"

"The engine is black, of course."

"Of course."

"And the caboose is red so the trains coming behind it will see it."

"Okay."

"And blue for my favorite color."

"And purple for mine."

"And—" Josh stopped when Ellen stood.

"Daddy's coming," she said.

Please, heart, don't make it difficult for me to breathe. Don't let me need anything from Aaron Hanaran. With her son's hand in hers, she approached the man she'd once vowed to love, honor and cherish—and sleep with—until death did them part.

"Hey, sport!" Aaron's grin was huge as he sped up the last few steps and scooped his son into his arms, hugging him tight. "I've missed you."

"I missed you, too," Josh said.

Ellen stared at those little arms clutching his father's neck. Josh needed this time with Aaron. He needed his father.

Then, with their son perched on his hip, Aaron's eyebrows drew together in concern as he looked at her. "How you doing, El?"

"Fine! Great!" The smile she gave him was genuine. "It's good to see you."

"You, too."

Then they stood there with nothing to say. There had been no big angry outbursts between them, no hatred or resentment or bitterness. Just a sadness that had infiltrated every breath they took together.

"I better get him through security." Aaron's comment filled the dead air. "Our flight will be boarding in fifteen minutes."

"Okay. Well, then..."

Aaron put Josh down. "We'll call you the second we land, El, I promise," he said, his gaze filled with the sympathy she'd learned to dread. "And you have my cell number. Call anytime. As often as you...need."

She knelt in front of Josh. "You be a good boy and listen to your daddy."

He nodded, tears in his eyes again.

"I love you, bud."

"I love you, too."

Ellen kissed him. Josh kissed her back. Like usual. Then the little boy threw his arms around her neck, clutching her in a death grip.

Ellen couldn't breathe. Without thought she jerked the boy's arms apart, stopping herself in time to keep from flinging those tiny arms completely away from her. She held on to Josh's small hands, instead, squeezing them.

The boy didn't seem to notice anything amiss. A glance at Aaron's closed face told her his father had witnessed her reaction.

She gathered her son against her, close to her heart, and held on before finally letting go. "Now, have fun and remember to store up all kinds of things to tell me when you call," she said with a smile as she stood.

"'Kay."

She watched as the two men who used to be her entire world walked away, her jaw hurting with the effort to keep the smile in place in case Josh turned around to wave goodbye.

She made it outside the airport before she let the tears fall. But she let go for only a second. Josh was going to be fine. And so was she.

ELLEN WAS COMING AROUND the corner of Mesa and Lantana streets Tuesday afternoon, her second jog since Josh had left, when she heard the bike roar into town. Without conscious thought, she took stock of her surroundings. Ben and Tory Sanders' home was on the corner. Bonnie Nielson—owner of the day care Josh had attended the first four years of his life and would attend after school once kindergarten started the following month—had a home around the next corner. Bonnie and Keith wouldn't be home. Tory would be. It took only a second for the awareness to settle over Ellen.

Staying safe was second nature to her. She always knew, at any given moment, where her safety spots were.

She didn't alter her course, though. Not yet. Though she wanted to. But because she wanted to run for cover, she maintained her trek.

Slowing her pace, Ellen controlled her breathing with effort, her gaze pinned to the spot where the bike would appear—a stop sign at the corner. Waited to see who would roar past her.

Sam Montford had a new motorcycle. But it had a muffler, or something that made it run much quieter than the noise pollution she was hearing.

Sheriff Greg Richards had one now, too. He'd bought it as a gas saving measure. His bike was like Sam's— the quieter variety.

And there he was. A body in black leather on a black machine framed by shiny chrome. She didn't have to know anything about motorcycles to know that this monstrosity was top-of-the-line. It even had a trunk-looking thing that was big enough for a suitcase.

Ellen noticed, without stopping. Shortening her stride, she jogged. And watched.

Black Leather was not from around Shelter Valley. Of that she was certain. The bike and black leather were dead giveaways. The ponytail hanging down the guy's back was advertisement for *outsider*.

Tensing, Ellen paused, jogging in place at the end of

Tory's driveway. If the guy turned onto this street, she was running to the front door.

If not, she'd continue with her run. Her day. Her life.

Her mother was having a family dinner tonight—Rebecca and her husband, Shelley and, of course, Tim, who still lived at home—and Ellen was bringing brownies for dessert. Brownies that weren't yet made.

She also had to stop by the Stricklands' house to collect the mail. And she wanted to call Josh. It was an hour later in Colorado. Her son would be in bed before she got home from her mother's.

With his feet on the ground on either side of his mammoth machine, the biker mastered the weight between his legs, seemingly unaware of the disruptive noise he was emitting along the quiet and peaceful streets of Shelter Valley.

A light blue Cadillac drove by. Becca Parsons—the mayor. Becca was Martha's best friend. Ellen's youngest sister, Rebecca, was named after her. Ellen could see the woman's frown from a block away.

Hot-rod engines simply didn't belong in Shelter Valley.

BLACK LEATHER DIDN'T SEEM to see the car at all. He sat there, gunning his motor with a gloved hand, unaware that within minutes Sheriff Richards would be all over him.

Or at least, right behind him, finding a reason to stop him and determine his business in town. And if that business wasn't just passing through, Black Leather would be on the radar. The heroines of Shelter Valley—the core group of women whose strength and nurturing of each other and everyone else in town were the glue that held Shelter Valley together—would convince him so sweetly to exit their borders, he would never know the departure wasn't his idea.

That was how it worked around here. The people of Shelter Valley would help anyone. They were compassionate. Welcoming. And anyone who didn't emulate the town's values and ways was encouraged to find happiness elsewhere. That's what kept Shelter Valley what it was—a town that embraced and protected in a balance that was even enough to create a form of heaven on earth.

At least most of its residents, including Ellen, thought so.

Black Leather picked up his feet, his gaze locked straight ahead as Becca drove past. He yanked on his throttle one more time.

Ellen watched the thirty-second episode, her chest tight, and wondered at the man's audacity. Wondered why she didn't simply go say hello to Tory. Ask how the kids were doing during this last hot month of summer.

"Ellen? You okay, sweetie?"

Tory's soft voice floated to Ellen from the front steps. The thirty-one-year-old stay-at-home mother looked as put together and beautiful as always.

"I'm fine," Ellen called with easy assurance, staring down the street.

Black Leather leaned. He was turning in the opposite direction. She breathed a little easier and with a wave to her mother's much younger friend, resumed her course down the street. As she increased her pace, Black Leather glanced her way, pinning her with a stare that struck at her core.

Then he was gone.

But the memory of him wasn't.

The man had guts. And the seeming intelligence of someone who would house bulls in china shops. Fortunately, he was not her problem to worry about.

HE'D SPENT TIME IN MORE boring places. But Jay Billingsley couldn't remember when. Or where. He was ready to leave. Every place and every activity the quiet desert city had to offer he'd already been to and done. And he'd been in town only twenty minutes.

Didn't bode well for his future, since for the foreseeable part of it, he was here—living in the furnished home a few blocks from the clinic where he'd be working part-time at a job that satisfied him. He'd already made arrangements to rent the property on the edge of Shelter Valley on a month-to-month basis. The hours he wasn't at the clinic he'd be hell-bent on completing the tasks that had forced him to come to Shelter Valley.

He'd driven by his new place. Didn't try the key he had in his pocket because the boxes he'd had shipped weren't due until tomorrow morning. The pool in the backyard was pristine with a rock waterfall. And there was a fire pit for grilling. For once the real thing was even better than the picture.

Really, it wasn't Shelter Valley's fault that he was in a rank mood. Wasn't anybody's fault. Not even his.

Not many guys would like being forced into distasteful situations.

Best get on with it. His life's motto. Which was why an hour after he'd driven into—and around—his latest home base, Jay showed up at the clinic looking for Dr. Shawna Bostwick, the psychologist who had so effusively accepted his offer to practice clinical massage under her auspices. She had a small room at her clinic ready for him to use and some patients to refer to him.

"You're Jay Billingsley?" The young woman's shock wasn't carefully enough disguised.

"Yes, ma'am." He bowed his head, his hands crossed in front of him, standing the way he'd learned while waiting in the mess line during his eighteen months on the inside.

Back to the wall and cover your balls, as he privately described it. Those months had taught him other life lessons. *Accept what you can't change. Don't expect anyone else to watch your back. Being still is the best way to assess the opposition. Adopting a subservient stance is the fastest way to disarm others' defenses.*

Eleven years on the outside and, whenever he was being negatively judged, he still reverted to the man he'd become while doing time for drug possession.

Some lessons lasted a lifetime.

"You, uh, ever been to Shelter Valley?" The pretty blonde seemed to be somewhere around his own thirty-two years.

He waited until she looked him in the eye and said, "No. I'd never heard of the place until a month ago."

Her smile, though tentative, seemed genuine. "You might be in for a surprise."

"I doubt it," he said easily. Then something about her, or about the damned town, had him adding, "I'm good at what I do, Dr. Bostwick. I'm in this business because I care. Because I want to help people. You can rest assured that I won't let you down."

She grinned at him. "I've read your résumé. I'm not worried. But I do think you might want to get your hair cut. And lose the vest."

"My only transportation is a motorcycle." He told her what she'd find out soon enough anyway. Who would have believed he would find a Western town without a Harley dealership? Or any other signs of motorcycle ownership? "Leather deflects bugs and is more impervious to wind."

"And the hair?"

He shrugged. He could have cut it, if he'd wanted to give a false first impression. Jay was who he was. A free spirit. A man who didn't conform to social pressure. His hair told people that up front.

And it reminded him every single day that his freedom was in personal expression and belief, not in the making of his own laws—either moral or physical.

"It's taken me eleven years to grow it." That was all the explanation anyone would get.

Jay noticed the doctor's firm backside at the tail end of the blue blouse that hung over her jeans as he followed her down the hall to his new space. The room would suit and, once his table arrived tomorrow, he would set up quickly.

He'd only been in town an hour and had already seen two very fine-looking women—a jogger and his new professional sponsor.

Too bad he wasn't in Shelter Valley to have sex.

JAY SWAM IN THE NUDE. His temporary backyard was completely enclosed by a cement block privacy fence. He had to traverse the entire length of the pool four times to get what he determined to be one lap. Somewhere around forty lengths he lost count.

The cool water sluicing against his skin was like the wind pulling at his hair when he rode full-out. A communion between nature and man—raw life. Something he could trust. Count on.

When his body was tired enough to stay put on the stool awaiting him inside the house at the breakfast bar, he hauled himself out of the deep end and grabbed the jeans he'd left in a pile on the patio.

Zipping the pants with care born of practice, he grabbed a cola from the fridge and glanced at the neatly stacked folders awaiting him. Usually his investigative skills itched to be used. This time, Jay was reluctant to begin.

Finding the man who'd deserted him—who'd walked out only weeks before Jay's mother's murder—was on his top ten list of things he most wanted to avoid. Right up there with going back to prison.

Or ever again being out of control of his mental faculties.

His aversion to the task at hand was the only reason he was glad to hear the knock on his front door. The uninvited intrusion delayed having to open those folders.

He wasn't so sure he hadn't jumped from the frying pan into the fire when he saw a uniformed lawman standing on the front porch.

"Jay Billingsley?"

"Yes."

"I'm Sheriff Richards."

Greg Richards, Jay read the official identification the man held out. "What can I do for you, Sheriff?"

He hadn't done anything wrong.

"You have a second?"

As many of them as he wanted to have. "Sure." Jay stepped back, leaving Greg to come in, close the door behind him and follow Jay to the second of the two bar stools at the kitchen counter.

He offered the lawman something to drink, retrieved the bottle of water Richards requested from the fridge. The sheriff perched on the stool, both feet planted on the floor. The man's hair was dark. Short. Proper.

"I had some complaints about that motorcycle of yours."

Jay met his gaze head-on, drinking from his can of cola while he did so, his bare feet resting on the silver metal ring along the bottom of his stool. "There a law against motorcycles in Shelter Valley?"

"No. I've got one myself," Richards said, and Jay reminded himself that those who judged prematurely generally ended up making asses of themselves. "But we do have noise restriction laws."

"No semi engines after six o'clock?" Jay guessed.

"No excessive noise within city limits, period."

"Who defines excessive?"

"I do."

Jay nodded. Less than twelve hours in town and he was already being run out. If only the sheriff knew how happy Jay would be to oblige....

"I'll run my machine on low throttle in city limits."

"I'd appreciate it."

The lawman hadn't opened his bottle of water. And he wasn't leaving, either.

"There something else?"

"I talked to Martin Wesley. He says you're renting this place month to month."

Jay had found Martin's rental ad on the internet. "That's right."

"He says you're a medical massage therapist working with Shawna Bostwick."

"That's right." And if Jay was a betting man, he'd put money on the fact that Richards had already been in touch with the pretty doctor for confirmation.

"We don't have a lot of call for that around here. Seems like you'd find more work in a city like Phoenix."

"Or Miami," Jay agreed, "which is where I've lived a lot of the past ten years."

"So why here? Why now?" The sheriff's expression wasn't unfriendly. But he wasn't making small talk, either.

"I've got some business in the area." Until he knew what he was going to find, his father was his secret. "Personal business."

"And when you've completed your business? What then?"

Shrugging, Jay took another sip of cola and tried not to get depressed. "Who knows?" He wondered what the hell his life would look like when he was through messing it up.

"Is a life here in Shelter Valley among the choices?"

At least he could put one man out of his misery. "No."

"You did some time in prison."

Were there laws against that in Shelter Valley, too?

Jay didn't respond. There was no point. Richards had access to Jay's records. The man knew what he knew and he'd make of it what he would.

"Possession with intent to sell."

Those were the charges. He hadn't had a hope in hell of proving his innocence. Mostly because he'd been high on cocaine when the cops raided the frat party he'd been attending.

It didn't help that his so-called friends had all been rich kids with daddies—or more importantly, daddies' lawyers—who made sure that Jay, the scholarship kid without family, took the fall.

Still, he'd made choices. And he'd deserved to pay for them.

"I hope that it's just coincidence that you've chosen to work in a clinical environment." The sheriff's words threw Jay for a second. Until he put it all together. Clinics had drugs, giving him potential access to them.

"I was arrested at a frat party. We were doing cocaine. No one there was making a living off the stuff," he said. "My professional record is as available to you as is my criminal one, Sheriff. You're welcome to take a look at that, too. I don't use drugs, nor have I been caught with any in my possession."

"I've seen your professional résumé. You come highly recommended. In the field of medicinal massage, but also as a private investigator. I'm told you've done some impressive work assisting detectives with cold cases."

"Mostly volunteer."

"You don't make a full-time career at anything."

"I'm not a white picket fence kind of guy."

"Most people who can't settle down have something to hide."

"Criminal types, you mean."

"You said it. Not me."

"I did my time. And I learned my lesson. I do not make choices that could send me back to prison. Ever."

"I'll bet that makes your mother happy."

"My mother was killed during a home invasion when I was a baby."

"Your father then. Grandparents. Siblings. Whoever was hurt when you were sent to prison so young."

"No one was hurt." At this rate Jay was going to need another fifty or so laps in the pool to calm down enough to get to work. "My only living relative—the aunt who raised me—passed away during my freshman year of college."

"You ever been married?"

"No."

"What about girlfriends?"

"No one serious." Not that it was any of this man's damn business.

"Any close friends?"

"Not that I can think of offhand."

"You have no one at all."

Jay felt exposed by the shock in the sheriff's voice. And forced himself to answer the question, too. "No."

Now the other man knew Jay's dirtiest secret. He was completely alone in the world. No meaningful relationships. He'd never had anyone with whom he felt close. Had no idea how to be a member of a family unit. Let alone the head of one.

"Any more questions, Sheriff?"

Jay's voice must have had more of an edge than he'd intended. Leaving the unopened bottle of water on the counter, Sheriff Richards stood and moved toward the front room. Before he reached the door he turned, a look of concern lining his face.

"We aren't unforgiving folks," he said, his hands at his sides. "Nor are we unwelcoming. We're just protective of our way of life out here. It's why we're all here, and not in some other place. The people of Shelter

Valley have chosen a lifestyle that makes them happy. It's my job to protect that as well as to protect them."

And an ex-con with long hair and secrets roaring into town on the back of a Harley didn't fit.

Jay couldn't agree more.

"We're a family here in Shelter Valley. A big, over-grown family sharing a homestead in the desert. We all look after each other's kids, and after each other. But I guess you wouldn't understand that."

No, probably not.

And he sure as hell wasn't selling his bike or cutting his hair to make them all happy.

At Jay's continued silence, Richards opened the door. "I'm sure I'll be seeing you around," he said. "Call if you need anything."

Jay had the oddest feeling that the guy's offer was sincere.

"Come back anytime," Jay offered in return. But only after he'd shut the door firmly behind the other man.

THE ROAD WASN'T WELL TRAVELED. Two dirt tracks was the extent of it. Ellen bumped along easily, breathing in the peaceful mountain air through the open window of her green Ford Escape, appreciating that the temperature dropped so drastically in mere minutes as she left behind the hot desert that she also adored.

Each time she made this bimonthly trek she felt torn. Part of her wished that Joe Frasier could open himself up to a move to town, to having more than only her and Sheriff Richards in his life. And part of her understood why Joe clung so voraciously to his mountaintop home. Life made sense out here.

Still, life was meant to be lived, not avoided.

Ellen slowed from the 15 mph she'd been going to climb the steep track to 5 mph as she pulled into the cleared bit of dirt in front of Joe's rudimentary cabin. He'd cleared the spot for her—had that been almost five years ago?—when Sheriff Richards had first asked Ellen to be his partner in this effort to assist the lonely mountain man who'd helped the sheriff find his father's killers.

"Joe?" Pulling the thin, short-sleeved button-down over the top of her shorts, Ellen climbed out of the SUV and stood.

Ellen was a trained social worker. Joe needed to be socialized in the worst way.

"Joe?" she called again. She wouldn't go any farther, take another step, until the fiftysomething bearded man appeared. If this wasn't a good day, she'd come back.

Joe knew that. He knew he could stay hidden.

He never had before.

They had something in common, Ellen and Joe. A shared awareness of the tragic effects of inexplicable violence against women.

"I've got your syllabus and textbooks," she called. Joe had a thirty-year-old degree in engineering. Once Ellen had discovered that fact, she'd started planting the seeds of him upgrading his courses with the hope that a love of learning would be able to do what five years of visits had not—get him out of the hell he'd thrown himself into after his wife's death.

She had bags of groceries, too, as always.

"Where's the sheriff?" Joe's gruff voice came from somewhere behind the one-room log cabin he had built by hand over thirty years ago.

Ellen and Greg usually made this trek up the mountain together. But not always.

"There was a traffic accident out by the highway."

"You shouldn't be here without him."

"Of course I should be," she called, completely without fear. "Sheriff Richards knows I'm here. And you need your groceries."

Besides, Joe would never, ever do anything to hurt Ellen. Ever.

Now if she had been meeting Black Leather, as she'd come to think of the man she'd seen roaring through town the other day, she would have—

She simply wouldn't have done it. Period.

"Can I come sit by the window?"

He'd built a seat for her there when she'd first started visiting him. Greg would sit in the cruiser and Ellen would counsel with Joe in plain sight but out of hearing range of the sheriff. Then somehow things had changed and Ellen and Joe had been more friends than social worker and hermit.

"Wait."

She heard a rustle of grass then saw the thin, slightly stooped man, dressed in baggy overalls and a flannel shirt, skirt around the front of the house and inside. He promptly latched the door with the board Ellen knew he used to lock himself in.

"'Kay." She only heard the word because she'd been waiting for it. Listening.

Leaving the cooler in the back of the Escape, Ellen grabbed the blue book bag she'd purchased at Walmart the same day she'd bought Josh's and headed to the house.

With her back to the building, she pulled out a folder of papers and rested them on the windowsill.

Joe's fingers didn't come close to brushing hers as he gently tugged the folder away from her.

"It's all there. Dr. Sheffield is glad you're in her class. And she hopes she gets to meet you before the semester is through." Classes didn't officially start for another couple of weeks, but Phyllis had agreed to send along Joe's work early. Ellen figured her mother's friend shared her wish that the studies would interest him enough to get him off the mountain and into the classroom.

"If it was anyone else but you, I'd think there was a trick here. Psychology class. Like I need psychological help."

"You probably do."

"Not up here, I don't." It wasn't the first time they'd had the conversation.

"I have an ulterior motive, Joe," Ellen said, as honest with him as always.

Their ability to speak openly was one of the things she valued most about their peculiar relationship. Conversation with Joe was stripped of most social graces. Or pleasantries.

"I hope that you love the class enough that you'll need to take more of them." She chose her words deliberately.

Joe grunted. He didn't believe himself capable of feeling anything as alive as love.

"How's Josh?"

"Lonesome." Just thinking about her son hurt her heart. "But I think he's having fun, too." This was their first time apart for more than a few days.

"How are you?"

"Fine. Busy. Mom and David have had me over for dinner twice this week. And I've been going to work in the evenings. I'm helping some of the residents cheer up their rooms. We're doing collages, mobiles and photo mosaics. I'd like to paint the multipurpose room, too."

"How many dates have you been on?"

Josh was her usual excuse for not dating.

"None."

"You're not fine."

She sighed. "Mostly I am, Joe. I'm busy at work. I love the center. How could I not? I get to spend my days helping senior citizens enjoy life. And Josh and I have a new house that I love. We even have a pool. And..." She fiddled with the hem on her shirt. "I'm really okay. I'm running every afternoon. I'm going to do a 10K with Randi Foster in November."

"In Shelter Valley?"

"Of course. Montford is sponsoring it."

"Is Randi training with you?"

"No. She runs at school." Randi was the athletic director at Montford—and baby sister to the university president, Will Parsons, Mayor Becca's husband.

"Who are you training with?"

"No one."

"You're running alone."

"Yes."

"You shouldn't be running alone."

"I'm careful. I carry pepper spray. And I'm not going to be held hostage to fear."

"You shouldn't be running alone."

He wasn't going to be convinced. She understood

that. And even understood why. But she was still going to run.

Because it was something she had to do for her. Whether Joe understood that or not.

She could so easily end up like him.

"You should be dating."

"You've done fine on your own."

"It's different."

"How?"

"I— My... She was the one."

"Maybe Aaron was, too."

"You really think so?"

She had. At one time. Then...time...had changed things. Less than sixty minutes of it had changed everything.

Forever.

And that was something that Joe Frasier understood all too well.

CHAPTER TWO

BEFORE DAWN FRIDAY MORNING, Jay left his motorcyle in the short-term parking lot at the Phoenix Sky Harbor International Airport. He caught the shuttle for the off-site car rental place he'd phoned the night before.

Half an hour later he was on I-10, his six-foot frame chafing beneath the seat belt in the Chevy Impala. He'd never driven in Phoenix before, but at that early hour there was little traffic and he'd studied maps. He also had a sense of direction that could get him from one dark hole to the next without a spot of light.

Mostly what he wanted to do was remain inconspicuous. As inconspicuous as a long-haired, broad-shouldered man could be. He'd shed his leather vest and figured his white T-shirt blended in as well as anything might.

He'd signaled his exit and followed his preset route to his destination. The neighborhood, once he got to it, was a nice one. Elegant. Expensive. The best.

He'd expected nothing less.

The gated entry slowed him not at all. Saying he was surprising his sister with a visit, he'd coaxed a garbage guy down the street to give him the service code.

Jay had been investigating those who didn't want to be found too long to let things like gates stop him.

Not that this particular jaunt had anything to do with

him finding someone who didn't want to be found. No, this time it was him who didn't want to be seen. Not yet. All in good time.

"HOW DO YOU FEEL WHEN Josh hugs you?"

Ellen didn't want to answer Shawna's question. She didn't want to answer any more questions ever again. Period. Questions made her feel like a freak.

And…they helped.

Which was why she was in counseling again.

She took a deep breath and forced herself inside, where the truth she was seeking lay waiting for her. "Sometimes his arms around my neck, his little body close to mine, is like what I imagine heaven to be. Light and free and so good you need to cry. With overwhelming joy. Other times, I feel peaceful."

There. All true. And as normal as it got.

"And?" Shawna peered at her over the reading glasses she always wore when she had Ellen's file on her desk in front of her.

Ellen, hands folded across her stomach, met the older woman's gaze head-on.

She and Shawna had been together, on and off, since before Josh was born.

"And sometimes, most particularly when he comes at me when I'm not expecting it, I have to fight the instinct to tear his hands away."

And then she quickly added, "But my patients at work hug me all the time and I'm fine with that. I love it." She was fine. Healthy.

She just wasn't dating.

And while no one but old Joe Frasier was on her

about it, Ellen didn't want to spend her life alone, raising her son alone, watching him grow and succeed alone.

She didn't want to sleep alone for the rest of her life.

"How many of them come at you unexpectedly?" How could Shawna's question come out so quiet when her voice sounded so firm?

"None."

"Are there times when Josh hugs you, when you are expecting it, that you feel cramped?"

Oh, God. Was she a horrible mother? "Yes," she barely whispered.

"Hey." Shawna leaned forward, her blond hair falling over her shoulders to her desk. Ellen focused on the hair. "It's okay."

She met Shawna's gaze and listened intently.

"You're fine," Shawna said. "Look at you, Ellen, you live independently. You have a successful career that you love. From what I can tell, everyone in town, young and old, comes to you for assistance because they know they can rely on you. You go out alone all the time."

Of course she did. She was alive. She lived.

She just didn't date.

"You're going to have hard times. We talked about that five years ago. I told you to expect them. And to know that you would get through them."

But...

"And you have gotten through them, haven't you?" Shawna asked.

Ellen thought to the time when she couldn't be in a room alone. When she couldn't leave her mother's house.

It had taken her two years to walk into Walmart.

She thought of the years when she hadn't slept through the night—any night.

"Yes," she finally said.

"You'll get through this, too, if that's what you want."

Because she could do anything she set her mind to. She knew that. Believed it.

And yet...

"Listen, I have a suggestion..." The way Shawna sat back, her words trailing off, got Ellen's attention.

"What?"

Studying her, Shawna remained silent, then glanced at Ellen's file and seemed to come to some kind of decision. "There's this new guy in town. He arrived this week. His name's Jay Billingsley."

Black Leather. Ellen's mother and most of the heroines of Shelter Valley—as Ellen secretly called the ladies who officially met for lunch once a month to solve the world's problems, but who spoke to one another almost every day—had assured Ellen last night that they were going to have him out of town in no time. Not that Ellen had asked for, or needed, the reassurance.

She didn't doubt the heroines' prediction for a second—though she was half rooting for the bold man who had the courage to roar through their quiet town without apology.

"I heard he's a massage therapist."

Suddenly, considering that Shawna might actually be about to suggest that Ellen use massage as therapy for what ailed her, she decided this Friday-morning visit was unnecessary after all. She was happy not to be dating. Who had time for it?

When she met the right guy...

When she was ready...

"That's right." Shawna folded her hands on her desk. "I hired him."

"Why?"

"He's a medical massage therapist, and a good one. His reputation is above reproach. He works with elderly people, volunteers his services a lot of the time, and his success stories would keep the Hallmark Channel in business for years."

"What kind of successes?"

"Patients with broken hips facing being bound to a wheelchair walking again. Stroke victims brushing their teeth, feeding themselves, learning to talk. A cerebral palsy patient taking his first step at seventy-two."

"I don't have a muscular disability. Nor am I geriatric."

"No, but he's also done quite a bit with trauma patients. Soldiers suffering from post-traumatic stress disorder, and abused women and children."

"He helps them walk again?" She was defensive. She knew it. She just couldn't help it. She wasn't getting undressed for some biker guy. No way. Even if she was half rooting for him.

"No, he helps to retrain their instincts, teaching them to trust sudden physical movement in their space and, eventually, accept touch to their skin. He's assisted women who couldn't tolerate any kind of physical contact. Apparently several of them have invited him to their weddings."

"Abused women. You mean women who were beaten? Like domestic abuse."

"Yes."

"What about rape victims? Has he ever had a rape victim for a client?"

"Not that I know of."

She was off the hook then. "I don't see—"

"What you're going through, this aversion to being touched, even in a completely noninvasive, trusted situation, is the same thing many abused women experience." Shawna's words hung in the air. Echoing around the small office. Getting louder by the second.

Or so it seemed to Ellen.

"Fine," she blurted to silence the sound. "I mean, what does this guy do? If you think I'm suddenly going to want a massage because a good-looking biker wants to give me one—" Heat flooded under her skin.

"You've seen Jay."

"Maybe."

"Were you afraid of him?"

"Not as much as I would have expected."

"Good. He's got a way about him."

"My mother and her friends don't think he should be trusted."

"It's not like them to judge by appearances."

"I guess David invited him to the men's group at church Sunday night and he said no. No excuses, just no, thank you."

Shawna didn't dignify the comment with a response.

"And Ben and Tory invited him to dinner. He turned them down, too." Why Ellen felt compelled to defend the heroines wasn't clear to her.

"Jay's personal life has nothing to do with his skills as a therapist," Shawna said. "I think you know that."

Ellen didn't always agree with some of the more narrow-minded opinions espoused by the heroines of Shelter Valley, as Shawna was well aware.

"If you see Jay, I'll insist on being a primary player in

your treatment. So far, with the few clients I've referred to him, Jay's insisting on that, as well. I'll want to speak with him first, but from what I know about his methods, the treatment will be completely noninvasive."

The repetition of the word *noninvasive* set Ellen off. "What does that mean?" The words were out before she had a chance to take a deep breath. Temper her reaction.

"It means you'll be fully dressed at all times."

Oh. Well, then. She relaxed her fingers from the edge of her chair. "Where?"

"Here. I've given him a room right down the hall."

She'd known she had to seek all the help she could get the second she'd pulled her son's arms from around her neck five days ago.

She had a month to fix herself.

CHAPTER THREE

JAY HADN'T PLANNED TO spend the entire morning sitting
in a car. It was a school day, Friday—what crazy school
system started at the beginning of August?

With the academic year barely under way, why in
hell hadn't the kid left his house to catch the bus with
the rest of the junior-high-aged kids?

There had been five of them. Three girls and two
boys. Jay could describe them all in detail. He knew
which houses they'd come from, too.

But he hadn't seen the boy he wanted to see.

Only to see.

Without being seen.

At ten o'clock, after three hours of surveillance, he
gave up. Either the boy was sick, cutting school, had
spent the night at someone's place or was in juvenile
detention.

Hoping it wasn't the latter, Jay made a couple of calls
to be sure.

Satisfied with the news that Cole MacDonald—
his primary reason for being in this state—wasn't
in custody, Jay spent the rest of the morning at the
Department of Vital Records and the library accessing
newspaper archives tending to the other reason he was
in the godforsaken desert when he could be watching
waves hit the sand. Before he could offer anything to an

out-of-control boy, he had to find his father. Find some answers about his life, about himself.

Cole apparently needed a strong hand—and stability. Jay had an aversion to being tied down. Shied clear of emotional attachment to the point that he'd never had a committed relationship beyond the kind but emotionally distant one he'd had with the aunt who'd raised him.

Jay's father had had an aversion to family ties, too.

Was Jay a chip off the old block? A man who couldn't be counted on to hang around? Was his need to be a free spirit hereditary?

Jay had no idea whatsoever how to be a part of a family and that couldn't be all by his choice alone. Was there something genetic that precluded the ability to have close relationships?

One thing was for certain, he wasn't about to contact Cole until he was convinced his presence in the boy's life would mark an improvement.

A call rescued him from the archives—in the library and in his mind—shortly after noon. Stepping outside to answer, Jay quickly agreed to Shawna's request he take an afternoon appointment in Shelter Valley. He returned the car, collected his bike and hightailed it out of town.

All in all, the first half of his day had been a total waste. Good thing he wasn't being paid for his private investigative work.

SHE SHOULDN'T HAVE AGREED to this. At the Shelter Valley Medical Center for the second time that day, Ellen studied the pamphlets on the bulletin board to the right of the reception desk in the lobby, waiting for her appointment with Black Leather—Jay Billingsley.

She would much rather be at Big Spirits, the retirement center and adult day care where she worked as a social worker and activities director. They were a relatively small operation—only fifty beds—and some days it seemed as though Ellen was a jack-of-all-trades, between the counseling and the planning and implementing activities to keep the seniors busy, challenged, healthy and happy. Still, she loved her job. Loved the people she cared for. They had so much wisdom. And many of them possessed an inner peace and acceptance that she would give much to obtain.

Even more than wanting to be at work, she would rather be with her son, who would have been playing happily at Little Spirits, the day care that was attached to the facility where Ellen worked. Had he been in town, that is.

"Ellen?"

Heart pounding, she spun around. *Black Leather.* He'd snuck up on her.

Not a good sign.

"Come on back."

No. She didn't think so. At all.

He smiled. Not a guy smile. Or a doctor smile. A… smile smile. Like what a stranger would give to another stranger passing in the hall. No threat. No invasion of her space.

Taking control of herself, Ellen stepped through the door with him, intending to tell him in private that Shawna had made a mistake, that this treatment wasn't a good idea. Maybe Ellen would soften the blow by agreeing to reschedule.

Probably not. She had no intention of coming back. And she wasn't duplicitous.

"Shawna says you work at Big Spirits."

"That's right." She stayed a step behind him as they passed mostly closed doors that housed Shawna's office, a weight-loss clinic and an eye doctor.

"I've got an appointment with a client there in the morning."

Why didn't Ellen know about that? Those were her people. Every one of them.

Not that she had a thing to do with their medical needs. She was their social-emotional captain.

No one needed her permission to call a massage therapist. Nor did anyone have to inform her when someone was having a medically prescribed procedure unless it related to something Ellen had planned. Or limited a resident's participation in activities.

But they usually did let her know.

The man in front of her slowed.

A vision of Josh's face as he'd turned around to wave goodbye to her at the airport flashed before her eyes. In the last minutes she'd been with her son, she'd pulled his arms away from her.

She had to get well.

For him, if nothing else.

Black Leather opened the door second from the end. The one Shawna had taken her to earlier that day.

Ellen knew exactly what waited inside. A padded table with a headrest extending from one end. There was a small table, too, with a box of tissues and an MP3 docking station. Next to that was a cloth-draped cart with drawers and a couple of shelves filled with white sheets and towels. The top of the cart was covered with various bottles filled with liquids.

She couldn't go in there. Not even for Josh. Well, to save his life, she would. She'd die for him.

But Josh's life wasn't in danger.

Black Leather, who wore black denim jeans and a white lab coat with black leather boots that made no noise when he walked, turned in the doorway to see her standing several feet away.

"Wait here," he said, when she'd already formed her lips to blurt out her unequivocal refusal to go any farther down the hall toward that door—or with any treatment he might have in mind.

Ellen stood there, the refusal to enter any room with him still hovering. She felt caged, staring at the ponytail hanging down his back as he strode away from her.

This was her chance to leave. She could have Shawna make her apologies. Shawna was the one who had put her in this spot so she could be the one to get Ellen out of it.

Not entirely fair. Ellen had asked Shawna for help. And Shawna thought Black Leather could help. He had training. History. Previous successes.

He liked old people.

So did Ellen.

He exited Shawna's office carrying a chair. Was he intending to use it? Or to have Ellen use it? Didn't much matter to her. She was not going in that little room alone with this man.

Not today anyway.

Not while she was in the middle of a panic attack.

She recognized the symptoms. The tightness in her chest. Butterflies in her stomach. Foggy thoughts that wouldn't land.

"Try this." Black Leather set the chair at the end of the hall and pointed.

"You want me to sit there?"

"Sure."

"Out here?"

"Yes."

Okay. Well, her knees were a little shaky. Maybe her symptoms were more obvious than she'd thought. And it wasn't as though he could do anything in the middle of the hall.

Granted the area was in a corner of the medical center. And not one soul had come or gone in the minutes she'd been there. But still, someone could. At any moment one of the other doors could open and someone could walk out.

Ellen sat.

"Shawna tells me you're suffering from PTSD."

Ellen had negotiated with Shawna and they had finally settled on her releasing only that information to him. It was all he needed to know to be able to treat her.

Stiff and ready to bolt, Ellen stared at him—as if he were a train wreck. She had to survey the damage. To see the suffering.

"You look too young to have been in the service."

"I'm twenty-six." Not young at all.

"Were you in the service?"

"No."

His gaze made her uncomfortable. Could the man see the quaking inside her? Better that than having him see the dark shadows in her mind.

"The idea here is to teach your body that physical touch is nonthreatening. And to teach your mind that physical touch will bring you pleasure. To get you to the point where your automatic reaction is to welcome touch because you associate it with pleasure. To retrain you to expect it. Does that make sense?"

She wasn't a moron.

And he wasn't going to get her in that room.

"I'm going to start out with one hand. I'll place it lightly where your right shoulder and neck meet. You naturally hold tension there and we want to relieve that tension."

He was not getting her in that room.

"You ready?"

Ellen glared up at him. "What? Out here?"

"Yes." He met her gaze head-on.

And the honesty, the understanding she saw there reached through her haze of panic.

"Just one hand?"

"Yes."

"You promise?"

"Yes."

"Only in the one spot?"

"Yes."

He didn't move.

She tried to prepare. To imagine his hand on her neck. To brace herself for how that would feel.

"Are you just going to lay your hand there, or what?"

"I'm going to start with three fingers. I'll take them away then touch again. I'll repeat that until your body accepts the contact."

"How will you know that?"

"You'll let me know."

She had to do something? The butterflies were swarming fiercely.

"What if I don't?" Did that mean he'd keep touching her? And claim that she hadn't told him not to? Because she'd—

"You will. Your muscles will tense up—their way of responding to unwanted contact."

Oh. Right. As a massage therapist, he knew all about muscles. Was probably trained to "listen" to them in ways Ellen didn't even know about.

What else would he be able to understand about her if he touched her?

"That's it then? You touch with three fingers— lightly—and that's all?"

"Once your body accepts it, if we get to that point, I'll apply light pressure—something meant to feel really good. I'll give you plenty of warning before I change a process. That's how this works. No surprises. And nothing without your explicit agreement. Okay?"

She wanted to date.

She didn't want to sleep alone for the rest of her life.

She was not going to spend her life—even one aspect of it—hostage to what that bastard had done to her.

Josh needed her to be healthy.

Ellen nodded.

"Look at me please."

She did.

"Okay?"

She nodded again.

"I need to hear you say it. This is totally your call."

"Okay." She tensed.

Black Leather waited then moved slowly to her side.

"Three fingers," he said, holding them about a foot in front of her so she could see them. "I'm going to touch. On top of your hair. Ready?"

"Yes."

She sensed more than heard his movement. "Touching now…"

Emotion exploded inside of Ellen, a volcano that rose from her stomach and took her breath away. Sight blinded by tears, she turned the corner of the hall before she even realized she was out of the chair.

And she didn't stop. Not when people called her name. Not until she was in her car with the door locked. Not until she was driving down the road, heading toward…she had no idea where.

That hadn't gone well.

CHAPTER FOUR

JAY HAD NEVER BEEN ONE to leave well enough alone. He had this cursed inability to turn his back and walk away. Even after the trait had landed him eighteen months in prison, he continued to let it drive his actions. And now he couldn't leave Ellen Moore to handle the fallout of their afternoon session alone.

But she'd disappeared—had been out of the parking lot before he'd been able to grab the keys out of the locked drawer in his table. Although he'd driven around the entire town, he hadn't spotted her.

Jay knew better than to ask people if they'd seen her. Or to hope they would direct him to her. She was a daughter of Shelter Valley. He was the outsider.

He called Shawna, knowing the counselor would have a hell of lot more luck at locating Ellen than he would, but reached her voice mail and left a message for her to phone him as soon as possible.

He had nothing to do this afternoon except wait for that call and tend to the one aspect of his life that he'd left completely alone.

His father had deserted him and his mother. The man was weak and irresponsible. He'd loved his mother enough to marry her, but not enough to stick around after she'd had Jay. And Jay had seen nothing worth pursuing in that situation.

Then Kelsey Johnson, now Kelsey MacDonald, had contacted him a month ago. They had known each other in college. He'd had sex with her. She'd married one of Jay's ex-frat brothers. And twelve years later, she confessed he had a son.

A delinquent son. One her husband was tired of dealing with. Apparently, MacDonald had known all along that the boy wasn't his. So out of the blue, Kelsey wanted Jay to take responsibility for Cole.

A man couldn't very well expect to father a troubled teenager when he had his own father issues. Jay didn't trust fathers. Or families.

He had no idea how to be the first. Or to be a part of the second.

To make matters worse, Jay, who knew what it was to be abandoned, had unwittingly put his own son in the very same position.

Damn Kelsey for putting him in this position.

The idea that he had a son was not sitting well with him. Despite having had four weeks to come to terms with the news, to make the plans that uprooted his entire footloose and fancy-free, lay-on-the-beach-whenever-he-wanted-to lifestyle, the existence of a boy with Jay's blood in his veins still seemed completely unrealistic.

He sat at his computer, intent on searching various databases he had access to for any mention of Jay Billingsley, Sr.

He had a copy of his mother's birth certificate and death certificate, which had been listed in her maiden name—his aunt's doing. She'd wanted to eradicate any mention of the man who'd deserted her baby sister.

Jay had his own birth certificate, too. But he couldn't connect Tammy Renee Walton to Billingsley. He couldn't find any record of his father at all. Not even on his own birth certificate. Even though they had been married, his mother had chosen to list her maiden name and leave the father blank.

He knew the man's name was Jay Billingsley. He knew he'd worked at a car dealership in Tucson—as a salesman his aunt had said—that had long since gone out of business.

With those three pieces of information, it should be easy enough to trace the guy. Jay had always thought he could find his father in a matter of hours if he'd really wanted to do so.

Apparently not.

This morning, when he'd attempted to access his mother's marriage license, he'd been told there wasn't one. The records clerk who had been helping him suggested that his parents might have been married in another state.

Just damned fine.

Like the majority of U.S. states, Arizona was a closed record state, which meant that without the man's name on his birth certificate, Jay had no legal way of accessing his father's records—other than those that were public such as birth date, marriage or death. He couldn't find any public records for the man in Arizona.

For all he knew, Jay Billingsley, Sr. could have been born in another state, as well.

Maybe he'd died at some point, too.

Jay had other avenues to check. He hadn't developed the reputation he had for ferreting out the most hard to find facts in order to solve cold cases without learning a few hundred tricks.

But he hadn't expected to need them this time. He'd

figured he'd make a few simple inquiries, do a stake-out—similar to the one he'd done that morning—then, depending on what he found, plan his next move.

Typing usernames and passwords on various internet public document reporting agencies Jay searched U.S. marriage, birth and death records.

Surprised as hell, Jay came up with another dead end. Jay Billingsley, Sr. had obviously lied to Tammy about his real name. That could explain why the man had taken off without a backward glance.

Had he been in trouble?

A member of the underworld?

Living a double life with a wife and family else-where?

Or simply a scumbag con man?

Trying a different tactic, Jay gathered the articles he'd located this morning. He opened a can of soda and sat back to spend the time before preparing his poolside dinner of grilled shrimp with news stories from the *Tucson Citizen* and the *Arizona Daily Star* dating back thirty-two years ago.

Maybe a birth announcement would shed some light on the latest irritation in his life. Or maybe a piece of school sports trivia would. He already had the few brief pieces that had been printed about his mother's death before the records had been sealed from the press.

There was no mention of his father having been on the scene at any time. During his years-long inves-tigation to find his mother's killer, he'd looked for any mention of his father. The only family listed had been his mother's sister—the aunt who had raised Jay. The same woman who had told him that his father had abandoned Jay and his mother before she'd been murdered.

It was conceivable the man might not even know about the heinous crime that had robbed Jay of any semblance of a normal life.

He'd known about Jay, though. That much was quite clear. Billingsley, Sr. had put it in writing, giving sole custody of his son to Tammy Walton Billingsley. Jay's aunt had kept the letter in a lockbox. Jay had it now.

But just because his father wasn't mentioned at the time of his mother's death, didn't mean that the man hadn't made the news in some other fashion. Jay had done the obvious—searched for any mention of Jay Billingsley—so now he was going to do the more tedious part of an investigator's job. Read through layers and layers of unrelated detail attempting to find that one piece of information that would click with something he already knew but didn't yet know was pertinent.

The man had lived in Tucson. That much was certain. His aunt had also mentioned—let slip was more like it—that his father had had some later ties to Shelter Valley.

The sooner Jay found his father, the sooner he could contact Cole's mother and determine exactly how the next phase of his own life would unfold. It wouldn't be a white picket fence in a small town—or anywhere. He knew that much. But if Cole's mother had her way, the kid could end up living with Jay.

He picked up a sheet of paper with a shrunken newspaper page copied to it. He took in the details of reported life in Tucson, Arizona. On January 13 some thirty years ago, Dr. Paul Fugate, a botanist and park ranger, left his office to check out a nature trail and never returned. Thumbing through pages, Jay found many references to the search for the bearded National Park Service employee, but couldn't find any reference to the man being found.

Could the man's disappearance have anything to do with his father? Could the man be his father? Sure... except for the name, and the age.

But what if his aunt had been mistaken about his father? What if Tammy Walton had been involved with, married to, an older man?

At his computer he typed the name *Fugate* into a secure database for public records. There was nothing linking Tammy Walton to any Fugate.

He searched the name *Paul Fugate*—and found an article dated 2010 about a memorial service for the man who had never been found. His wife, a woman who looked to be near seventy, had been in attendance.

Another dead end.

Jay's day had been filled with them.

As his thoughts trailed over the past several hours, the obstacles he'd encountered at every step of his day, in his mind's eye, Jay saw a set of eyes. Brown. Filled with panic.

His newest client.

He'd catapulted her into a very bad day.

When he'd given Shawna his word that he'd do all he could to help Ellen Moore, Jay's goal, his purpose, was to help her feel better.

And because that hadn't happened during their first encounter, he was worried about her. Did anyone outside of him, Ellen and Shawna know about the session? Would she seek help? Or comfort?

From what Shawna had told him about the woman, he suspected not.

He'd seen Ellen jogging the other day at four o'clock. It was almost four now. A person suffering from post-traumatic stress disorder often relied on the sameness of routine and schedule to maintain a sense of security. And that person might exercise religiously to relieve stress.

He knew at least a portion of her route and could figure out the rest. The town wasn't that big.

Still, it was Friday. She probably had plans. A beautiful woman like her—she probably had a date.

Taking the chance that she'd take her run regardless of later plans, Jay decided to find her.

ELLEN HEARD HIS MOTORCYCLE as she turned the corner past Tory's house. He must live nearby.

She stopped. But she didn't even think about turning back. Or trying to avoid the man who pulled up to the curb beside her and turned off his engine.

In fact, she walked toward the bike, studying the chrome while she willed her heart and her breath back to normal range. If he'd come looking for her, she would deal with him.

If he hadn't, then she'd extricate herself from the awkward position with the dignity and class that were her trademark—or so she'd been told dozens of times.

Dignity and class had been embarrassingly absent when she'd bolted from her appointment with Black Leather earlier.

"Nice bike." She walked around it, pretending she knew what she was looking for. Or at. It was a motorcycle, all right. And it was shiny.

"Thanks. You ride?"

"Nope."

The seat behind him had a backrest and arms.

"Ever?"

"Nope."

"You've never been on a motorcycle?"

Was the concept really that hard to comprehend?

"No, I've never been on a motorcycle." Proud of the even tone of her voice, Ellen forgave herself for feeling like a backwoods hick thanks to his incredulity. "You might have noticed, there aren't a lot of biker types in this town."

The jeans he'd worn at the clinic looked different astride his bike. He'd donned the black leather vest, too.

In her bike shorts and running T-shirt, Ellen wore far less than she had before. But standing on the curb—her curb in her town—she felt twice as covered. Because she had fresh air on her skin, the air of Shelter Valley wrapping her in a loving cocoon—and she was wearing the gazes of anyone in town who passed by, or watched through a window.

"Have you ever had a massage?"

"No." He wasn't going to unnerve her. She'd had time to realign herself.

"Are you afraid of me?"

"No." The answer came quickly…and rang true. Surprisingly true.

"I came looking for you."

Ellen held her ground. "That wasn't necessary."

"I thought it was. You were obviously upset when you left."

It wasn't the first time she'd had a breakdown.

Wouldn't be the last. But they were fewer and further between.

"As you can see, I'm fine now."

"Can we talk about it?"

"I'm not coming back."

"I don't intend to talk you into it."

"Then what's the point of talking about it? We tried something. It didn't work." She was fine. Healthy enough. No one was perfect. She didn't need help. She only needed to focus on who she was—Ellen Moore, social worker, activities director, mother of a five-year-old bundle of energy who was away for the entire month visiting with his father and the model girlfriend.

"I'm not good with failure."

He was Black Leather. A man who had popped into her thoughts on more than one occasion since he'd roared into town—quite a shock, considering she was a woman who avoided thoughts of men because of accompanying feelings of fear, revulsion or inadequacy.

"Has anyone asked you to leave town yet?" she asked.

"Of course not."

"They will."

"They'll be disappointed."

She didn't think so.

And she hoped so.

"Do I offend you?"

"No." He fascinated her. In a distant sort of way. A train wreck sort of way.

With both hands still on the handlebars of his motorcycle, Black Leather sighed then looked straight at her. "I'd really like a chance to sit and talk with you," he said, his voice surprisingly soft. Gentle. "I think I might be able to help."

No didn't spring immediately to her lips, which unnerved Ellen a little bit. "How?"

"I'm not sure." He shrugged and she appreciated his honesty. "Obviously there are a lot of things about you, about your situation, I don't know. I agreed to see you with only a minimal amount of information but I now think that was a mistake and a disservice to you."

"That's not your concern." He was a biker massage therapist. And not long for this town.

"I think it is. Most particularly if I have inadvertently made the situation worse."

Two cars she recognized had driven past. Becca Parsons again. Ellen often passed the mayor during her run since Becca left work at the same time each day in order to have time in the pool with her kids before dinner. Ellen had been in high school when Becca had finally, after more than twenty years of failed attempts, carried a baby to term. The whole town had watched that pregnancy, but no one more than Ellen's mother—best friends with Becca since grade school.

The other car that passed was Keith Nielson's, Bonnie's husband. Josh would have been at Little Spirits, Bonnie's day care, waiting for Ellen to pick him up. If he was in town...

"I have to go."

"Can we set up a time to talk about what happened today?"

He really seemed to want to help. Seemed to believe he had something to offer.

Was she honestly ready to give up? To accept who

she was, as she was? To be forever held hostage to a past she couldn't change?

She looked at Black Leather. She wasn't afraid of him.

"Do you ever braid your hair?" It was longer than hers. And absolutely none of her business.

"Nope."

She wanted out of the cage her past had trapped her in. She wanted to be able to date. Marry again. She wanted her son to be able to hug her without having his arms wrenched away.

She'd been through counseling—individual and group. She'd exhausted all of the conventional channels and, seven years post-attack, was still struggling to accept being touched. Shawna thought this man could help her.

As a social worker, a counselor, Ellen knew that a huge part of the success—or failure—of Jay's therapy rested with her. If she was going to do this, she had to be open to him. Completely. No matter how hard that might prove to be.

Considering this afternoon in the clinic, she didn't think she could be that open.

But she knew something else. If she didn't at least explore the possibility one more time—by speaking with him—she'd feel as though she'd given up on herself.

"Can you meet me tomorrow morning? Around ten?" Her stepfather, David Marks, was expecting her to help with the church bulletin before that.

"Yes. Where?"

Ellen suggested the Valley Diner.

"You want to be seen in the middle of downtown, sitting at a table with me?"

"Yes, I think I do."

She wished she could explain to herself why that was.

CHAPTER FIVE

Jay made it to the diner a few minutes ahead of schedule the next morning and went in to use the restroom. By the time he'd returned, Ellen was already seated in the last booth, her back to the wall. He recognized her first by the ruler-straight set of her shoulders then by the distinctive natural blond hair that hung freely down her back.

He knew even before he slid onto the bench opposite her that she wouldn't be wearing any makeup. Nothing about Ellen was made-up.

Hidden, maybe, but not made-up.

"Did you order already?" he asked in lieu of a greeting.

"No, I waited."

He picked up the menu, decided on the first thing he saw—a man-size stack of homemade pancakes—then returned the plastic-coated sheet to its place along the wall.

Ellen watched him, her hands folded on the table.

"Ellen?" The waitress, a middle-aged woman, approached, staring, not at the woman she'd addressed, but at him.

"Hi, Nancy. How are the kids?"

"Good. You know that Cameron starts at Montford this fall, right?"

"Yeah. And Leah will be following next year, I'm sure." Ellen ordered a diet soda, oatmeal and toast and waited while Jay asked for coffee, black, and his pancakes.

"Have you eaten here yet?" Ellen asked as Nancy, pocketing her notepad, walked away.

"Nope, this is my first time in." Glancing around, he figured he could have described the place accurately without the visit. Hometown diners looked the same the world over.

But as diners went, this one was one of the nicest. It was clean, of course, but the decor was...fresh-looking.

And it fit right in with this family-based town.

Jay focused on the woman he'd agreed to help, wondering about her. "Do you have siblings?"

"Three."

"Younger or older?"

"Younger. I'm the oldest."

"Are they all here in town?"

"Yep. Shelley's twenty-three, working toward her doctorate in music at Montford. She had her bachelor's at twenty and finished the master's program last year. Rebecca's twenty-two and married. No kids yet. Tim's just turning twenty. He's at Montford, too, playing baseball. And his interest is definitely more on the field than in the classroom, though he's planning to go to law school."

The woman was beautiful. He stared at her mouth, watching the way her lips moved as she talked. Her features were soft, almost innocent in their allure. Yet her eyes held secrets. And a sadness directly offset by the straightness of her spine.

He liked sitting here with her. Wanted to be here.

He noticed the uniformed man walking toward them. "Sheriff." He nodded acknowledgment.

"Ellen, you okay, sweetie?" Greg asked.

"Hi, Greg. Yes, I'm fine." Ellen's tone, her smile, was almost that of a child humoring a too protective parent. "Have you met Jay Billingsley? He works at the clinic."

Greg Richards glanced Jay's way, nodding, but the smile on his face didn't quite mask the concern lining his forehead. "Yes, we've met."

"The sheriff paid me a visit my first night in town," Jay said easily. "I invited him in and we—"

"Sheriff Richards. You did not go over and search this man's house simply because he rode into town on a loud motorcycle." Ellen's grin was filled with a disbelief that could only be genuine.

"No, he didn't," Jay asserted. If Ellen didn't already know about his police record—and shocking lack of family—then he preferred she not find out now when he needed her to feel comfortable with him. "He introduced himself and let me know that he was around if I needed anything."

The sheriff had crossed Jay's path twice since then and had been respectful. Jay responded in kind.

"Does your mother know you're here?" Sheriff Richards wasn't letting Ellen off the hook.

"If she doesn't yet, she will soon." Ellen's slight derision wasn't lost on Jay. And he didn't think the sheriff missed it, either. "I'm okay, Greg, really. David knows I'm here. And why."

David?

"Oh, well, okay then. Enjoy your breakfast." With

that, the man was gone as quickly as he'd arrived. Whoever this David was, he apparently had clout with the sheriff.

"DAVID IS MY STEPFATHER," Ellen said as soon as Sheriff Richards had left her peripheral vision. Opening up about her family, about her life, with an outsider went against deeply ingrained instincts.

Still, he might look like a Black Leather kind of guy but he was a professional. Shawna trusted Jay. Ellen trusted Shawna. Ellen wanted to get better. Therefore, she had to confide in him. She should have let Shawna fill him in to begin with and saved herself this awkwardness.

"You a churchgoer, Mr. Billingsley?"

"Call me Jay. And no, can't say that I am."

"I didn't think so. Otherwise you'd know David. He's the preacher here in town."

"And your stepfather."

"Yes. It's been seven years and he and my mom are still crazy about each other." In some ways it was hard to believe that much time had passed. In others, it seemed an eternity. "He's also one of my best friends."

Let Jay make of that what he wanted.

Nancy reappeared with breakfast.

"I thought you had an appointment at Big Spirits this morning," she said as she spooned hot oatmeal from the side of her bowl.

"Yes. At eight."

"How did it go?"

"Good."

The man kept the confidence of his clients. A point for him.

"I met with a mother and daughter from Phoenix yesterday," Ellen told him as they ate. "They were looking at the center as a possibility for the mother's brother."

"I thought the residence was full."

"It is. But there are a couple of rooms that have been used for storage that can be converted. After the meeting yesterday I volunteered to do the painting and decorating to prepare the rooms."

"They can't afford to hire a painter?"

"Yeah, they can, but I've got the time right now, and the rooms could be available by next week, which would work for those women. The man is being released from six months of rehab for a broken hip."

"So his stay will be temporary?"

"No." Ellen opened a packet of mixed fruit jelly. "He broke his hip when he ran a red light and was sideswiped. His wife died in the accident. His sister wants to take him to live with her, but the man is twice her size and she still works full-time. She can hire a nurse for home care, but she's afraid he's going to mourn and not improve. She heard about us and came for a tour. She has to make a decision this weekend."

"That's gotta be tough."

"Yeah." People had real problems. Much worse than an aversion to being hugged. "I gave her my cell number in case she had questions or concerns."

"You're committed to your job."

"I love my job."

He stopped eating and looked at her. "Why?"

The question was intrusive. Penetrating.

She held the slice of jelly-covered toast. She could do this. She could talk to him. "I have an affinity for old people. I think in part because they have so much wisdom." She silently fought the internal battle to flee. "The kind of wisdom you can't learn from books—or even always put into words. They teach by example. And I'm a sucker for that kind of lesson."

"So how do I teach you by example?"

She dropped the toast, the beginnings of a cold sweat coming on.

"I'm not— You're not—" She couldn't do this. She'd tried, but...

Jay wiped his mouth, put the used napkin in the center of a pool of syrup on his plate, then picked up the bill. "You ready to go?" He stood and pulled a couple of bills from a wad in his pocket and dropped them to the table.

She nodded then followed him outside. "Thank you for breakfast."

Every single person in the diner had watched them walk out. She slid her hands into the front pockets of her jeans and resisted the urge to run.

"I'm not giving up on you."

His quietly spoken statement slowed the cacophony inside of her. He wasn't giving up on her. Was she?

"I have a son." Josh. If she couldn't do this for herself, she had to do it for Josh. "His name's Josh. He's five."

They were standing on Main Street on Saturday morning. Attracting looks.

Shelter Valley protected its own—most particularly Ellen. She'd been in the papers. Everyone knew who she was.

"Did you talk to his father about your session with me?"

"No. Josh's father lives in Colorado now. He's got

a live-in girlfriend. Josh is with them for the month of
August."

"Oh."

One word, but it seemed to mean more than a professional collection of knowledge.

Or she was overreacting.

"How long has his father been in Colorado?"

"Three years. He left us to take a job there."

"I'm sorry to hear that."

"Me, too, for Josh's sake."

"Not for yours?"

Ellen shrugged. "Not so much. By the time Aaron
left, our divorce was almost a relief."

He didn't ask any more. But she could see the questions in his gaze. The battle raging inside her—*run,
get away, protect, protect, protect!* on one side and *you
need help, you'll be imprisoned for life, you'll never
be normal!* on the other—was overwhelming her. She
couldn't hear either side clearly.

But she could picture her son's face.

"Do you have time to take a drive with me?" She
was losing it. She couldn't be doing this. Couldn't be
contemplating opening up any more to this man.

She had to do something.

"In your car?"

"Yeah. I drive or we don't go."

"I have no problem with that."

She did, but she wasn't going to let that stop her. She
lived life. She didn't run from it.

CHAPTER SIX

JAY HAD NO IDEA WHAT, specifically, was going on. But he knew it was significant. In her jeans, Ellen looked about eighteen behind the wheel of her mini SUV as she drove beyond the city limits and approached the highway entrance ramp. He glanced at the steely set of her chin.

From there he watched the road. And waited.

Past the ramp, she turned into a parking lot full of potholes and in need of repair. He'd ridden by the seedy-looking motel turned studio apartment rentals any number of times. At least fifty years old, the place had clearly seen better days, and he had thought it closed before he'd seen a car parked outside one of the rooms earlier in the week.

Judging by the way she drove in without hesitation, Ellen had been there before. She pulled up in front of door fourteen, then put the Escape in Park.

Surely she didn't live here?

Even if she did, she wouldn't be taking him inside. The car was still running.

"How much time do you have to talk?"

The question wasn't what he'd been anticipating. At the least, he'd expected an explanation of why they were here. The trashy place with its peeling paint and filthy windows wasn't the setting he'd pictured for the intimate conversation he'd been hoping to have.

"A couple of hours. I've got a client at two." In Phoenix. Because work would initially be slow in Shelter Valley, Shawna had asked if he would be willing to do a few sessions in Phoenix. He was using the space of another medical massage therapist who didn't work weekends.

But right now, Ellen was all that mattered to him.

"I had the perfect life growing up," she said. "Parents who loved me. A safe town where people care about each other. Enough responsibility to shape me into a contributing member of society, enough freedom to learn from my mistakes, enough material comfort to more than satisfy my needs and enough time for fun."

Jay listened. He stared at the ugly door and didn't kid himself that he and Ellen were simply getting to know each other. Something was coming.

The life Ellen described didn't cause PTSD.

She was narrating her life with the detachment of a stranger. As though she had no connection to the woman about whom she spoke. She was speaking analytically, like a counselor discussing a client.

"All that changed when I was nineteen."

That young. Damn.

The four was crooked, as though the nail had come loose.

She glanced at him. "I'm sure you've seen Montford." She named the college around which Shelter Valley was built. Around which the town orbited.

He nodded.

"My father was a professor there."

"What field?"

"Psychology."

So it probably wasn't her social work degree alone that had given her understanding about life. "Did he share his insights when you were growing up?"

"Yeah." She smiled, and the warmth that flooded her gaze knocked him for a second. "He was the greatest, always explaining why things were the way they were. From rules they laid down to feelings we'd have in given situations."

"My father made life bearable, not because he took care of our problems for us, but because he sought always to teach us to take care of them for ourselves."

The softness disappeared as quickly as it had come.

She was suffering from PTSD. She was so locked up inside that the mere touch to her neck yesterday had unhinged her. This behavior from a woman with a degree and training in dealing with life.

"David says that Dad taught us to fish rather than giving us fish." Derision dripped from her tone. And he knew it was directed at the man who was both stepfather and best friend to her.

"You don't agree?"

"Oh, no, I agree," she said, glancing at him briefly. Her hands were still on the wheel. She wasn't really gripping it, but she didn't let go, either.

"David thinks we need to focus on the good that Dad brought us and forgive the rest. I don't agree."

Holding on to the anger would bring bitterness. But bitterness served a purpose. Sometimes it was the key to survival—until one was strong enough to survive without it.

"Not about forgiving him," Ellen added. "I can do that. My father is a weak man. He can't help that. What

I don't care to do is build him up as some kind of great guy, either. Because he's not."

"Because he's weak?"

"Because he walked out on his responsibilities. Because he lacks moral character."

If the man had walked out on his family, Jay couldn't agree more with her assessment. She'd summed up his own bottom line. A man who abandoned his responsibilities lacked moral character.

But he was not getting to know Ellen the way a man gets to know a woman. Even if, personally, he found her interesting.

He wasn't here to discuss philosophy. Or his own views. He was here to understand what troubled Ellen so he could help her.

"I was at class the night my father told my mother he was leaving her. She tried to hide it from us kids at first. I guess she thought maybe they could fix things. They were high school sweethearts. He was the only guy she'd ever dated. And they'd been married more than twenty years."

"Had they been having problems?"

"Not that she'd thought. They'd grown apart, but no more so than a lot of couples with four kids to raise."

"Is he here in town?"

Maybe in room fourteen? Surely Ellen wasn't rejecting touch because her father had deserted them. She was far too self-sustaining, confident, aware for that.

"No. When he told Mom he was leaving, he didn't mean he was only leaving her. He was leaving all of us. Permanently. To move East and marry a woman who was a couple of years older than I am. She was his student at Montford. They have two kids now. I've never met either one of them. And he's never been back."

He agreed with Ellen. The man lacked moral character. In a big way. Jay had a few less acceptable words to describe the guy. But he kept those to himself.

"My father deserted me, too." Sometimes you helped others by sharing a bit of yourself. College hadn't taught him that.

Life had.

Telling other victims who had experienced the repercussions of criminal actions about his mother's death had allowed them to trust him, to open up to him, and give him the information he'd needed to help bring them closure. And peace.

"He left right after I was born."

She looked at him fully then and the compassion in her gaze struck him. In ways that he was rarely struck. Jay didn't need her compassion. He didn't need anyone. Never had.

She was a potential client. Someone he was trying to help. Business as usual.

"Have you ever had contact with him?"

"Nope."

"Did you ever try?"

"No."

"You didn't want to?"

"No."

"What about your mother?"

"She died when I was a baby."

"Oh, my gosh, Jay, I'm so sorry."

He shrugged. "I had an aunt, my mother's older sister, who took me in. She loved me. It's the only life I knew." So he'd minimized the situation. His history wasn't important here. Understanding of the effects of a father's desertion was all that he'd meant to contribute.

JAY MIGHT LOOK DIFFERENT than anyone she'd ever known. He might turn his nose up at Shelter Valley convention, at the town that was as much a part of her as her arms and legs. He might reject the hospitality that had been offered to him. He might not be a churchgoer. But he had suffered. He knew what it was to feel pain.

To be alone.

He wasn't just a professional anymore. He'd become a person. Ellen wasn't sure if that made trusting him easier or harder.

"My father left my mother with four teenage children to raise. She had to find a job so that we could keep our house. She'd quit college to marry him and have us so she had no real training. But the new job he'd taken didn't pay nearly as much as Montford and the child support just wasn't enough.

"I had a job and helped out with my brother and sisters as much as I could, but I wasn't him, you know?"

Jay's nod, the way he looked at her, as though he understood completely, helped her to continue.

"One night, shortly after my father called to say that he and his new wife were expecting a baby, I ran out of gas on my way home from work. I'd been running the kids around a lot and hadn't paid close enough attention to the gauge. I was pretty upset about my father and not thinking as well as I should have been. I knew I had to figure this out on my own. I'd gotten myself into the situation and had to get myself out. I was dating Aaron, Josh's father, but he was busy. I couldn't call Mom and add to her burdens. She hardly had time to eat and was getting only a few hours of sleep a night."

"You're being a little hard on yourself. You know that, right? You were nineteen. You'd been driving at most three years. Adults run out of gas. It happens. And when it does, they generally call someone."

"Hindsight's twenty-twenty. As it turned out, it would have taken Mom far less time to come and get me."

The sequence was still so clear and, as she relayed it aloud, it unfolded in her mind as though it was happening for the first time...

SHE AND AARON HAD HAD a fight earlier. He'd accused her of not trusting him. She'd overreacted.

But she did trust Aaron. It was just men and life she was having a little trouble believing in. She hadn't told him about her father's last phone call, about the new baby on the way. Or about how frequently she heard her mother crying in her room when she thought they were all asleep. She didn't know what to do, what she could possibly say that could ease her mother's pain. In the end, she cried, too.

She didn't care what Pastor Marks said. Sometimes life sucked.

And now her car wouldn't start. Ellen turned the key a third time, pumping the gas pedal, but nothing happened. And she knew why. She'd used the last of her gas to flood the engine. The gauge had been below empty when she came into work but she'd decided to fuel up on the way home so she wouldn't be late.

She should have gotten gas after she'd left college this afternoon, before picking up her sisters and brother from school. There was a station around the corner from Montford. She knew that.

Head on the steering wheel, she promised herself she wouldn't cry. She'd never run out of gas before. Wasn't sure what she should do.

Except not call her mother. There was no way she was going to add anything to her mom's already over-flowing plate. The gas station was too far to walk. Besides, there was no guarantee they'd even have a gas can to loan her. And she couldn't call Aaron. Not after the way she'd stomped off.

This was her problem. She'd gotten herself into it. She could get herself out of it.

Filled with resolve, feeling better, stronger, by taking control of her life, she climbed out of the car and headed for the highway ramp at the front of the Walmart parking lot. She'd noticed girls hitchhiking there before and they always seemed to be picked up almost immediately. That didn't surprise her. That's the way things were in Shelter Valley—there was always someone nice willing to help out.

Purse in hand, she reached the road, stuck out her thumb with uncharacteristic boldness and waited. She'd ask to be dropped at Aaron's dorm. First she'd beg for his forgiveness because that was all she really cared about at the moment. Then, if he accepted her apology, she'd tell him about her car. He'd know where to find a gas can. And he would drive her to her car without ever telling her how stupid she'd been to run out of gas in the first place. That was Aaron's way.

It was only one of the hundreds of reasons she loved him so much.

So lost in thought about the boyfriend she couldn't

imagine living without, Ellen almost didn't notice the brand-new Lexus that pulled up beside her. It took the open passenger door and the call to get in to garner her attention. She didn't recognize the car—or the older man at the steering wheel—which was a surprise in Shelter Valley. But she certainly recognized that the suit he was wearing was expensive.

He must be a friend of the Parsons. As president of Montford University, Will was always entertaining rich and important men from Phoenix. And Becca, the new mayor, knew her share of rich folk, too.

Or maybe he was some friend of the Montfords— descendants of the town's founder. They were richer than Becca and Will.

"You heading into town?" she asked, holding the edge of the door as she peered at him.

"I am." He smiled. "If you'd like a ride, hop in."

With a lift in spirits that had been plummeting all day, Ellen did as he bid, thanking him and giving him directions to Aaron's dorm. "It's this side of the main light in town," she told him. "It's not far out of the way."

Finally something positive was happening. It was like Pastor Marks had said. If you can get through the challenges, and if you do all you can do to help yourself, there's always good on the other side.

"Have you ever been to town before?" she asked the man who had a friendly look about him.

"Nope."

"It's a great place. You'll like it."

"I'm counting on it," he said, smiling at her again.

"The turn's right ahead."

He nodded.

"After that next group of trees."

He nodded again, tapping his thumb on the steering as he drove.

"There," she said quickly when it looked as though he was going to miss the road.

He drove past.

"That was it," Ellen said, sorry that he was going to have to turn around, that she was costing him more time than intended. She'd tried to be so clear.

He didn't slow down. Didn't turn around. Didn't even appear to have heard her.

"Excuse me," she said. "Did you hear what I said? You missed the turn." Did he have Alzheimer's or something? She'd heard Becca talking to her mother about one of the ladies at the new adult day care in town and how her family had had to take away her keys because she'd gotten in the car and forgotten not only where she was going, but most of the rules of driving, as well.

God, please don't let him wreck. Her mom would die if she were to get a phone call that Ellen had been in an accident. It was a parent's worst nightmare. Everyone knew that.

She tried a couple more times to get his attention.

He didn't say anything, just smiled at her and nodded.

But on the other side of town he slowed and Ellen breathed her first sigh of relief. She would get out as soon as she could, find a phone and call Aaron. Even angry, he'd come to get her. And call for someone to help the old man, too.

Not that he really appeared old enough to have Alzheimer's, but it did hit some people in their fifties. And no one she knew had ever acted this odd before.

"This isn't anyplace you want to be," she told him, knowing he was out of it for sure when he pulled into the parking lot of a run-down boardinghouse that used to be a motel during the early gold mining days.

The man was scaring her.

Especially when he pulled up to a door and grabbed a key from the console between them. *"Let's go."*

"Go where?" Was he crazy? She wasn't going anywhere with him.

"Oh, so that's the game you want?" he asked, not sounding crazy at all. He held her wrist as though being used to getting exactly what he wanted.

Which was what? The man was rich. Dressed nice. Driving an expensive car.

"I don't know what—"

"Let's go, sweetie. I don't have a lot of time before my wife expects me—" He frowned, as though he'd said too much, but he did let go of her wrist.

Ellen didn't even think. She wrenched open the door, intending to run as fast as she could to the nearest sign of humanity. Wherever that was.

With one foot out of the car, she propelled herself forward, trying to figure out which direction would be the safest bet. She had the sick feeling she might only get one chance.

Her second foot got tangled up between the seat and her leg. She started to fall.

Except that the man was there, catching her. *"So you like it rough, huh?"* He sounded excited in a way she'd never heard before, but still recognized. *"They didn't tell me that."*

"No!" She pulled at his grasp, unable to feel anything

but the urgent need to escape. His words made no sense to her.

His grip made no sense to her.

Aaron! Her heart screamed, even as her mind refused to work. Something terrible was happening and she didn't know why.

She had to get away. For Aaron. For Mom. For herself. She had to do something.

The man had her body in an iron clutch, carrying her to the door a few feet away. She kicked him. Hard. On his shins. Over and over. She tried to reach higher, but he had his legs too close together.

"You little bitch," he said, but he didn't sound mad. Somehow she seemed to be pleasing him.

Oh, God.

Ellen screamed. So long and hard the sound ripped at her throat. There was no one around to hear. He covered her mouth with his own, eating up her sound, but not the burning in her tonsils.

She had to vomit. She bit him to make him release her.

He bit her back, sliding her along his body to hold her between his legs while, with one hand on her swollen mouth, he unlocked the door with the other.

Then, with his hands on her breasts, his body pressed against her backside, he pushed her ahead of him into the room and kicked the door shut behind them.

CHAPTER SEVEN

"HE RAPED YOU." JAY'S words cracked the silence that had fallen between them. He couldn't look away from Ellen—almost as though he could prevent anything bad from happening to her with the force of his gaze. As though he could somehow turn back the clock and prevent the horror she'd lived through.

"Yes." She wasn't looking at him.

He asked the first question that occurred to him. "Josh?"

"Is Aaron's son. He was born almost two years later."

Right. She'd told him her son was five.

The anger roiling through him wasn't going to help. It wasn't normal for him, either. His work put him in contact with abused women on a regular basis. And with victims of crimes when he researched cold cases. He knew how to distance himself. He knew how not to let it get personal.

But Ellen... She reminded him of feelings he'd long since put away. For some inexplicable reason, this woman he barely knew *was* personal. And what had happened to her...

He recognized the way he was feeling. The helpless, debilitating rage was something he'd dealt with several years ago. When he'd finally found his mother's killer. A random home invasion, rape and murder. The man had committed a slew of similar crimes across the Southwest.

His mother had been the same age Ellen had been when she'd been—

He had to help Ellen.

That's what this was all about. Why he was getting tangled up in emotion. Because he was meant to help Ellen. There was simply no other reason Jay would be feeling so much of…anything. He wasn't a touchy-feely kind of guy.

"DID THEY CATCH THE GUY?"

Ellen had expected the question. And she wanted this done. No more questions. No more need to answer. Done. She'd moved on.

She didn't like the conversation, but she didn't have a problem with answering him. She was capable of talking about what had happened to her.

So she stared straight ahead at the door that no longer appeared in her nightmares and said, "Yeah, they caught him. I testified at his trial. He was convicted of felony kidnapping and several charges relating to the rape and is serving fifteen years to life."

"Was he from around here?" His quiet, steady tone unnerved her a little bit. What generally came across as morbid curiosity in others was more like a genuine need to know coming from him.

"No." This was the hardest part—the anger that still surfaced sometimes at the senselessness of it all.

David hadn't given up. He was certain that someday her heart would find peace. On this one count, Ellen wasn't so sure.

"He was chief operating officer of a large corporation

in Phoenix, making half a million dollars a year. He had a wife and three kids—all of whom were in college—" She swallowed.

"And in his spare time he raped innocent young women?"

"No, in his spare time he hired prostitutes to role-play with him so that he could act out the dark fantasies that didn't fit into his prestigious world."

"But…"

Ellen looked him straight in the eye. "He mistook me for the woman he'd hired. She was supposed to meet him around the same area and surprise him with her pickup line. She was there, too. But neither of us saw her and she didn't see us. He saw me hitchhiking and thought I was the one. Wrong place at the wrong time."

"I'm surprised, with his money, he didn't find a way to use that to his advantage during the trial."

"He did. But I was crying and telling him no. Even if he'd paid for sex, it became rape the second I said no. Same with the kidnapping. I got into the car of my own free will, but he forced me into the room. The fact that I'd asked him to make turns in the car that he'd failed to make didn't help his cause any. Frankly, I don't think he cared whether I was his girl or not. He was ready and there was no turning back."

"He was ready?"

"He'd taken something that guaranteed it."

And David thought she'd find peace?

"I want to ask a personal question."

What did he consider all the questions he'd already asked?

"I might not answer it." She should be starting the

car. Taking Black Leather back to town. And painting trains on the wall of her son's room.

"You got pregnant with Josh after the rape. Were you able to have normal relations with Josh's father?"

If it was possible to have no intimacy when discussing sex with a sexy man, then Ellen supposed there was no intimacy in the question.

He was speaking as matter-of-factly as a doctor would have done.

Had done.

As Shawna had done.

She told herself that was why she answered him. "I did okay. I didn't respond as I had before, but I didn't fall apart, either."

"Did your husband's touch scare you?"

"No. But I didn't find…pleasure…in it."

"And now?"

"I haven't seen Aaron in a couple of years."

"I meant now, as in, with other men."

She'd run from his touch. "I think you know the answer to that."

"Is that why Shawna referred you to me? So that I could help you find pleasure in touch?"

She was hot all of a sudden. Too hot. But she didn't want to be so obvious as to roll down the window. To be anything other than cool and composed and fine.

She already had one episode of crazy to eradicate.

"She said you've helped victims of domestic violence."

"I knew what I was dealing with."

"She thought the noninvasive touch might help."

"It probably will if we're working together honestly."

Ellen was filled with conflicting emotions. But still

sitting here. Still not putting the car in gear and driving away. "I told Shawna the only way I'd agree to meet with you was if she didn't tell you why."

His nod was slow. Easy. "I know. She told me." Those warm brown eyes of his...they captivated her. There was no judgment there. No pity, either.

"I'd like to help."

She wasn't surprised. And she was scared to death to let him. Scared beyond the possible negative reactions his professional touch might raise in her. Her emotions were more intense around this man. All of them. As though she was a little less in control.

Which seemed dangerous.

"Give me one more try," he said. "I have an idea and if it doesn't work, we shake hands and part ways."

"What's your idea?"

"You seemed interested in my bike."

"It's hard to ignore."

"I'd like to take you for a ride."

That sounded personal. Like a date or something. No way. Uh-uh.

Yet...his motorcycle. It intrigued her.

"How would that help?"

"It's not a new idea," he said. "The practice was suggested by a therapist I worked with in Florida and I have had some success with it. When you're on my bike you have to be close to me, touch me, but you don't have to face me. My hands are occupied at all times. And my safety would also be at risk if I did anything untoward."

"You could take me anywhere you wanted to go. Stop the bike and turn around and—"

"Not if we call Sheriff Richards and have him ride along with us."

She couldn't believe she was listening to this. That she was still sitting here. But she wanted to be normal, right? Prided herself on being as capable as any other woman her age.

And what woman with blood in her veins wouldn't jump at the chance to go for a ride on the back of Black Leather's bike? Ellen might be a bit uptight, but she wasn't dead. Or blind.

"Your natural inclination is to resist other people touching you," he said. "So we put you in control. And hopefully, after a bit, you begin to trust me enough to move on to more traditional therapy."

She didn't hate the idea. Except…

"I don't— Everyone in town…they think I'm… They don't know I'm still struggling. I don't want them to know. Because mostly I'm fine. And if they knew…"

The way they had treated her following the rape… They made her feel as much a victim as the bastard who had raped her—although in a completely different way. The coddling made her feel weak. Incapable.

"So what are you saying?"

"If…we…do…this…I don't want you to call Sheriff Richards."

She was considering the idea. Excitement and fear collided inside her, making her wish she hadn't eaten breakfast.

There was something about this man. Something different. And dangerous.

And yet…she felt safe with him. As long as…

Shawna had done background checks. He had a great

reputation. This is what he did for a living. And he was really successful at it.

"You call the shots, Ellen. If you don't want me to call the sheriff, we won't. You tell me where to drive, that's where I drive. You want to stop, come back, we come back. You want to carry pepper spray, you carry pepper spray…"

Ellen stared at him. Not at the ugly door in front of them. At him. This rogue of a man with his long hair and black leather. He knew she felt safe as long as she was in control.

And he was handing over control.

"When?" The word, struggling past the dryness in her throat, made her cough.

"Tomorrow morning?"

Because he didn't want to give her time to chicken out? To rethink?

He didn't know her very well. When Ellen said she would do something, she did it.

But she hadn't said she was going to do this.

"I have church."

"Tomorrow afternoon then?"

With Josh gone, she had the whole day spread before her. And if she didn't have anything to do, her mother and David would expect her to spend the day with them. They would want her to.

"I'll meet you in the Walmart parking lot." The parking lot where her car had sat, out of gas, all those years ago. "And we head away from town."

She would have her cell phone. The man had credentials. He'd been referred to her by a medical professional. If she was going to be normal, she had to trust.

"You got it."

Yeah, she probably did have *it*. She only wished she knew what *it* was.

And, more importantly, she wished she knew if there was a cure.

AFTER HIS TWO-O'CLOCK appointment, Jay returned to Shelter Valley and spent the afternoon at Montford University Library, going through microfiche and computer files of yearbooks, newspaper and magazine articles, newsletters—church, school and community—anything he could find where a former occupant of Shelter Valley might have been mentioned.

He skimmed. Read. And made copies, too.

"Anything I can help you with?" The middle-aged librarian stood over his shoulder. If Jay wasn't mistaken, the man had read everything on the screen he was perusing.

"No, I've got what I need, thanks."

"You interested in knives?" A Damascus and Pearl D/A filled the screen. With its jagged and multifaceted blade, the thing looked lethal just sitting on the page. It also looked like something a dangerous biker dude might own. Jay had never seen one in real life. And had no need to, either.

"I'm interested in the knife show," Jay said, clicking the back button to show the previous page of the article. Then he clicked forward to the page following the picture. It showed a shot of the crowd attending.

Jay was currently focused on articles about functions of interest to guys. The knife show had been in Tucson the year before he was born. Maybe his mother had attended with his father. Maybe there had been mention of a name, a caption on a photo, anything that would resonate when he happened upon it.

"Well, if there's anything I can help you with, let me know," the man said. He stepped back, but he stayed in the vicinity, and Jay figured he'd be reporting to the local sheriff's office.

Just before five o'clock he had one of those moments that made months of research worth every second. In a newspaper article about a men's doubles tennis match between Montford and the University of Arizona in Tucson in May of 1978, there was a crowd shot. It captured a woman—the expression on her face was priceless, as though she was entranced. The woman was Tammy Walton.

To the man who had known his mother only through a few pictures, the clipping was priceless—a new link to her.

But to the investigator, the picture mattered for an entirely different reason. There was also a man in the picture. Behind his mother. The man had his arm around her and was leaning into her in a way that made it obvious they were close. Very close.

The man's face was only partially displayed and he was not named.

But unless Jay had lost the instincts that had seen him through more than ten years of successful cold case investigation, he was looking at Jay Billingsley, Sr. The man who had fathered him.

CHAPTER EIGHT

IT WAS HOT AS HELL OUTSIDE by noon on Sunday. But Jay changed into a pair of jeans without complaint. The white T-shirt—the kind most men wore under dress shirts—and black leather vest followed. Not usual work attire, but then not much about Jay's life had ever been normal.

He spotted Ellen's Ford Escape the second she pulled into the parking lot five minutes before their appointed meeting time. He'd already been waiting fifteen minutes. He wasn't giving her the chance to claim she'd shown up and he hadn't been there. Nor did he want to take the chance that she'd get scared and take off if she had to wait on him. He didn't want her to talk herself out of the advisability of his brand of healing.

He would be fine having her talk herself out of this if she was able to get healing elsewhere. But Shawna had led him to believe that he could be Ellen's last hope.

Sitting on his bike, he waited for her to park and approach.

She wore jeans and a T-shirt, too.

"I was kind of hoping you weren't going to show."

"I had a hunch. This is for you," he said, staying seated while he handed her the helmet he'd pulled from his trunk.

"You don't have one."

"I ride at my own risk. You don't."

Taking the helmet, she studied it for a second and then put it on, working the strap latch. With anyone else, he'd have offered to help.

"Ready?" he asked as soon as she'd secured her head gear. He didn't want to risk saying something that spooked her—or give her any excuses to end the session.

Ellen nodded, but she was frowning.

"You're going to have to come closer if you intend to ride on the same bike I'm on," he said. "I've got it steady. Put your foot here—" he pointed "—and hop on."

It took almost a full minute, but she managed to mount without coming into contact with his body.

"Push the button on the side of your helmet," he told her, turning his head so she could hear him. At the same time, he secured the wireless headset he'd also pulled out of his trunk.

"Can you hear me now?"

"Yes."

He heard her clearly.

"Anytime you need anything—to stop, turn around, anything—you let me know. There's a mic in your chin piece. If you start to get upset, say so."

"Okay."

He gave her some brief instructions about moving with him, leaning and not leaning, general principals of keeping the bike balanced.

"Where do I put my hands?"

"On me," he said, staring straight ahead. "That's the point of this exercise."

"I know that. Where on you?" It sounded as though she was gritting her teeth.

"Your choice. You're the boss. For this exercise, my body represents your safety. It is fully at your disposal—like a tornado shelter in a storm or a fort during battle. Trust it."

"What about you?"

"What about me?"

"Who keeps you safe? I could do something nuts. Like panic and grab at you and—"

"Ellen. It's a bike ride. And you're a normal, rational woman seeking treatment for an ailment. If you start to panic, you'll let me know and we'll pull over."

"You didn't answer my question. Who keeps you safe?"

If it took ten tries on ten different days, he wasn't giving up. "You do."

"You're that certain I'm going to be okay? You're willing to risk your life with me back here?"

"Yes."

"Okay then. Let's go before someone sees me and we end up with a caravan behind us."

Her touch wasn't much, a light resting of her fingers on the top of his shoulders. As soon as he felt it, he started the bike and put it in gear.

They'd been riding about ten minutes at a slow enough speed that she could have maintained balance without holding on. He wasn't going to keep her out long this first run. And he wasn't going to challenge her much, either. This exercise had to be a success for her or there wouldn't be a second chance.

He hadn't heard a sound from her. "How are you doing?" he asked.

"Fine."

"What do you think of motorcycles now?"

"That I might look into buying one."

"Pretty cool, huh?"

"Yeah. Just too loud."

"It's a Harley. It's supposed to be loud."

"Can it go any faster?"

"Of course."

"Now?"

"You sure you're ready?"

"I'm slightly nuts in my bad moments, Jay, but I'm not an old grandma who has to be coddled at every turn."

Her voice came through with a strength, a clarity, that spoke as much as her words.

"I don't want to push and end up with you running off again."

"I can hardly do that while we're moving and I thought the purpose of this exercise was to force me to associate touching your body with safety."

She was right, of course.

"Hold on." With a twist of his wrist he upped the throttle a notch. And received a slight increase of pressure on his shoulders.

"More," she said, five minutes down the road.

He'd told her she was boss. Jay let the bike have its way with the road a little more, and more again another mile farther. Ellen's inner thighs gripped him he took a curve. Her hands moved down to his waist, holding him securely.

He increased the speed once more and she laughed out loud.

And that's when the whole damn thing went bad. The

laugh, the touch of her hands, or maybe it was her thighs holding his. Whatever...Jay felt a nudge of sensation between his legs that started to grow.

ELLEN TURNED HER SUV onto the dirt path leading up the mountain, honking her horn as she did so. She'd told Joe she would stop by early in the week, but he probably hadn't been expecting her on Monday.

She needed to talk to someone, and it sure as hell couldn't be anyone in Shelter Valley.

He flashed a piece of cloth in front of the window as she pulled up so Ellen got out and made her way to her window seat.

"What happened?" The gruff voice didn't even say hello.

"What do you mean?"

"The look on your face when you walked up."

First him, then they could talk about her. "I wanted to make certain you're okay with the books and supplies. Do you need anything?" He couldn't give up on this.

"A pack of number two pencils."

"What about the other pencils I got you?"

"I keep breaking the damn lead on the mechanical ones. Never did see the likability in them. And ink means I can't erase."

He was taking notes?

"Of course," she said, trying to keep the excitement from her voice. "Is tomorrow soon enough?" She didn't want to push too hard.

"Next week is fine."

"Okay. Do you have anything for me to take to Dr. Sheffield?" Since the semester hadn't yet started, Phyllis wasn't in her office. But she'd asked about Joe so many times, Ellen knew she was itching to see something from him. Eager to help him if she could.

"School hasn't started yet."

"You aren't attending class, either. You're enrolled, but until you come down to class, she's creating a separate syllabus for you."

"I didn't realize I was causing trouble. I thought…"

"You aren't causing trouble, Joe." Ellen stared out at the dirt and trees between her and the path that led down the mountain to civilization. "Phyllis, Dr. Sheffield, has been after me for a couple of years to talk you into studying with her."

"Why?"

Ellen didn't usually talk to Joe about people in the valley. And certainly didn't want to leave him with the uncomfortable belief they were all talking about him. But maybe it was time for the old man to face some things, too. Maybe it was time to push a little.

Pushing a little was supposed to help her, so…

"The sheriff talked to her about you. After you helped him catch his dad's killer, he wanted to do what he could for you."

"She's a teacher. And I don't need help. Not much, anyway."

She knew Joe appreciated the groceries. Before the sheriff and Ellen had been making their treks up the hill, the man had hiked the many miles to town once a month to buy what would fit in the rudimentary cart he'd made.

Ellen had no idea how the man handled his banking. Joe paid her in cash for everything she brought.

"Phyllis is also a certified psychologist."

"I'm being poked at by a shrink."

"No! You're taking a psychology class. I'd like you to think about an English class, too. A friend of Phyllis's teaches several literature classes that I think you'd like."

"One thing at a time, young lady. Take this down to Dr. Sheffield. She might change her mind about this whole remote teaching thing."

Hearing the rustle of something sliding against the sill, Ellen reached behind herself to grab it. Joe had given her one of the spiral bound notebooks. Every single page was filled, both sides, from top to bottom with precise, neat handwriting.

Her plan was working. Joe needed more than his mountain could give him. More than anything, Ellen wanted to help the man find a way out of his prison. It was as though by helping Joe heal, she was also healing herself. If she could guide him to freedom, she was also setting herself free.

The past could only hold them hostage if they let it.

"Can I talk to you?" She'd thought about this a hundred times during the night.

"Depends."

"On what?"

"I belong here."

"Okay."

"Don't be thinking you're going to change that."

"That's not what I want to talk to you about."

"Then talk."

"I went on a motorcycle ride yesterday. And another one today."

"Didn't know you had one."

"I don't. I'd never been on one before."

"You were with someone else."

"Yeah."

"A man."

"Yeah."

"A date?"

"No! It was nothing like that."

"Too bad."

"He's a therapist. My therapist. The rides are part of my treatment."

"Don't fall for that, Ellen. You call someone. This morning. Before you get to town. Let them know about this guy. No therapist takes a beautiful young woman on a motorcycle ride."

"He works with Shawna. She referred him to me."

"She check his credentials?"

"Of course. He works with some of my people at Big Spirits, too. Remember Hugh? I told you about him."

"The cantankerous one. Won't leave his room until his kids visit and they won't because he was a controlling bastard their entire lives."

"That's their story." Ellen couldn't quite connect the hurting old man with tears in his eyes to the character Hugh's son had tried to depict. She suspected that the son was describing himself and wasn't going to be dictated to by his father who no longer had anything to contribute to his life—his son's words.

"Anyway," Ellen said slowly, "Hugh was so stiff from lack of exercise that he couldn't get himself to the bathroom last week. Jay had him walking within a couple of days. Hugh does whatever Jay tells him to do."

And she knew that Jay had stopped in to say hello to Hugh every single day. Including Sunday.

Jay hadn't mentioned the visits to her.

"Don't you be doing whatever he says. Motorcycle rides? How did he justify that one?"

"The idea is to put me in a situation where I have to touch someone to stay safe. But the experience has to be a good one so that I will associate the touch not only with safety, but also with pleasure."

Ellen relaxed when Joe remained silent. If he'd found no potential validity in the exercise, he would have blurted his concern without taking time for a breath.

That was Joe. Her watchdog. And hopefully she was the chain that could pull him out of seclusion and into the life he'd let go. He was alive. And deserved to live.

"How'd they go?"

"I loved the rides. They reminded me of a time when I was a kid and Dad was still home, in love with Mom. Shelley and Rebecca had been born, but we didn't have Tim yet. We all went to an amusement park and my father took me on this swing ride. My sisters stayed with Mom—they weren't tall enough. It was just me and my dad and it was the greatest thing I'd ever done. I felt wild and free and special and like I could do anything in the world. Like the world was perfect. I've never forgotten."

She was talking to the trees. Watching a mental movie. And smiling.

"Did you touch him?"

"Yeah, to hold on."

"And?"

"It was a little awkward. I mean, he's like a doctor to me and I hardly know him. But otherwise, no problem. I was in control. So that doesn't really mean anything, does it?"

"Therapy usually works in stages. I read about that."

In a Psychology 101 textbook? Or was Joe reading the other books Phyllis had sent? Ellen hadn't looked through the packet she'd delivered.

"He wants me to ride with him again. Until I don't feel any awkwardness at all."

"How does he look at you?"

"I don't really know."

But she thought she had noticed something when Jay got off the bike yesterday. Then he'd turned, occupied by storing their gear. She hadn't looked in that direction again, either.

"Did he come on to you? Ask you to his place?"

"I told you, it's not like that."

"You're sure?"

"About that? Yes."

"I don't like it."

"I'm not sure I do, either." Which was why she was talking to Joe. She certainly couldn't talk to her mother or anyone else in Shelter Valley. They would keep her under lock and key until they booted Jay out of town.

"I worry about you living alone every single day."

"I have Josh. Most of the time."

"A young child is no protection."

"I have a gun. Took self-defense. Carry pepper spray. You know that."

"And I know that you are a woman and a man's a man and one is genetically stronger than the other."

She hated when he talked this way. But she knew that if he was ever going to accept the world, ever rejoin society, he had to see that not every woman was in imminent danger of attack.

"There are ways to take someone down regardless

of physical strength." She knew them, and would use them if she had to.

"And when you're in bed at night, asleep, what then? What if you're taken by surprise before you have a chance to think of your techniques? You need a man in your house, protecting you."

"I want to marry and have a partner and…maybe even more children," Ellen said quietly. "But I do not need a man for protection."

"You need this therapy."

"I think so, too."

"You've told me about it. Now I'll worry. Keep me informed. Okay?"

"Yeah. And Joe?"

"What?"

"Thank you."

"Next time the sheriff's up this way I'm telling him about what you're doing with this guy."

She'd figured he would. And was glad for the protection. Even if she didn't need it.

CHAPTER NINE

JAY RECOGNIZED THE NUMBER on his phone Monday evening and answered immediately.

"Yeah."

"Jay, I haven't heard from you," Kelsey said.

He hadn't heard from her once in the twelve years his son had been alive—not even a birth announcement— and now all of a sudden there was a rush? "I know."

"You're not running out on us, Jay. Not again."

"I didn't run out on anyone before," he reminded her. He'd been the one left in the cold. Not one of the families who had opened their homes to him had had any qualms about letting him take the fall for them.

"You know what I mean."

No, he really didn't.

"You turned traitor. You're the one who made the call that sent you to prison. You did it to yourself and had no right taking everyone else down with you."

Yes, because saving a drugged girl from life-altering devastation was not the right thing to do.

"Was there a point to this call, Kelsey? I'm in Arizona. I told you I would be in touch soon and I will be."

"Cole cut school twice last week. He's back on pot. I'm certain of it."

Maybe if they didn't give the kid enough money to

buy the stuff, or maybe monitored his friends a little better, they wouldn't have this problem. But what did he know? He had no skills with this parenting thing.

"You said he was being tested regularly."

"He is."

"And?"

"The last two tests were clean, but after each test he's had this smirk on his face—the one that tells me he's up to something. I think he's found a way to manipulate his drug tests."

"You sure you aren't paranoid because you know what you got away with when you were growing up?" Jay couldn't resist the taunt. It helped take away the sting of concern for the son he'd never met. Despite all they'd done, Kelsey and her crowd had all turned out all right.

"I'm sure, Jay. None of us ever ended up in jail."

No, but not because they hadn't committed the crimes that would have put them there.

"You have to do something. Cole's out of control and we can't handle him anymore."

"I have some things to clear up," he said. "I told you I'd be in touch and I will be."

"When?"

"Soon."

"*Soon* is not good enough."

He wasn't sure he was going to be good enough, either. Hell, the last thing a troubled kid needed was a guy who had no clue what to do with him. If Cole was already riding on the edge, he couldn't afford a parental screwup. He couldn't afford to trust—or need—a guy who wasn't capable of being around for the long haul.

A guy who made a habit of moving rather than dealing with women who wanted more from him than sex.

Jay could tell Kelsey that. He could say no. Tell her to find someone else to help her kid.

If he were some other guy, maybe he could. But whether he was father material or not, Cole was his son.

"Soon is going to have to be good enough," he finally said. "It's all I've got."

JAY TOOK ELLEN OUT AGAIN on Tuesday. During the early-morning hours at her request. Early morning was good for him. He had things to think about as he rode. He focused on upcoming appointments, clients at Big Spirits and, when that wasn't enough to distract him from an awareness of the female body behind him, he thought about his father. He'd been searching for a week—perusing every document he could find—and he was no closer to locating the bastard than he'd been before he started looking.

If he didn't turn up some clue soon, he was going to have to ask Sheriff Richards for help. Though Jay hated to ask anyone in this town for anything, he needed more official resources and his access to them was in Miami.

He thought about his son, too—about the most recent call from Kelsey. Jay knew nothing about kids, living with them or raising them. He had no idea what she thought he could do to help.

Leaning to the left, he rounded a corner, comfortable with the powerful machine between his legs. He and the bike were one. Part of one body.

And thinking of bodies...

Ellen's hands were on his shoulders. Their third time out and her touch was still tentative.

She was enjoying the motorcycle, and, he hoped, learning to trust him so that they could move to the next stage of therapy—light massage. On top of her clothes.

"Can we stop a second, I'm getting a call." Ellen's voice came through the buds in his ears.

Pulling over to the side of the road, Jay guided the bike with his feet until they were far enough onto the shoulder to be safe.

Ellen shifted behind him. "It was my mother."

He couldn't miss the displeasure in her voice.

"I have to call her."

Jay pulled the buds out of his ears when they crackled with Ellen's movement as she removed her head gear. She got off the bike and he turned to watch her.

She pushed one button and paced while she held the smartphone to her ear.

"Mom?"

That was it, nothing else for what seemed an inordinately long time. He tried not to listen when Ellen eventually spoke.

"Yes, Beth was right. I'm riding on his motorcycle."

Beth? As in the sheriff's wife? Jay wiped at the chrome on his handlebars with his thumb.

"It's not like that, Mom."

Another silence.

"Mom, don't do this to me." Her voice was firm. "Yes."

More silence.

"Because I didn't want you to do exactly what you're doing. I made a decision. An educated decision."

Ellen paced in front of the bike. Then around it. She didn't look at Jay, but she didn't stray far, either.

"I know. But you have to trust my judgment. I'm a grown woman."

He'd had a lot of attractive clients. He'd never had trouble maintaining the walls between the therapist and the man. What was it about this woman that raised these uncomfortable feelings?

"Not anymore, I'm not. Besides, it's therapy. He's reporting to Shawna."

She was so damned beautiful and seemed completely unaware of that fact. Which had to worry her mother.

Beautiful women didn't usually get their hooks into him. So why did this one seem to be doing so?

Was it the town? The loving environment that was so foreign to him? Was it the knowledge of Cole? The possibility of a family on the horizon?

"I have to go. I had Jay pull over when my phone rang. I didn't want you to worry."

He tinkered with the key in the ignition, the back of his neck burning as her voice grew closer behind him.

"I know. But you undermine me when you don't trust me."

Ellen had her head on straight. Jay had already figured that out.

"I know," she said. "I love you, too."

He heard the phone click closed seconds before the bike took her weight. Securing his earbuds, Jay didn't turn around as Ellen fidgeted then said, "I'm ready."

"Everything okay?" he asked as he rolled the bike toward the road, checking for oncoming traffic.

"Yeah."

He didn't pursue the subject further. He had to trust that she knew the situation well enough to know.

"SO WHAT IS IT THAT you have to tell me?" Ellen stood in her mother's kitchen that afternoon, after work. She was still holding on to the joy of her day, reluctant to discuss anything that would crush it.

The residents at the center had been in particularly high spirits as they'd played bingo for brownies. And Hugh had joined them. For the first time since he'd moved in.

He'd won a brownie.

And, at one point, had laughed out loud.

"You want some juice?" Martha pulled a jar of pineapple juice from the refrigerator. A component of the diet she'd been on since shortly after Ellen's father left.

"No, thanks."

Wearing jean shorts and a T-shirt, Martha had come from the production room at Montford where she was now production manager of the university television station. Her mother had lost weight over the past seven years and looked as good as any of the students she helped.

"Hard to believe Josh has been gone only eight days."

"I know."

"Have you talked to him today?"

"Yeah, this morning. They were leaving for a trip to Boulder—going to a ski resort."

"What's a five-year-old boy going to do in a ski resort in the middle of summer?"

"I intended to ask Aaron that question, but Josh said Daddy and Jaime were in the bathroom getting ready. He was playing a video game."

"It better not be any of those violent things. You don't think Aaron would let him do that, do you?"

"Aaron is as determined as we are to see that Josh grows up without violence," she said. "He was playing some racing game with one of the educational characters he and I watch together."

Ellen didn't have nearly as much faith in her ex-husband as she once had, but there were some things that didn't change. She hoped.

"Still, I'll feel better when we have him back," Martha said, leaning against the counter.

The way her mother was looking at her, with the worried frown that she was trying to force into a smile, put Ellen off her mark. She knew the look from those hellish months following the attack. If not for Martha's watchful care, Ellen might not have made it through.

Her mother and David had saved her life. They loved her more than anyone possibly could.

"Tell me what you found out about Jay," Ellen said.

Martha had tried to tell her this morning during the ride, but Ellen had cut her off. She couldn't be in the man's company while listening to gossip about him.

She would rather not listen to it at all.

"He has a ponytail for heaven's sake, El. What kind of man wears a ponytail? Except one who's thwarting convention? One who wants people to know that he won't conform?"

"It's a ponytail, Mom. Maybe he's an artistic sort. Or has an aversion to scissors near his head. This isn't like you to be so petty."

"It's not just the ponytail."

"I didn't think so."

"I shouldn't be saying anything." Martha's voice had the tone the heroines used when about to say something negative about someone. Ellen's stomach knotted. The ladies meant well. The information they passed on was always true. And they passed it on only when they were attempting to help or protect someone they cared about.

Still…

"Greg talked to him, as you know."

Yeah, and he'd found out that Jay was a therapeutic massage therapist as he'd claimed. One with national certification by the medical board, and with a host of past clients who sang his praises.

"He has no intention of sticking around, Ellen. He told Greg that point-blank. Which means that if you get involved with him, you're going to get hurt."

"I'm not getting involved with him and have no intention of doing so."

"He's shunned every one of our attempts to get to know him better, every invitation. It's like he's hiding."

"He's a loner, Mom. It doesn't mean anything."

"Greg mentioned something to Beth the other day that she should never have repeated. But when she saw you on that man's motorcycle, she thought she had to warn me so I could make certain that you don't get hurt."

Ellen took a deep breath. "Mom, you can't protect me from ever being hurt again. Pain is a part of life. You—and all of the others—have to let me live or I might as well have not survived—"

"Don't." Martha held up a hand. "Don't ever say that."

Tightening her lips around her response, Ellen nodded.

"You're right," Martha said.

Ellen sank into a chair at the table that predated her. She could remember spilling her milk one night when her parents had invited Will and Becca over for dinner. The milk had seeped into the crack between the leaves and splashed on everyone's feet.

"We do have to let you live. My friends and I, the sheriff, David—we are overprotective. I know that. I see us doing it and every time I promise myself we'll stop. But we don't."

Martha reached over and ran her hand through Ellen's hair, separating the strands with her fingers as she'd done so many times over the years. When Ellen had the flu and the chicken pox. The time she'd lost her bid for class president in high school.

When she had confessed she was divorcing Aaron.

"You're a remarkable young woman, Ellen. Sweet and kind and nurturing, and you didn't deserve—" Martha met Ellen's gaze. "I'm a mom. My job is to protect. And you…you've always been the child who I could most relate to. The one I most understand. When you got…hurt…"

"I know, Mom," Ellen said, feeling tears build. She wasn't going to cry. But she couldn't back down, either. "I'm a mom, too. I get it." She paused. "But I can't allow it. I have to make my own decisions or I'll become more and more dependent. More and more powerless."

"He's a private investigator, Ellen," Martha said. "He works on cold cases—disappearances and murders. He's looking for something here in Shelter Valley. And he has a way of getting information that no one else can find. He has underhanded methods. Uses people and…"

Martha continued, giving details of cases as Beth had repeated them to her. Ellen listened, but she was thinking about something Hugh had said. She'd asked him how things were going with his therapist. It was outside the bounds of her job—regardless of whether she knew the therapist or not.

"He wanted my help. First time anyone has needed me for any damned thing since I got old, and I couldn't help him," Hugh had said.

"Wanted your help?" Ellen had asked, sliding a marker on the B-14 square on Hugh's bingo card.

"I've been 'round these parts since before grass got here. Didn't think there was anyone here I hadn't at least heard of. But I don't know the name of the guy he's lookin' for."

Jay was looking for a guy.

He was a private investigator and had never said a word to her about that. What was he investigating? For whom?

He really was a therapist. But that didn't preclude him from using the people of Shelter Valley to serve his own purposes. People like Hugh.

And her? Was he using her to get something on someone in Shelter Valley?

Ellen couldn't stand duplicity. Not on any level. And she also couldn't stand the fact that she'd been starting to like him. To hope that he could help her.

She'd actually felt an inkling of attraction.

She'd given him her deepest, darkest confidences.

All the while he'd been keeping secrets.

She was done with the man. Period.

CHAPTER TEN

JAY WAS GETTING READY to leave the house Wednesday morning to pick up Ellen for her daily ride when she called to cancel.

"Is everything okay?" he asked, wishing he was a bit more surprised—and less disappointed—to discover that her mother's obvious disapproval of their endeavors was stronger than Ellen's belief he could help her.

"No, everything isn't okay."

Ellen was more than a job to him. She'd been presented to him for a reason—he had to help her.

"What's wrong?"

"You're a private investigator."

It wasn't a secret. It also wasn't common knowledge. But then, this was Shelter Valley. News that never surfaced in Miami wore traveling shoes around here.

"In my spare time and usually volunteer."

"Are you working on a case now?"

"Yes."

"Why didn't you say so?"

"It has nothing to do with you."

"Does it have to do with Hugh?"

"No."

"But you tried to use him as a source."

"I spontaneously asked him a question. It wasn't premeditated. I'll explain if you give me a chance."

"You don't have to explain yourself, Jay. I just think it's best if we end our sessions."

"I *want* to explain myself. And I'm not giving up on you, either," he said. "We're making progress. You aren't physically afraid of me."

"I don't deny that."

"Then don't give up, Ellen. At least not until after you've heard what I have to say."

"This investigation you're working on…is it why you're in town?"

"Yes."

"So working with me, with the rest of your massage clients…we're a cover and—"

"Whoa!" Jay responded to the accusation in her tone. An accusation that, if he were to examine it, went beyond the bounds of therapist and client. "Absolutely not. I'm a massage therapist first and foremost. I do not give any less attention or commitment to my work because I also investigate. That work…it started out as a onetime thing. A personal quest. Turns out I'm good at it. So I help out when I can. That's all."

"You aren't working for, like, the CIA or some other branch of the government? You aren't here on some official business?"

"Of course not."

"How do I know that? If you are working for someone, you'd lie to me. You'd have to as part of your job."

"How about you give me a chance to explain?" He was going way beyond professional obligation for this woman. "I'll show you what I'm working on, explain the case to you. Then you decide if you still trust me."

"When?"

"Tonight?"

"What time?"

"Seven."

"Where?"

"If you want to see my files, you'll need to come to my place. If you only want to hear what I have to say, we can meet anywhere you'd like."

"What I'd like is for you to meet me at my mother's. I want her to meet you. Then we'll go to your house to see these files of yours."

"Are you sure she'll be okay with that?"

"I'm sure she won't be, but she'll agree, all the same."

In his opinion, Ellen's mother—and everyone else in Shelter Valley, as far as he could tell—as well-intentioned as she was, actually was part of Ellen's problem. She was never going to feel safe if people made her feel as though she had to be watched over. Protected, as though she couldn't protect herself.

He asked where her mother lived. Took down the address. "I'll be there."

And for your sake, Ellen, I'll even put on the one nice shirt and pair of pants I own.

ELLEN, MARTHA AND DAVID were in the kitchen when they heard the bike. Ellen remained with her mother while David answered the door, but she could hear what was being said.

"Good evening, son. Come in." David used his most patriarchal voice. One his parishioners rarely heard.

"I'm Jay Billingsley, Pastor Marks." Jay's voice sounded as easy as always. "You stopped by to invite me to church, but I wasn't home. You left a card."

"Call me David. I also called to invite you to a men's group. You declined."

"I'm not much of a church man."

Ellen exchanged a glance with her mother. She smiled. Her mother did not.

"While I am a servant of God, I am also a man and I will not stand calmly by and allow anyone to hurt my family."

"You have an entire town backing you up, sir."

"Then we understand each other. Fine."

Hearing the footsteps approaching, Ellen took a couple of steps forward. She didn't quite meet Jay's eye when he entered the room, but she did note the unfazed expression on his face.

Then her thoughts snagged on the man's attire. Instead of jeans, he wore a pair of expensive-looking black pants with a white, long-sleeved shirt.

And dress shoes.

Wow. If she were sexually healthy, she would be drooling.

"Mom, this is Jay," she said quickly to cover her momentary loss of focus. "Jay, this is my mom."

He put his hand out. "Hello, Mrs. Marks. Nice to meet you."

Ellen held her breath, afraid her mother was going to reject Jay's overture.

Martha's hand moved slowly, but she did shake his hand.

"You know we're watching you," she said.

"Yes, ma'am."

"And you don't care?"

"I have nothing to hide."

"We might be small-town folks, but we aren't fools."

"I realize that, ma'am."

"Ellen…she's special—"

"Mom," Ellen said, with a warning tone in her voice.

"I'm trying to help Ellen overcome an issue that has arisen as a result of her attack. That's all." Jay's voice was so certain, so calm. Confident.

Ellen wished he hadn't lied to her. Even if only by omission.

"I know. She told us Shawna referred her to you."

"Ellen is struggling with trust issues. Your lack of trust in me isn't supporting her in any way."

"Okay, I'm right here, folks. And don't much like being talked about as if I wasn't." Ellen did appreciate that Jay spoke about her frankly without revealing any personal details.

"Oh, baby, you're right. I'm sorry," Martha said. Jay and David remained silent, squared off on either side of Ellen and her mom.

"Fine, now that you've all met, let's go." Ellen nodded toward Jay then led the way to the front door.

"You're going to his place now?" Martha asked as David planted himself between them and the door.

"Yes."

"If she doesn't hear from you within the hour, the sheriff and I will be at his house," David said.

Ellen smiled. For some reason David's protectiveness right now didn't cramp her. Or make her feel weak. "Thank you." She leaned forward to kiss her stepfather on the cheek, then left.

"I'll follow you," she said to Jay, then climbed behind the wheel of her car before he could argue with her.

But she knew he wouldn't have. He didn't seem to have a problem with her giving all the orders.

Of course, his calm acceptance could be a facade. And Ellen could be making the second biggest mistake of her life.

JAY KNEW THE SECOND ELLEN was inside his front door that he'd made a mistake—crossed a line he shouldn't have. He'd never had a client in his home before.

Now he had a choice to make. Tell her to leave. Or continue to embed himself in a situation that could become professionally unethical.

There was no law that said he couldn't be personally interested in one of his clients. And he really believed he could help Ellen.

"What is it you had to show me?" She stood in the foyer, unself-consciously attractive wearing khaki shorts, a black T-shirt and black flip-flops.

"Over here, on the table." And that easily his choice was made.

He wasn't going to tell her to leave.

He slid around to the far side of the oblong oak table as she approached. Her gaze was directed at the piles of file folders spread around the table.

"Have a seat." He took it as a good sign when she did so, then he pulled out a chair for himself.

When he'd blurted out his willingness to share his business with her, the idea had made sense. He'd seen it as his chance to maintain her as a client—to help her.

He hadn't considered how difficult it would be. Few people in Jay's post-prison life—aside from the detectives he'd worked with—knew of his past. Until this stint with Shawna, his massage therapist work had all been on a consultant basis. No one hired him full-time so there had been no background checks. And beyond work, no one got close enough to need to know.

The folder marked Photos was in front of him. He opened it and studied the grainy black-and-white image of his mother.

Regardless of his reservations, this was the right thing to do. He slid the photo toward Ellen.

"Who is she?" she asked after a minute.

"My mother."

EVEN THOUGH THE PICTURE was grainy, Ellen could see that the smiling woman had been beautiful. "She looks so happy."

"I'm fairly certain the man in that photo with her is my father."

"Where is he now?"

"That's what I'm trying to find out."

"The investigation you're working on is to find your own father?"

"He left a few weeks before she was killed." The twist of his lips reminded her of a similar one she'd seen—many times—on the faces of her siblings when her father was being discussed.

"Did he come back for you?"

"You're kidding, right?"

Jay slid a folder in front of her. "The night he took off, he left my mother a letter. They were married. Had a kid. And he leaves her a damned letter. She read it so many times, cried so many tears over it, it's hard to read, but there's enough of it there to make the message clear."

The folder contained a single sheet of notepaper encased in a protective plastic cover. Written in narrow script using dark ink, the letter was nearly illegible in places. But she could read enough to understand that someone signed away his parental rights to a baby, J. J. Billingsley. One phrase kept popping out at her: "I'm not fit to be a father."

Ellen couldn't make out the signature. It was in the middle of a fold and mostly torn away.

Her mind couldn't grasp that a parent would forfeit his child. She knew it happened—she was a social worker, she knew families broke down. But as a mother, loving her son as fiercely as she did, it was impossible to comprehend.

"So you've never heard from him? In all the years since?"

"Nope."

"What's his name?"

"Jay Billingsley, same as me. I was raised by my aunt—she was older than my mother by a decade—who, understandably, detested my father. One of the few pieces of information she shared with me was that I was named after him—at my mother's insistence. According to my aunt, my mother was besotted with the man to the point of losing all common sense. My aunt rarely spoke of my father. Rightly or wrongly, she blamed him for my mother's death."

Ellen reached for the next folder. "May I?"

Jay nodded, and she started to examine the evidence he'd compiled until he held up his phone.

"You need to call your folks or we're going to have visitors."

Hard to believe almost an hour had passed. Grabbing her cell phone, Ellen called her mother, told her that she was fine, and that she'd call her when she arrived home.

"And, Mom, it might be a little while," she added as warning for her mother not to panic.

"You've got a lot of dead ends here," she said to Jay.

"He worked at a car dealership in Tucson—Dolby Dodge." He'd rolled his sleeves up and undid the top couple of buttons of his shirt. "I found a used Mustang there when I was sixteen, wanted to buy it. My aunt wouldn't sign for the car and forbade me from ever going back. When I pushed, she told me why."

Ellen tried to picture a sixteen-year-old Jay and failed.

"I've never heard of Dolby Dodge." Not that she was all that familiar with Tucson.

"It went out of business eleven years ago," Jay said with a sigh. "There's no record I can find of a Jay Billingsley, other than myself, ever having lived in Tucson during that period. I can't find a marriage license for my mother in Arizona, or any other state, either."

"You have her social security records." Ellen had glanced through them.

"I'm next of kin. And as you see, there's no record of a name change. The IRS reports no joint filings, either."

"So maybe they weren't married."

"My aunt sure thought they were—and I have my mother's wedding ring. At this point I have to consider that they might not have been. At least not legally."

"Is your aunt still alive?"

"No. She died from kidney failure fourteen years ago—during my first year of college."

Ellen couldn't imagine being so young and without family. Hell, she couldn't imagine being without family at any age.

"I've been alone in the world ever since."

So he'd never married. She'd wondered.

He picked up the photo he'd first shown her. "I have to find this man," he said, pointing to the guy who'd been standing next to Tammy. "Based on when the picture was taken, that has to be my father. She wouldn't have had time to end one relationship, start another and have a baby."

"Did you show the picture around Big Spirits?"

"I asked Hugh. He mentioned Dolby Dodge one day when he was talking about all of the cars he'd owned over the years. And yes, I showed him the photo."

"But he didn't remember anything about your father."

"No."

Sitting back, Ellen pondered his situation. "If your folks lived in Tucson, why are you looking for him in Shelter Valley?"

"When I was looking at colleges I wanted to apply to Montford. My aunt had heard that my father had moved to the Shelter Valley area and she refused to help pay for college if I applied here. That photo was taken at Montford. There's a connection here. I simply haven't found it yet."

"Why was your aunt so against you running into him?"

"I think she was afraid he'd do to me what he did to my mom—reel me in with promises to be a real father to me then abandon me. That would not have stopped me if I'd wanted to see the man. I didn't. Wherever he was, I wanted to stay as far away from that place as I could."

That, Ellen understood. She had no desire to be around her father ever again, either. A parent who couldn't be one was like a stomach that couldn't process food—unnatural, debilitating and terminally painful.

"So when you find him, what then? You move on?"

The expression on his face was odd. "I don't know." He flipped the edge of one of the folders. "I go where investigative cases take me, picking up massage work anytime I'm in one place for a period of time. And when I'm not investigating, I gravitate toward the beach. Mostly in the Miami area."

"How many cases do you do a year?" Not that it was any of her business. At all.

"Depends. One year I did six. Usually one or two."

"And you never looked for your father?"

"Nope."

"So why now?"

His glance was pointed as he assessed her, as though trying to make up his mind about something. "I got a call last month from a woman I slept with in college."

"That's an odd way of putting it."

"I'd say a woman I dated, but we didn't really date. We hung out in the same crowd. And we had sex."

"Did she have something to do with your father?"

"No, she told me I am one."

"What?" Ellen sat forward, her mind spinning over what she knew about him. His aunt had died fourteen years ago during his first year of college so that would make his child at least eleven. "You didn't know she'd had your child until a month ago?"

"That's right."

"How could that be?"

"I…left…college after my junior year, which was when Kelsey and I slept together. After that she married another guy in our crowd and passed off the kid as his."

"She didn't tell him that the child was yours?"

"I don't know if she did or not. He knows now. And I assume that he's known for some time based on what Kelsey has said."

"Is she still married to him?"

"Oh, yeah. The marriage isn't at risk. The kid is."

"At risk, how?"

"He's twelve years old and has already been arrested twice. For drug use and petty theft. That's why Kelsey called. She says Cole's problems are my fault and it's time I deal with them."

"How can they be your fault if you didn't raise the kid? And how are you supposed to deal with him?"

"I guess that's up to me."

"Where is he now?"

"Living with his mother and stepfather in Scottsdale."

So he was close. Scottsdale was an upscale town on the northeast side of Phoenix, less than an hour from Shelter Valley.

"Does he know you're his dad?" The social worker in her kicked into gear.

"Not yet."

"I'm assuming you've met him?"

"Not yet."

He'd known that he had a son for an entire month and he hadn't met him yet? Ellen would have caught the first flight to the boy's doorstep.

"Aren't you anxious to meet him? Even a little bit?"

"Sure, I want to meet him. Who wouldn't? But not until I'm prepared to take on an at-risk kid. He's already in trouble—and that's with the supervision of two parents. How am I, a single person, going to keep a better eye on him than they could? How can I trust myself to be able to be there for him long-term? Thus, my search for my father. I need to know why he left. And find out if I'm like him. Find out if he had wanderlust, too. If he discovered he couldn't coexist with family life. My lifestyle suits me. Maybe there's a reason for that.

"I have no family to offer a kid. Have no idea how to be a member of a family. There's no one to fall back on if we run into a problem. Until I have some kind of solid plan, it can't possibly be good to uproot the kid."

As a certified family counselor, she agreed with him there.

"You've obviously thought this through."

"I've thought of little else since Kelsey dropped her bomb on me."

It occurred to her he hadn't answered her other question. "So why does Kelsey think Cole's problems are your fault?"

"I'm surprised Greg hasn't already told you."

"What does the sheriff have to do with it?" Still trying to assimilate everything he'd shared, Ellen couldn't see how Greg fit.

"I spent eighteen months in prison for drug possession."

HE WAS WHAT HE WAS. And if the sheriff had told his wife about Jay's private investigating, it was only a matter of time before the drug bust came out, too.

To be fair, Greg seemed like an ethical man. And it was Jay's responsibility to tell Ellen the truth if he wanted her to trust him.

"I got in with a crowd of rich kids at the University of Arizona." Merely thinking about those days and the choices he'd made had him slouching in his chair. "We had all the drugs and alcohol we wanted and we partied hard. My aunt had just died, and I couldn't resist being welcomed into the group. These kids had families. Not just parents and siblings, but aunts and uncles and cousins. I could join in and forget for a while that I didn't have anyone. They invited me on a Christmas cruise to the Mediterranean, a ski trip to the Swiss Alps, weekend jaunts to Vail, a summer in the Bahamas.

"It was great until the night a couple of the guys thought they were entitled to drug a girl and rape her because she'd told one of them that she wouldn't sleep with him if he were the last guy alive. I called the cops.

"Problem was, we were all high on cocaine—had plenty of it in the house. Fortunately for them, they had their daddies to bail them out of jail and hire them top-notch attorneys. Me? I wasn't so fortunate and spent eighteen months behind bars as a result."

"And the girl? Did she know what you did for her?"

"I have no idea. I hadn't seen her before and haven't heard of her since. She wasn't raped that night. That's all I know."

"That's when you left college."

"Right."

"Kelsey was pregnant with Cole when you went to jail."

"That's what she says."

"Are you sure Cole's your son?"

"I have no reason to believe he isn't. It's easy enough to check these days, and Kelsey knows that. She knows I'm a private investigator. She's not going to lie to me about it."

"But you're going to have a blood test done, to be sure?"

"Of course. At some point. When the boy is ready."

When Jay was ready, was more like it. Whatever course of action he decided upon, he knew there would be no turning back. Yet he had no idea how to move forward.

It wasn't as though he would be able to ease into parenting, learning the easy stuff such as how to change a diaper and stick a bottle in the kid's mouth.

"I'd like to help." They were the last words he'd expected Ellen to say.

"Help how?"

"Let me ask around to see if anyone has heard of your father. Maybe show that picture. People trust me so they might tell me something they wouldn't share with a stranger. I mean, did you talk to Becca or Will Parsons? He's the president of Montford and she's the mayor."

In another town he might have gone to the college president or the mayor. In a metropolis used to accepting all kinds of people. In Shelter Valley he hadn't pushed that far yet—hadn't figured he'd get much cooperation. But if Ellen did the asking...

"I'll agree on one condition," he said.

"What?"

"That you come back to the clinic and try therapy again. We can go slowly. Light touch only. Fully clothed. When you need to stop, we stop."

"I liked the motorcycle riding better."

"We can do that, too. It might help to keep things from seeming too threatening to you."

She stared at his folders, but he had a feeling she didn't really see them.

"Okay," she said. "I'll try, but I'm making no promises."

"Understood."

"When should I come in?"

"Tomorrow morning too soon? You start work at nine, right? I can meet you at the clinic at eight."

"Fine." She was frowning, and stood to leave. She asked for a copy of the photo she'd be showing around town. He agreed to have it for her in the morning.

Then she left.

All in all, they'd done a good day's work.

CHAPTER ELEVEN

EVERY MUSCLE IN ELLEN'S body tightened the moment she entered Jay's clinic room. The space was too small, the walls too close. The table was too skinny and the mechanism for the headrest seemed vaguely sadistic. The lighting was too dim.

The entire space was open. Nowhere to hide.

She hated everything but the soft music playing.

"Here's the photo." Jay grabbed a manila folder from the counter to hand it to her.

Taking it, Ellen calmed herself. Right. She was in control here. Helping him. And allowing him to try to help her, too. He was Black Leather. Motorcycle Man.

He'd met her mother and given her nothing to complain about. Except the ponytail, of course.

What's he trying to say with that ponytail, El?

Strangely enough, rather than bringing her to her senses as her mother had hoped, the comment had only made Ellen smile.

"You ready to get started?" he asked.

Her mental smile faded. Along with the calm.

"Not really."

"You want to talk about it?"

"No." She wanted to be normal and able to get a massage. The heroines of Shelter Valley treated themselves to spa days in Phoenix. They went as a group.

She wanted to be normal and have a healthy spousal relationship.

But she didn't want to be touched.

"I'm going to leave the room for a couple of minutes. Take your time. Listen to the music. When you're ready, get up on the table, lie down on your stomach, with your forehead against this pad, and cover yourself with this sheet."

"I'm keeping my clothes on."

"Just as we discussed," he agreed. "And you'll be covered with a sheet."

She wouldn't be exposed. She'd be a shadow under a sheet.

Nodding, Ellen watched him go. And prayed that he wouldn't go too far. She didn't know how long she could hold out against the urge to run.

Afraid to be caught uncovered, she pushed her purse under a table in the corner and climbed onto the massage table, then arranged herself as he'd instructed. Through an opening in the headrest she could see the floor, but her features were protected from view.

She could cry and no one would know.

Reaching back to grab the sheet, she pulled it around herself and settled into position. She'd made it. Was fully covered. Not exposed.

The low lights were nice. Kept her hidden. And the music...if she concentrated on it, went where it wanted to take her, she could almost leave the room. She followed it to a field. The grass was long and soft and green. A slight breeze cooled the warmth emanating from the sun shining in the blue sky above. The music took her to a flower garden filled with deep red tulips, brightly colored marigolds and lilacs. They were in full bloom, and the air was filled with heady sweet scents....

The door opened and Ellen tensed.

Jay didn't speak as he entered. If not for the soft rustle of his steps against the linoleum, she wouldn't have known he was there.

The same as on the motorcycle. He was the driver and yet, remained...unobtrusive. He let her take her own journey on that bike. Let her touch or not touch as she saw fit. He followed every directive she'd given him.

He was there for her. To help her. She wanted help.

The sheet moved and she felt immediate panic.

He pulled the sheet up, covering her neck.

Okay. She was safe. She tried to focus on the music. Violins played. Flowers were there, in the periphery of her mind, but she couldn't access them.

What was going to happen next? Would she bolt? Would he tell her what he was going to do?

She was a freak—lying here on the verge of explosion.

The touch on her shoulder was light, a stroke. One, then another. One side, then the other. So soft that it seemed a flower caressed her. Not a human being. Not a man. Just a flower. Lightly brushing her shoulder.

She heard music. Not breathing. Saw a floor so dimly lit she couldn't make out the design in the tile. She saw shapes. Like clouds. Maybe soft white clouds in the blue sky above her flower garden.

She could almost smell the lavender. Or was it lilac? The roses were distinct. She could have orchids, too. It was her garden. Anything could grow there.

Strokes along her shoulders led naturally to strokes at her neck. And along her back. Ellen accepted them.

Became one with them. Gentle touches delivered peacefully in a perfect garden of peace.

The sound of footsteps was disturbing, but not upsetting. Abrasive to her lethargic state, but not alarming.

"I'm going to step outside." A low voice pulled her from her garden. "Take as long as you need. I'll meet you in the hallway."

They were done? That was it? She'd made it?

She waited a full minute after she heard the door close before she moved. Sliding off the table was easy. Focusing, finding the energy to walk, to pick up her purse was more difficult.

When she opened the door, the light in the hallway was almost blinding.

Jay stood there, his brown eyes focused solely on her, a crease in his brow. "You okay?"

"Yeah." She sort of smiled. "I think I am."

"Good." He walked with her. "If you have any residual effects, feel free to call."

"Residual effects?"

"If you get scared, start to feel uncomfortable thinking about the session. That sort of thing."

She hadn't considered that. "Okay."

"I'd like you to come back tomorrow," he said as they rounded the corner into the waiting room.

Several people filled the chairs lining two walls. Allison Everson—a girl Ellen had graduated from high school with who had married a boy from their class—was there with her two toddlers, both whining. Ellen also recognized an older guy who worked in the janitorial department at the university. She'd seen him there many times, although had never actually met him.

A woman she'd worked with once was engrossed in a magazine. And an older couple she knew from church were hunched over a clipboard apparently filling out a form. The anxiety she expected to feel at having so many familiar faces witness her conversation with her therapist never appeared.

"My recommendation would be daily sessions for a while," Jay said. "You did great today. The more often we repeat, the better chance we have of your psyche cooperating."

She felt more relaxed than she could remember being in…forever. "Okay." She smiled at Allison. They had lost touch after the rape. Ellen had lost touch with most all of the friends her age after the rape. No one had known how to treat her. And she hadn't known how to treat them.

"Same time in the morning?" Jay asked.

"Okay," she said again and, nodding at Natalie, the receptionist who knew to bill her insurance for the appointment, Ellen walked out into the warm Arizona sunshine.

JAY WAS SITTING AT A booth in the diner late Thursday morning when a tall, lean man with thick silver hair approached and asked if he could join him.

The tone of his voice, the set of his face commanded respect.

"Sure," Jay said, watching as the man slid onto the bench opposite him. This was no friendly, welcome-to-town visit. Jay knew that. But his curiosity won over his annoyance.

"I'm Will Parsons."

"Nice to meet you," Jay said, not bothering to put down his fork for a handshake.

Will studied him, and Jay returned the assessment.

"We'd like you to know that we appreciate your desire to help Ellen," Will said after a time.

Jay took another bite of the delicious ham and cheese omelet he'd ordered. Nancy placed a coffee cup in front of Will and filled it.

"We know you mean well. You just don't know her."

The cheese was cheddar, not American, not processed. And the ham cut in chunks, the way he preferred. The eggs were fluffy. Overall, a perfect breakfast.

"She's special, our Ellen. One of those rare individuals who truly puts others first. Thinks of others first. She's got a heart of gold, that girl."

Jay would rather get to know Ellen on his own, but refrained from saying so.

"Always offering a helping hand. Not only to her sisters and brother, her mother, the church, but to anyone and everyone who might need a little assistance."

He wondered how many people took advantage of that fact. Even in Shelter Valley.

"The thing is, she's learning to trust again. Any breach of that trust could set her back five years in her healing. I'm sure you can understand how even the thought of something like that happening to her, after all she's been through…"

Jay waited for Will to finish what he was saying.

"Bottom line is, we'd be extremely grateful if you'd stay away from her."

Fork hanging midair, Jay looked at the older man. How grateful were they prepared to be?

Not that it mattered to him. After three sessions, Ellen was making real progress. She smiled at him when she entered his clinic room. And chatted easily as she was leaving. He wasn't giving up on her.

Period.

"Also, I wanted to let you know that we'll find your father for you," Will said. "If he was ever in this area—and it appears from the university photo that he was—someone around here will know. Greg and I, Ben and Zack, Matt Sheffield, Sam Montford and all of the women, we'll canvas the entire town. We'll go through every photo album we have, every scrapbook— whatever it takes. We'll find him for you."

"If I leave Ellen alone." The implication was clear.

"I didn't say that."

Of course not.

"I'd appreciate the help, sir. I'm about to ask for the sheriff's assistance. While I'm confident that I'll find my father eventually, I don't have all the time in the world."

"Because of your son, Cole, right?"

Ellen had told his secrets. Or at least part of them. He shouldn't be disappointed.

He hadn't told her in confidence. Not explicitly. He'd allowed her to ask around about his father—giving implied permission to speak of his personal business.

He was disappointed anyway.

"Right. I have to make some decisions regarding his future."

"We'd like to help."

"I'd appreciate that."

"And you'll stay away from Ellen? We'll make certain that if she needs a massage therapist, she'll get one."

If she *needed* a therapist? Implying that the work Jay was doing might not really be necessary? That it was somehow up to them to determine what Ellen needed?

And if they decided that massage therapy might be good for Ellen, after all, then what? Would they find a nice safe woman to help her?

A woman wouldn't be nearly as effective as Jay was going to be. Not unless they wanted Ellen to feel safe only with a woman's touch. Her problem wasn't with women. A woman hadn't attacked her.

"I have a question," Jay said, placing his silverware in the middle of his half-empty plate before tossing his napkin on top.

"What's that?"

"Who's this *we* you keep referring to? Because I don't think Ellen is included in this request."

Without waiting for an answer, he stood, grabbed the bill and said, "You all, whoever you are, do Ellen a disservice even speaking with me like this. You belittle her, make her into something less than a fully competent human being capable of running her own life. If Ellen wants to stop seeing me, she'll tell me so. Until then, she is my client and I am her massage therapist."

With that, he turned his back on Montford University's president—and one of Ellen's mother's best friends—paid for his breakfast, then went back to work.

CHAPTER TWELVE

ELLEN LIKED VISITING the garden. She now understood why the heroines of Shelter Valley were so passionate about their spa days. Why the folks at Big Spirits praised Jay as if he were an angel sent from heaven.

She'd seen Shawna on Thursday and told her about the sessions with Jay. Her counselor had smiled, said she wasn't surprised and encouraged Ellen to continue.

But on Friday morning, lying on the table in the semidarkness, Ellen could hardly wait for the session to be finished.

"Relax." Jay spoke for the first time during the session.

"I'm trying." The padded metal dug into her chin.

"What's bothering you?"

"Nothing."

"Is my touch upsetting this morning?"

"No, not at all." It was the same as the day before. Flower strokes along her shoulders, neck and back.

But this morning the music didn't take her away.

He moved silently for another few minutes then she heard him walk toward the door. "I'll meet you outside."

Ellen waited about two seconds, long enough for the latch to click shut behind him, jumped down, grabbed her purse and followed him out.

"Can you come in tomorrow?" he asked.

"Yes."

"It's clearly time to ratchet things up a notch."

"Fine." She was committed and proving she could handle it.

"Fine?" He started down the hall and Ellen walked beside him.

"Yeah. But...do you have a couple of hours this afternoon?"

Frowning, he glanced over at her. "Sure. Why?"

"I—I'm not sure. I don't want to get your hopes up... but I think I found your father. Well, I didn't find him myself. Not really. I'm not sure quite how the chain went but someone who knew Sam Montford's wife, Cassie, knew of someone whose son played tennis for Montford in the day and... Anyway, Cassie says this couple knows who the guy in the photo is. They can meet with us this afternoon."

Jay stopped, turned, and the vulnerability in his gaze melted her from the inside out. "Did they say if he still lives around here?"

"I don't know. If they did, I didn't hear about it. And no one is likely to tell me if they do find your dad. Most of the folks around here are encouraging me to stay away from you. But Cassie..." Ellen tried to find the right words to describe Cassie. "She's different. She gets locked up inside, sometimes, too. Her house is full of TVs. I think she uses them to avoid having to think too much about the past. She's why I'm careful not to turn mine on unless I'm watching a specific show for a specific reason."

Ellen was talking too much. But she felt better than she had in years. And she really wanted this to be right for him. Jay had given her so much and she wanted to be able to help him, too. To give as much as she took.

"Anyway, Cassie called me to set up a meeting with you. She didn't say if the man in the picture would be there. We both thought it would be easier if you had someone to make the introductions. If you're okay with it, I'd love to go with you."

"I'm okay with that."

"Good. How about if I pick you up at three?"

"You think it would be better to arrive in your SUV rather than on my bike."

"I didn't say that."

He grinned. "You didn't have to." Then he sobered.

"What?" Ellen moved aside so the person who had exited a room across from them could get by.

"You do understand that, as much as I need to find my father, I have no feelings of affection for him, right?"

"You pretty much hate the guy," she translated. She'd been the last holdout with her own father. The last of her siblings to cling to faith in the man who had replaced them with new babies as if they were worn-out clothes rather than people.

"Close. Get rid of the *pretty much* and you're spot-on."

"I called my father after the...attack." Ellen heard herself say the words, as if from afar. She avoided talking about that time in her life with anyone but Shawna. She'd moved on. Didn't want anyone, including herself, to dwell on it.

She leaned against the wall and Jay stood in front of her, as though protecting her from anyone who might approach. She should have felt closed in, claustrophobic, trapped by his proximity. All she felt was...gratitude toward him.

"I begged him to come home. Only for a few days. I needed him so desperately. He was my daddy. I'd always felt so safe with him and I was so damned scared. Scared to sleep. Scared to wake up. Scared to leave my room. To go to church where other men would be close to me."

She had never told her counselors about that—never described the depths of her fears.

"He said he'd like to, but his wife was having morning sickness and he was sure I'd understand that it wasn't a good time for him to leave her."

Jay's lips pursed, the muscles in his chin and jaw bunching as though he was gritting his teeth.

"I called him a couple of days before I had to testify, too. His excuse then was that the baby had colic."

That was when Ellen finally saw her siblings had been right—and she'd finally given up on him, too.

"Anyway, the point is, I get how you feel about your dad. I also appreciate how important it is for you to find him. For your sake. And for Cole's."

"Just so you aren't picturing some grand reunion—"

"I gave up on grand dreams years ago." Ellen straightened. "These days I'm happy with peaceful gardens."

He couldn't possibly understand the reference, but that was okay. He didn't need to.

JAY WASN'T A GREAT PASSENGER. It was something he hadn't mentioned to Ellen. Sitting in a vehicle subject to the driving skills—or lack thereof—of someone else, having nothing to do, was a mild form of torture. Add in thinking about possibly seeing his old man for the first time, and this trip was damned near excruciating. This situation was not for a guy who craved the freedom of his bike, the wind whipping around him and no family ties whatsoever.

The couple they were going to see, Daniel and Elise Black, had a place in the desert, about ten miles outside of Shelter Valley heading toward Tucson.

Jay noticed his leg bobbing. And concentrated on relaxing his muscles one by one. His leg stopped, but his thumb tapped the doorjamb. That came to his attention only after Ellen glanced over several times.

She looked cute in her blue shorts, sleeveless white top and matching blue-and-white flip-flops. She wasn't wearing any makeup or jewelry. Nothing flashy to attract a man's attention.

She had Jay's anyway.

She didn't say a word, didn't chatter or engage him in a conversation he couldn't keep up. She simply was... with him. A new experience. One he didn't hate.

Jay handled life—and it's challenges—on his own. He always had. Because he liked it that way.

But today was different. And no small part of the reason was Ellen.

"The house should be up ahead," she said, slowing after having made a couple of turns. "I've been on this road. A girl I used to know in high school lived out here. But I'm not exactly sure which place is the Blacks'."

The houses were spaced about five acres apart. In the middle of the desert. Jay couldn't figure out why anyone would want to do that to themselves. Live in the middle of cactus needles and drought. Not to mention the poisonous reptiles and insects.

He couldn't figure out a lot of things at the moment and didn't like feeling this way. His jeans stuck to his ass against the leather of the seat. The back of his T-shirt was soaked, too, in spite of the cold air blowing from the vent pointed directly at him.

"If my old man's there, I want you to step outside."

"Okay." Checking the address, she drove on. "Can I ask why? I mean, you know all my stuff, it hardly seems fair that—"

"I'm you're therapist."

"Massage therapist."

"Nationally licensed medical massage therapist." He was being a prick. And wasn't proud of himself.

"I'm a certified family counselor."

"Not mine."

"So you get to know my stuff and I don't get to know yours."

"Right."

"Then you're no longer my therapist."

What kind of crap was that? "Ellen."

"No, really. If I'm not good enough to give back to you, then—"

"Fine. You can stay. But don't blame me if you don't like what you hear."

"I won't."

"And no canceling tomorrow's session because of it."

"Fair enough."

"Good." Life wasn't fair—but he chose not share that tidbit.

She turned into a driveway before Jay had realized she'd found the house. The woman did things to him.

After they parked and had gained entrance, Jay

assessed Elise and Daniel as introductions were made. He would guess the couple was in their mid-fifties. Their welcome, while reserved, was polite and they motioned Ellen and Jay toward the living room.

Another man sat in an armchair in the corner of the room. He could be in his fifties, too, although his sun-weathered skin and sunken eyes made it hard to tell. His mouth hung open, his lips pulling inward over what appeared to be toothless gums.

Jay almost puked when he saw him. This gray-haired, wrinkled man was his father?

Could reality be worse than the nightmare he'd lived with for most of his life? He'd pictured a weak man. A selfish one. But one who had lived with a measure of success. A man who had made something of himself, after leaving Jay and his mother in his dust.

"Have a seat," Elise said as Daniel pulled a couple of wooden rocking chairs closer to the couch.

"That's Harry," Daniel said, pointing to the guy in the corner. "He used to work for us, helping us with the horses. Harry took a hard fall about ten years ago, and when it was clear he was never going to be himself again, his wife left him. Elise and I felt it was our duty to take him in."

Jay looked again at the man, noticed the straps holding him upright, and accepted the shame that swamped him. He'd prejudged. He knew better.

Approaching Harry, Jay took in the lost look in the man's eyes, the lethargic set of his shoulders. "How you doing?" he asked softly.

Harry blinked. Smiled. But said nothing.

"We're not sure how much he understands." Elise brought in a tray of cookies. "But he's easy to care for.

Easy to please. Doctors say he's not long for this world. We want to make certain that, for as long as he's here, he's comfortable."

She placed a cookie in Harry's hand. It took the man several seconds to get it to his mouth.

Jay sat in the rocker next to Ellen and surveyed the room. Though rustic, the place was clean, the wooden floors covered with large woven rugs.

"A buddy of mine used to play tennis for the university," Daniel said. "I was at every match. I was there the day that picture was taken—Montford was about to make Arizona tennis history with number of consecutive wins. Bleachers that were normally half-empty were filled to capacity. Students came from as far as Flagstaff to watch."

Jay nodded. He'd read the statistics. Montford lost that day to the University of Arizona. That was the school his father had apparently attended, although Jay could find no record of a J. Billingsley on the student roster that year. Or the years directly preceding or following it, either.

"The guy in the picture is Bob Scott—he's on his way. Our friend tells us the woman is your mother."

"That's right."

"I didn't know her," Daniel said. "But Bob and I go way back."

"He's still lives around here?"

"If you consider Phoenix around these parts. He's a lawyer."

An attorney. Anger built in Jay. His father was an attorney? Picturing a well-dressed professional man with his own thick hair and long legs, Jay's blood started to churn. How dare the man desert his mother—a young woman not even out of her teens—make something of his life, but never look back? Did Bob Scott know that Tammy was dead? Did he know the circumstances?

Did he care that Tammy had left an infant son behind?

Not sure that he would be able to hold his tongue when the man walked in the door, Jay took a long swig of water, praying that it would turn into beer between his lips and his throat. And when that failed to materialize, he prepared to meet the man he'd spent his entire life hating.

CHAPTER THIRTEEN

ELLEN'S SENSES WERE ON full alert. She heard the sound of tires on the gravel drive and straightened, ready to… what? Dart in front of Jay and save him from himself when the Phoenix lawyer walked in?

"That'll be Bob," Daniel said, standing. Elise rose, too, getting a glass and bottle out of a sideboard. Pouring a healthy portion of amber liquid into the glass, she added a splash of water and stood behind her husband.

Ellen's focus was on Jay. Her academic training told her the myriad of emotions he could be experiencing as his moment of reckoning approached. She noted his sudden stillness. The clenching of his jaw.

Jay might look tough—he might be capable of tough—but he was also a very gentle man. A man who would rather go to prison than see a girl, a complete stranger, be hurt.

His hands could control that monster machine of his, but they could also bring sweet solace to a body taut with fear, braced for attack.

"Daniel, Elise, good to see you. Ah, thank you, dear." Ellen could not yet see the man, but she saw his hand take the glass. "Now what's this about a picture?"

When the attorney came into view, Jay twitched, as though a fuse had been lit. The man was tall, like Jay, with thick salt-and-pepper hair and a receding hairline.

He was trim and obviously fit. The glass Elise had poured was already half-empty.

A man who played hard? He reminded Ellen more of a high rolling poker player than a member of the professional elite.

He assessed Jay and Ellen, a smile on his face.

"Bob, this is Ellen Moore, a friend of a friend from Shelter Valley. And this is Jay."

"Jay, Ellen." Bob nodded, but didn't approach or attempt to shake hands. "Nice to meet you."

Ellen nodded. Jay didn't say a word.

"Some folks in Shelter Valley have been showing around this photo," Daniel said, handing a copy to Bob. "Turns out that woman is Jay's mother. He wanted to ask you some questions."

"I'll be damned." Bob grinned. "I haven't seen this photo in years. Montford was about to set a state record for most consecutive singles wins." He peered closer at the image. "Yes, I remember this girl. Tammy something. She was one of those you don't forget. Had these big blue eyes. I was so busy staring at her as I climbed up to take my seat that I knocked over her drink. She got really upset so I bought her another one. Thought I'd stumbled on a new, if slightly hazardous, pickup line. Missed most of the match because of her smile."

Ellen hung on every word, hating the man on Jay's behalf, yet watching for the possibility of redemption. He wasn't all bad. He'd driven from Phoenix simply to meet with them.

Bob looked at Jay. "So what can I do for you?"

Jay's lips twitched. He set his bottle on the table. "How well did you know her?"

The attorney's eyes narrowed. His court look, Ellen supposed, imagining he could crack a witness's testimony with it. Despite the distance in his expression, he seemed genuinely confused, as though trying to put pieces together that didn't quite fit. "Not well, though not for want of trying. She was sweet. Funny. In the space of an hour I was hooked."

Jay's shoulders heaved. He locked his hands behind his back. "And then?" The words were barely civil.

"And then, when I asked her out, she started to cry."

"Cry?" Ellen spoke up, though she hadn't intended to. "She cried over being asked on a date?"

"Yeah. She said it wasn't my fault. Told me that she wasn't...free...to date anyone. Then she left."

"And that was it?" The words were still staccato, but Jay's tone had less bite to it.

"That was it. I never saw her again."

"Did she tell you anything else about herself? Anything at all?"

"Just that she was eighteen. And from Tucson."

"Was she in college?"

Tilting his head to the side, the lawyer pursed his lips. "I'm sorry, man, I don't recall. She seemed to know a lot about the game. As I remember it, I spent the match trying to make her laugh. What's this about? Did you just find out she's your mother?"

"No, I've known that. She died when I was a baby. I'm looking for my father."

"Your— You thought..." Bob looked at the photo once more then put it on the table. "No, sorry. I didn't even get as close as holding hands."

"You have your arm around her."

"I helped her after she stumbled."

"Was she at the match alone?"

"Seemed to be. She didn't talk to anyone else. And as far as I could see she left alone."

"Did you see where she went? The parking lot? Toward campus?"

Bob bore Jay's questions with equanimity, giving each one thoughtful consideration.

"Now that you mention it… Yeah, it was odd. She went toward the tunnel where the visiting tennis team congregated. I figured she knew someone on the team. I'd forgotten that."

"She didn't say that, though? During the match?"

"I don't remember. It was thirty years ago, you know? I remember the girl. That's about it."

"Did she seem to cheer for anyone in particular?"

"No. She actually wasn't cheering at all. Just watching. Studying. Like she was a coach, or a student of the game. She was pretty focused."

"Did you find it odd that she was at the tennis match alone?"

"Not really. If she was a student, she could have been there to support the school. It was an exciting time— possibly putting Montford on national news."

"Where were you in January of the following year?"

"Boot camp. I was a poor kid at Montford on scholarship. The money ran out and I joined the army reserves so I could finish my education."

"You never attended the University of Arizona?"

"No."

"You ever heard of a guy named Jay Billingsley?"

"No."

"And you never saw Tammy Walton again? Never met up with her in Tucson?"

"No."

Ellen swallowed tears as she watched Jay grill a guy who was obviously not his man. His thoroughness didn't surprise her. Neither did his lack of ability to let go.

What did surprise her was her own personal attachment to Bob's answers. As though what affected Jay affected her. What mattered to him mattered to her. She had to stop that. Now.

"You ever hear of Dolby Dodge?"

"No. But if it would help, I'm willing to submit to a DNA test to prove I'm not your father."

He wasn't the man they were looking for.

"I'M SORRY."

Sitting in the passenger seat again, his long legs stretched out in front of him, Jay watched the desert passing by. Ellen's voice reached inside him, settled there.

He had to dislodge it.

"Yeah, I guess I am, too. I don't look forward to facing the man, but I'd just as soon get it over with. Still, I'm a bit relieved," he admitted. He was tired.

"That's understandable," Ellen said. "You're only looking for your father because you feel like you have to, not because you want to. And you've been given a reprieve."

"What I've been given is another dead end. The photo's out."

Nothing added up. Jay existed, ergo, there was a father. But there was no evidence of a man in his mother's life. No evidence of her having friends. Going to college. Or high school even. No evidence of a job. Or any life at all other than her time with his aunt.

"Maybe not so dead," Ellen said slowly. With both hands on the wheel, she was focused on the highway.

"What do you mean?"

"I've been thinking about what Bob told us. Trying to visualize it all. Putting myself in Tammy's position. Why was she there alone? Based on the things we know about her—her lack of friends, absence of any high school records—it's odd that she was at that match let alone by herself. So it makes sense that she was there to watch someone. She probably knew someone on one of the teams."

He'd come to the same conclusion. Had planned to find out what he could about every member of both teams in attendance that day. He had an entire folder of articles and pictures of that day gleaned from the public Montford University archives.

"But something else is sticking with me. She cried when Bob asked her out. Not really cause for tears. The only reason I can come up with for a woman to cry at the drop of the hat is because she's hormonal."

"PMS?"

"I was thinking pregnant."

Jay did the math back from his birth date. "If she was, it was just barely. Four weeks at the most. There weren't tests that could have told her that conclusively—"

"Of course there were, just not available over the counter. She could have had a free blood test at any Planned Parenthood clinic. She also could have been further along. You might have come late."

Had his mother been pregnant that day? Had his presence made her cry?

He had always assumed that his mother wanted him.

But what if she hadn't? What if he'd been as much a surprise, a hardship, to her as he'd been to his father?

"Was Planned Parenthood even around then?"

"Yeah. The first clinic in Arizona opened in Tucson in 1934. Strange, the things you retain from college."

And strange, the things that didn't add up. Such as why his possibly pregnant mother, a resident of Tucson, had been in Shelter Valley at a tennis match alone.

But the strangest of all was the way the woman sitting next to him made the dead end, his lack of answers, seem…manageable. Ellen Moore made life okay.

AN HOUR LATER, JAY STUDIED his copy of the photo he'd left with Bob. He'd asked to keep the picture and Jay could think of no reason to refuse.

As he sat at his dining-room table, he concentrated on his mother. The photo was grainy—not as clear as others he had, compliments of his aunt.

Grabbing his photo viewer, he examined the photo inch by inch, as though he could see the shape of the embryo—him—she carried. As if he could somehow discern his genetic makeup there, find the Y chromosome that contributed to his existence and discover the identity of the donor.

He was good at ferreting out the most obscure information. He saw what others did not.

Usually.

He picked up the phone, vaguely surprised that he was reaching out to someone. Very unlike him.

Ellen answered on the first ring as though she'd been holding her cell. Awaiting his call.

He was being ridiculous. If she had been, it was past

time for him to hightail it out of town. The last thing Jay ever wanted was a woman waiting for his call.

"Scott said my mother had big blue eyes."

"That's right."

"None of the pictures I have of her make that clear."

"Doesn't it say so on her birth certificate?"

"No. Eye color isn't checked."

"Well, apparently they were blue."

"Mine are brown."

"So you think your father had brown eyes."

"An educated guess."

He was staring at the photo while they spoke, his eye to the photo magnifier.

"I'll be damned."

"What?"

"The photo. She's wearing a ring on a chain around her neck. I can make out the indentation under her shirt."

"What kind of ring?"

"I can't tell, but it looks plain. A wedding ring maybe?"

"Like the one you have from your aunt? Your mother's wedding ring?"

"If she was married, why would she be wearing the ring around her neck?"

"I have no idea. If she was further along in her pregnancy, I'd say maybe her fingers had swollen, but she's thin."

He didn't know the whys, but… "The important thing is, she was wearing it. She told Bob Scott she wasn't free to date. Because she was already married? But if so, where was her husband?"

"Maybe he'd already left her."

"My aunt said he left just after I was born."

"I'm beginning to think what your aunt said and what really happened might be two different things. From what you've shown me, it seems like none of her facts can be substantiated."

LATER THAT NIGHT, JAY was thinking about what Ellen had said. She was right, of course. He would have reached the same conclusion much sooner if he'd been on the outside looking in—investigating a life other than his own. But this was his aunt. The only family he'd ever known. And while she maybe hadn't been the ideal parent, to the best of her ability she had been both mother and father to him.

The murder of her adored baby sister had taken its toll. She hadn't trusted anything or anyone—including Jay, some of the time. But he'd understood. The tragedy—and the police's inability to find the perpetrator—had imprisoned her in bitterness and distrust. She'd lost touch with friends. Quit going to church. She'd lost all sense of joy. Their home, while clean, had been stark. They'd had only the bare necessities to sustain life. No cable television. No computers.

His aunt's life had been work and Jay.

She had monitored his every move. There had been no spoken affection between them, but she *had* listened to him. Considered his thoughts. She encouraged him to discover his interests and talents. To study hard and to believe that he could be anything he wanted to be.

And when he'd taken steps that she hadn't approved of—such as trying to buy that Mustang from Dolby Dodge—she stopped him cold.

Now he had to contemplate how untrustworthy she was. How much of his life had been a lie?

He'd intended to find his father so he could lay the past to rest and decide how to proceed into the future with Cole. Instead, Jay was finding out that he had no idea who he really was.

This revised view of his aunt took Jay back several steps in his investigation. Sure, it opened innumerable new doors, as well, but he had to retrace his work.

And to top it off, he was feeling emotions he'd never felt before. A peculiar attachment to Ellen that defied definition or explanation. Was it a response to her uniquely needy and at the same time nurturing nature? The fact she'd suffered from a crime similar to his mother's? Some chemical sexual thing?

Whatever it was, Jay was drawn to her. And that didn't sit well with him.

CHAPTER FOURTEEN

ELLEN WAS LOOKING FORWARD to Saturday morning's session with Jay. Afterward she had a hundredth birthday party at work, and then was scheduled to meet with a family about enrolling their mother at Big Spirits. Whether someone was better off living in residential care or not, there was no way that she knew of to make the transition easy for the families. Or the residents. A not so fun part of her job.

She had talked to Josh that morning. He was off to Las Vegas to play at Circus Circus. Ellen had never been to Vegas and wasn't particularly thrilled to have her five-year-old son exposed to the city of sin.

She wanted her son home in Shelter Valley with her. Where they both belonged.

But as only one of Josh's parents, she couldn't prevent him from going. Not when he was on his father's time.

All in all, half an hour in her peaceful garden sounded fabulous.

Jay was in the waiting room, motioning her in before she'd scarcely cleared the door.

"How are you?" she asked quietly. She'd thought of him all night long. Wishing he'd had a friend to share the darkness with him.

Maybe wishing she could have been that friend.

"Fine."

"Did you find anything in the tennis team archives?"

"No."

Taking her cue, Ellen remained silent the rest of the way to his room. He left her, as usual, telling her to take her time getting ready.

She went through her now-familiar routine and was waiting for him after a few moments.

It took him a full five minutes to return.

"I'm going to do a bit of light massage today," he said softly. "The same thing we've been doing with a little bit of kneading." His low voice, speaking slowly, blended nicely with the music.

He pulled the sheet up to her neck. "If you have a problem, please let me know immediately. We'll try to talk our way through it."

She settled in and let the music take her to her special place.

Jay's touch was soothing, gentle, his fingers working her muscles with a light, rhythmic pressure. The music was there. She could hear it. And the dimly lit floor looked the same in a comforting way.

Pressure against her shoulder at the base of her neck.

The walls moved a little closer.

Ellen tensed.

"You okay?"

Jay's voice.

"Yes."

More pressure. Jay's hands. She could see his thumb, tapping rhythmically against the car door yesterday. He'd been a grown man...and a little boy, too.

A human being trying to understand how a parent could desert him. Parents were partial to their kids. Parents loved their kids more than anyone on earth.

Parents were security in a changing world. Safety in the midst of danger. Reassurance during sickness and encouragement in health. It was the natural way of things.

Pressure. Pressure. Pressure.

Jay had missed all of that. No safety. No security.

She could see him in her car.

She cared.

His hands moved lower, edging along her spine next to her shoulder blades.

He was her therapist. Not a man she cared about.

Pressure. Kneading. Like she was a loaf of bread.

She wasn't a loaf of anything.

Josh was going to Las Vegas.

Jay. His hands. His hurt.

She cared.

More kneading.

She could handle it. This was Jay. She had her music. Her flowers. The private garden in her mind.

Peace.

Kneading. Kneading. So much needing.

Life was hard.

Strains of music filtered in. Speaking to her. All she wanted was peace.

"Let's talk about it."

She couldn't talk. She was sobbing.

She wanted to go home.

"Try, Ellen. Talk to me. Talk through it."

He stroked her lightly. As he had on other days. Gently stroking. Back and forth. Bringing peace.

Invading her space.

She didn't want to be touched.

But she couldn't tell him. Telling him would mean failure. She was normal. She wanted a normal life.

Tears dropped to the floor.

She heard his steps as he moved away.

"Take as long as you need."

She waited for the click of the closing door. Then curled into a ball on the table and sobbed.

JAY STOOD OUTSIDE HIS treatment room. Strategizing. Planning. Determined to make Ellen like other clients he'd helped through difficult times—determined to focus on the job at hand.

Tension built from the inside out. He couldn't fail her. Couldn't stand here and watch her walk away. If she came through that door and told him she was done, he couldn't not go after her.

Five minutes passed. She was always out within two. Seven minutes. No sound emerged from the room.

Eight minutes and Jay's hand was on the knob. He turned it slowly. Gave her time to notice. To stop him. To claim her privacy.

Ellen wasn't standing. Or even sitting in the chair where she'd left her purse. She was still on the table, huddled like a child.

In that moment he knew this woman would never be just another client to him. She was a client. She meant that much.

But so much more.

He'd known her only a matter of days yet it was as though he'd known her his entire life.

Her sobs tore at him and he approached the table, even though his training told him to keep his distance.

"I'm here, Ellen," he said, keeping his voice soft, rhythmic. He didn't touch her. "Talk to me."

She hiccupped. Jay waited. There was nothing else to do. He wasn't going to leave her there alone.

"I'm a freak."

"You are not a freak."

"I—I am."

Talk her through it, man. Work. Do your job. "What makes you a freak?"

"I— People love…massages. I can't…even make it… through one." Her voice was muffled against her hands.

"You know why. You were hurt. We're healing that."

"What if it doesn't work? What if I never get better?"

What-ifs were no-win situations. Once allowed, they would insinuate themselves into every corner of the mind and eat it alive.

"Tell me about today. What happened?"

"I don't know."

"When did it go bad?"

"I don't know."

"We need to talk through it. To take the sting. To take away the mystery. To take away its power over you."

She moved, unbending the slightest amount. She was still curled, but her head was not pushed so tightly against her chest.

"I couldn't relax. From the beginning," she said, her voice calmer. She had stopped crying.

"Okay, do you have any idea why?"

"No. I found out this morning that Josh is going to Las Vegas with his father."

"And that upset you?"

"Well…yeah. I mean, it's Sin City and he's only five."

"Okay." He didn't push her. Let the music and the dim lighting do their work.

"I—I can't handle a simple massage and Josh is going to be in Las Vegas."

She was afraid and feeling powerless. He understood that. But he couldn't quite put the Las Vegas part together with the reaction.

"Let's talk about the massage," he said. "Can you tell me when the touching went bad for you?"

"I don't know."

"How did you feel?"

"Like the walls were closing in. Like I had to and I didn't want to and I couldn't do anything about it."

"Did I hurt you?"

"No."

"Did it feel good?"

"I don't know. I— My mind wandered and I got confused and...I don't know. It all went bad."

"Do you want to take a break?" He wasn't going to give up on her. But pushing too hard could do more damage than good. "Try again in another week or so?"

"No." Ellen sat up, her voice firm. "I'm not going to live like this my entire life. I hate having you see me this way. I'm an ugly freak and I don't want to be. Not anymore. So I'm not going to run away."

His hand moved before his mind did. With the tips of his fingers he pushed the hair from Ellen's face, wiping her eyes then her cheeks with his thumbs. "You are not ugly, Ellen Moore." Those teary brown eyes gazed at him with such longing. "For the first time in my career, I find myself struggling to ignore how beautiful the woman on my table is."

What in the hell was he doing?

Ellen stared at him and something entered her eyes, her expression. Something he'd needed to see.

But she closed her eyes, and turned her face into the palm of his hand.

She didn't push herself into him. Didn't so much as move her lips. She simply rested against his palm. A moment. Two.

She slid off the table, and quietly collected her purse.

Next time she was there he'd have her take off her shoes. Only her shoes. A slight disrobing. He'd do her feet. And nothing else. The plan presented itself to him as she moved toward the door.

"Thank you." She glanced at him over her shoulder for the briefest second then she was gone.

But he knew she'd be back.

He knew something else, too. He had to have a talk with her before he worked on her again.

He'd crossed a professional line that he shouldn't have. He had to tell her.

Then Ellen had a choice to make: to trust him to be able to help her heal.

Or not.

ELLEN THOUGHT ABOUT JAY for the rest of the day. Alma, the woman celebrating her hundredth birthday, cracked a joke that had the whole room laughing and Ellen wished Jay had been there to hear her. He knew Alma.

She chose a brownie over a vanilla cupcake and wondered if he would have made the same choice.

And when she counseled the Mercer family—a son, a daughter and a son-in-law—about admitting their mother, Joan, to Big Spirits because the woman kept wandering away from home and they were afraid for her life, she thought of Jay. Of the fact that he would never have to go through moments like these. Never have to face a family crisis.

She thought about how unfair life had been to him. How lucky the Mercers were to have the security of a family unit to lean on while facing life's challenges. And how lucky she was to have her family—both the blood family, and the adopted family she had in the people of Shelter Valley.

Jay had never had a home.

Ellen had never known a single moment without one. Even in her worst moment, she'd had a home to think about—and to eventually run to.

Jay deserved to know what a home meant. How it felt. What it stood for.

She had to help him find his father. Then, hopefully, he'd let her help him integrate Cole into his life, as well.

Beyond that she couldn't think. She had no idea where he'd be once he'd completed what he'd set out to do. One thing was very clear. He wouldn't be staying.

And she would never leave.

That impasse occupied her thoughts as she left her office following the session with the Mercers. She would meet with them early next week after they had considered their options over the weekend.

"Hey!"

Ellen stopped when she heard the voice.

Clara Larson was in her room, sitting in a chair adjacent the window. The ninety-two year old had family in Tucson. The same place where Jay's father had deserted him. Clara's family had all but deserted her, visiting only once a year. Did they have some nonfamily chemical contaminating their drinking water?

"You need something, Clara?" Ellen stepped into the room.

"I need to talk to you is what."

"Okay." Ellen pulled up a chair and took the older woman's frail hand, careful not to squeeze too hard and bruise her. There were more veins than skin visible these days. "What's up?"

"The new girl—the one they hired last month—I don't want her in here anymore."

"Tell me what's going on."

"My body is old and useless, my brain is not."

Smiling, Ellen said, "I can certainly attest to that." Clara had beat Ellen in a game of Scrabble a couple of days ago. They kept the game set up in a corner of Clara's room and Ellen played at least one word a day.

"The girl treats me like I'm a moron."

"And that's completely unacceptable," Ellen said. "I'm glad you said something."

"That's what you're here for, ain't it?"

"Yes, it is."

"So...you'll see that she doesn't come back in here?"

Ellen couldn't promise to choose aides' schedules based on the likes and dislikes of residents, but...

"Let me ask you this," she said. "If she apologizes, can you give her one more try?"

She knew the staff member—Lacey Barnes. A single mother with a two-month-old infant, Lacey was living with her parents and struggling to make ends meet. The job at Big Spirits worked for her because she could still breast-feed her baby who was next door at Little Spirits.

Clara didn't answer.

"I give you my word. If her behavior doesn't change

immediately, I won't ask you to be patient a second time."

She harrumphed. Then, with a petulant look, she nodded. "All right. But I want that apology."

"You'll get it," Ellen promised.

She sought out Lacey's supervisor to make good on her word as soon as she left Clara's room.

Back in her small office, Ellen packed up her bag then headed out the side door of the facility. At the same time, Jay walked in.

She stopped.

He did, too.

"You got a minute?"

He was still wearing the jeans and T-shirt he'd had on that morning.

"Yeah."

"I need to see Hugh. But if you'll wait, I'll be right out."

Ellen nodded. What did he need to see her about? She wasn't up for discussing her breakdown this morning. But maybe Jay had word on his father or needed her help.

She could have left. He'd allowed her time to leave. She didn't.

CHAPTER FIFTEEN

JAY FOUND ELLEN LEANING against a corner of the building, her phone turned sideways and her fingers moving along the screen as though she was playing a game. He had a touch screen MP3 player that kidnapped him anytime he picked it up. There was this bird game…

"Sorry. Hugh's playing the stock market with a hundred dollars and an internet account. He wanted to ask my opinion of some charts he'd downloaded."

"You know about the stock market?"

"Some. Not enough to give advice, though, and I told Hugh that. So that chat…" He cast his mind for a private place where they could talk—one that wouldn't distress her. He couldn't take her to his place and had no intention of going within half a mile of hers. Maybe a bench on Montford's campus.

"We could take the motorcycle someplace," she said.

"We could." Riding therapeutically was one thing. Having her on the back of his bike, stopping, having intimate conversation—intimate to him, at least—and then riding some more…

Could be a recipe for disaster.

"I know a place at the base of a mountain about thirty miles outside town," she said. "We could go there."

She was trusting him. Jay couldn't offer a negative response to that.

Leading the way to his bike, he unlocked the trunk case, pulled out the helmet Ellen used and handed it to her before climbing onto the bike and waiting for her to settle herself.

They were old hands at this part. Almost like a couple. Something they would most definitely never be. He'd suffocate in a town like Shelter Valley. Who was he kidding? Settling in any town would smother him.

And even if a woman was willing to freestyle it with him, he'd suffocate in a long-term relationship.

Which was why he didn't trust himself to help Cole.

"WHAT IS THIS PLACE?" Turning off the bike, Jay held it steady while Ellen climbed off. She'd guided him to an undeveloped, unpopulated spot. They'd taken the highway to a dirt road, then had off-roaded it for a short stint, until a path formed by tire tracks appeared, leading to a clearing that abutted the south side of the mountain. The area was surrounded by an unusually thick grouping of Palo Verde trees, enclosing it, hiding it from the rest of the world. Making it the perfect place for illicit activity.

He pulled out his earbuds and remained on the bike, his feet firmly on the ground. "What are you doing bringing me here? I mean, I'm glad you trust me this much, but a guy could easily get the wrong idea being brought here."

Hooking her helmet over the seat, Ellen crossed her arms over her chest and walked toward a rock face. Wearing that colorful pullover and jeans, she didn't look intent on seduction.

Even so, he couldn't seem to stop thinking about sliding his hands underneath her top.

What in the hell was wrong with him? He wasn't a predator. He was here to come clean with her.

"You said we needed to talk," she said, leaning against the mountain. "We needed privacy, which, in case you haven't noticed, is almost impossible for me. So here we are."

"For a woman with trust issues, this is pretty bold." He couldn't get off the bike. Didn't trust himself to get too close to her.

"You might think so...until you made one inappropriate move," she said.

Frowning, Jay wondered if the morning's session had taken a greater toll than he'd thought. Should he have called Shawna? Was he in way over his head? Hurting Ellen when he thought he was helping her? Sending her into a make-believe world because she couldn't deal with reality as it was?

"This place is called Rabbit Rock." She stepped away from the mountain and pointed upward. "Look at the formation—it's like a rabbit."

After a second or two, he saw the resemblance.

"When my parents were young, kids used to come here and make out. During Sheriff Richards's high school days they did drugs and hallucinated here. About fifteen years ago, this rock was used as a gang initiation site. Boys had to hijack pricey cars, bring them out here and ram them at full speed into the rock. Sheriff Richards's father was a victim of one of the hijackings. Got hurt pretty bad. The kids left him for dead but he lived another ten years—in a vegetative state."

Jay listened, still worried about her unawareness of the potential danger she'd put herself in.

"You see, the sheriff, my mom, Becca and Will, Tory and Ben, Cassie—they've all suffered through life's challenges. They've been hurt, and they've grown from it. Rather than becoming embittered, or mean, they've banded together to build a town where people can find peace and be happy."

Or a town where they could hide from the world. Depending on your perspective.

"And as for Rabbit Rock, I'm perfectly safe here." She resumed her position against the stone surface. "You should know me better than to think that I'd put myself at such obvious risk. Even with you."

He liked the *even with you* part—tucked it away for further examination later.

"We're being watched," she said.

There were in the middle of freaking nowhere. God, what if she was really losing it?

"Watched? Really?"

"Joe Frasier. A friend of mine."

To verify, he looked around. He would have known if they had been followed.

"Where is he?"

"Up there." She pointed upward.

"In the sky?"

Did she think angels were watching over her? Was that it? Did she think they would protect her from being hurt again?

"No, on the mountain," she said, her expression serious. "He lives out here. He's the one who told Sheriff Richards what was going on with the Phoenix gang. He's also a...client...of mine. Greg introduced me to

Joe several years ago. A couple of times a month the two of us bring Joe groceries and stuff. Sometimes I come alone."

Jay glanced around again and studied the mountain more seriously.

"You won't see him," Ellen said. "Joe's serious about being left alone. He's got a cabin not far from here, but he spends a lot of time exploring, too."

"How do you know he's watching us?"

"Joe hears every vehicle that comes anywhere near this place. He was probably listening to your bike ten miles out. Plenty of time to get to his lookout."

She didn't sound crazy. She sounded perfectly rational. Sane. And confident that she was perfectly safe.

"Does he have a gun?"

"Of course."

"Is he a good aim?"

"I assume so."

He'd heard about backwoods fathers on porches with shotguns protecting their daughters' virtue, but a hermit on a mountain?

"How old is this guy?"

"I'm not sure."

Or she wasn't saying. If Joe was her client, she couldn't talk about him. Jay respected that.

"He knows about you."

That didn't surprise him. Not around here. If anyone ever needed to be famous, all they had to do was ride a motorcycle into Shelter Valley and talk to Ellen Moore.

"I guess the sheriff warned him."

"No, I told him about the therapy. I...talk to Joe sometimes. I trust him. And I respect his judgment. After our first two bike rides I wanted a sounding board and knew that I couldn't talk to anyone at home about it."

Hmm. She had continued the therapy, so Joe couldn't be completely opposed. "He didn't warn you against such unusual therapy or me?"

"No, actually. He said I need the therapy. He wants me to get married."

Did this Joe want to be the bridegroom, too? Jay didn't ask. The answer was none of his business. It didn't have anything to do with her healing.

That led him to why they were here. Jay would rather ram a car into Rabbit Rock than tell Ellen that he was attracted to her.

"I have something I need to talk to you about." He couldn't work on her again unless she knew.

"Okay."

"Can we sit?" He indicated a large boulder in full view of the mountaintop. Ellen sat. Leaving several inches between them, he did, too.

What to say? Depending on how he handled the next few minutes, he could lose all chance of helping Ellen.

Despite this inability to stop thinking about her sexually, he still believed that he could be a part of her healing process. If he could send her into the world able to love fully, into the arms of a man who would cherish her and make her happy...

"Is this about your dad?"

It took him a second to catch up with her. "No." But he should have figured that she'd think so. And that was going to make what he had to say that much more shocking to her.

"It's about us."

"Us?"

He couldn't identify the tremor in her voice. Fear? Or something else?

"I'm struggling, Ellen."

"About what?"

The way they sat, they faced out at different angles, which made not looking at her a little easier, a little less like avoidance.

"The lines are blurring. I still believe I can help you—partly because you're so committed to helping yourself."

"I hear a *but* in there. If you're trying to tell me that you want me to stay out of your business, then fine. I'll stay out."

He should accept her offer. Instantly.

"I'm trying to tell you that I don't think of you as only a client."

The sun was hot, but this late in the afternoon, it was behind the peak of the mountain, giving Jay some relief. Dry heat was much better than air that hung with moisture, but it was still hot.

"How do you think of me?" He could hear the tremor again.

"I'm not sure." *Liar.* "I find you attractive. But it's more convoluted than that."

"How so?"

Sweat trickled down the back of his T-shirt. He thought of the guy watching them, and wondered if he was aiming his gun.

"I was there. I was asleep in my crib in the next room when it happened." An abrupt change of subject, but he wasn't sure how to get her to understand something he'd never articulated for himself. "A friend stopped by, heard me crying…found my mother— They called my mother's sister."

Her sharp intake of breath registered first. He could feel her gaze boring into the side of his head. Jay didn't move, didn't turn to meet her eyes. He couldn't say all that needed saying if he saw the compassion, the *pity* in her eyes.

"I know I was an infant, completely incapable of taking care of myself let alone anyone else. But…I have always wondered if I heard what was going on. Did I hear anything? Sense the danger? Did I know on some level what was going on? And if I did…if I'd cried sooner or something, could I have saved her?"

"What could you have done? Sure, you might have cried sooner, but who knows? And maybe it was for the best that you didn't. If the guy had known you were there, he might have gone after you, too."

"Possibly. In any case, I spent a lot of time thinking— especially in prison—about that day, wondering if I'd heard something. You have a lot of time on the inside, and I couldn't get away from the idea that I might have been able to make a difference for her. I was right there…"

"You couldn't have known."

"Of course not. But I determined that as soon as I got out, I was going to find my mother's killer. It was something I *could* do. I had some idea that I might subconsciously know something, or recognize something, that would lead me to him. I was the only witness."

"They never caught the guy?" Her question was barely above a whisper, so close to him he could almost feel her breath.

"They have now."

"And?"

"He's on death row here in Arizona."

Her breath caught again and he turned toward her. Ellen's compassionate expression, the open understanding in her gaze, grabbed at him.

"Because of you?"

"It took me more than ten years to track the guy down. In the end, it was a series of newspaper articles that put it all together. My aunt had gone on about this handkerchief that my mother had had. It belonged to their grandmother. My aunt claimed that handkerchief was missing. No one paid any attention to her. My aunt couldn't remember when she'd last seen it and nothing else was missing from the house. My aunt couldn't really even remember distinctly what it looked like. But she was insistent she'd know it if she saw it and was equally insistent that my mother would never ever have disposed of it.

"As I've told you, my aunt was a bit...odd. She tended to glom on certain things and, frankly, I agreed with the police that the missing handkerchief—if it really was missing—had nothing to do with my mother's murder. Then one night I was reading through other unsolved cases against young women in their homes in the United States—one of which had been in Wyoming. A newspaper article said something about a chain missing. Something that mattered a lot to the victim."

Through this part of his story, Ellen had maintained her stare. Jay didn't focus on her. He couldn't get lost in that gaze.

Because she was his client. And because, other than as a therapist, he had nothing to offer. She didn't need what he had to give. And he didn't have to give what she needed.

Neither fact stemmed his growing desire for her.

"I started looking through newspapers from all over the West and hounding police departments for any unsolved cases where something of emotional importance to the victim was reported missing. Turns out there were two others. One in Montana and one in Oregon. When I looked at all four cases, I was able to discover enough similarities and compile enough evidence from the four separate cases that, when put together, gave law enforcement officials sufficient evidence to find the guy."

"And they got a conviction."

"Eventually."

"Were you at the trial?"

"Every day. The day the guy was sentenced to death he blurted out in the courtroom that he wasn't sorry for what he'd done. He turned to face us, the families of his victims, and said that he'd told the women that he wasn't going to hurt them, that he only needed a safe place to hang out for a couple of hours then he'd be gone. He let each of them hold something that was meaningful to them to give them comfort.

"While they were holding their most precious item, he raped them, slit their throats, then stole their prized possession as a memento."

"Did you get the handkerchief back?"

"Yeah. Those mementos—found in a box in the trunk of his car—were what finally convicted him. There were others, there, too, indicating that the four women we know about weren't the fiend's only victims."

There were other families, other kids who had grown

into adults maybe, who were still as lost as he'd been
all those years without answers.

Jay felt for them.

His mother's handkerchief, the small square of white
linen, stained with his mother's blood, was in his wallet.
It went everywhere with Jay. Every single day of his
life.

CHAPTER SIXTEEN

THERE WERE OTHER MEMENTOES. Other women, victims of similar crimes. Victims of a serial rapist who had ravaged the West thirty years before.

Glancing toward the top of the mountain, certain that Joe was watching out for her, Ellen couldn't quell the nervous tension racing through her.

Just as Tammy Walton's friend had found her raped and dead, just as the other women had been raped and murdered, left for dead, in their own homes, Joe had come home to find his wife raped and dead.

By her best guess, Joe's wife had been murdered a year or two before Jay's mother had suffered the same fate.

Her mind leaped to possibilities, with her heart completely keeping up. What if the same man had killed both women? What if Jay had found the man who had killed Joe's wife? What if a memento of Joe's wife was missing? Would he know? Or had he left town before going through her things?

And if Jay had found Joe's wife's killer? Would closure help the man? Give him some sense of peace? Of justice? Just enough to get him off that mountain and into life?

"What about the other mementoes? Were any of the other victims found?"

"Yes. The FBI followed up, based on cold case files, and I was given some cases to investigate, as well. All in all we found a total of nine victims."

"Did you find them all?"

"No. There were fourteen mementos."

Five victims unaccounted for. Could one of them be Joe's wife? Her stomach churned, but Ellen said nothing.

"Were all the victims from the West?"

"All who were found. The national missing persons database was searched but no cases from the East or Midwest matched the evidence we had."

Joe's wife wouldn't have been listed as a missing person. And with Joe gone, there might not have been anyone pushing the Tucson police to solve her murder. What if her case had been left…unnoticed?

And what if, by stirring up the past, she sent Joe even further into his self-imposed isolation?

Ellen was being assaulted by the confusing and dichotomous signals from her heart, all of them somehow wrapped up with the man sitting beside her.

She couldn't get involved with him. She didn't want to get involved with him.

Yet her heart had leaped when he'd told her he was attracted to her.

She was afraid of the power he had to stir her. Yet filled with a need to make things better for him.

Ellen was a nurturer. And Jay needed nurturing more than anyone she'd ever met.

Whether he knew it or not.

"Is that why you work with victims of domestic abuse? Because of what happened to your mom?"

A few strands of hair had come loose from his

ponytail on the ride out. "It's why I feel so compelled to help you."

"So the lines that are…blurring… You're confusing me with your mother?"

That would make things safer. A whole lot easier. It wasn't easy waiting for his answer.

"No."

Her heart rate sped up.

"It only makes this more convoluted. I can't walk away from you because of her. Ever since you told me what happened to you I knew I had to help you—like I knew I had to find my mother's killer.

"But the way I'm feeling, the attraction, has nothing to do with my mother. And everything to do with you."

Ellen had absolutely no idea what to do next. What to say. His words excited her.

And that shamed her.

What in the hell was the matter with her? Because while the idea of Jay wanting her was, well, maybe a little exhilarating, she wanted no part of a physical relationship with him.

Or anyone—yet.

What kind of woman did that make her? That she wanted a man to want her with no intention whatsoever of giving him what he wanted?

"Where do we go from here?" she finally asked to escape her thoughts.

"That's up to you. I'm a professional. I do not, ever, cross the line between the therapy and personal while I'm working. You have my word on that. But I'll understand if you decide that you can no longer trust me to treat you."

Silence fell and Ellen closed her eyes, tuning in to

the warmth of the rock beneath her. The quiet of the desert. Searching for peace.

And finding the heat of the man sitting beside her. Her stomach churned.

Oh, God.

How could she trust a man to touch her nonsexually after he'd told her that he was sexually attracted to her?

Actually, no, he'd merely said he was attracted to her. He liked her. Maybe the way he liked his bike. Or a good steak for dinner. Maybe the lines that were blurring were between friendship and professionalism.

The desert's peace found her.

She was helping him find his father. It was reasonable to expect that he would rely on her a bit. To experience a sense of indebtedness. Or gratitude. To think of her as a friend.

"This man part of you, the part where the lines are blurring, you just…like me, right?"

"Define *like*."

"You appreciate that I want to help you find your father. My personality resonates with you in some way." Ellen flushed with embarrassment. Or Arizona's afternoon heat. She sounded like a textbook even to herself.

"I get turned on when I think of you for any length of time. And sometimes when I have a flash of a thought. If our situation was different, if I wasn't your massage therapist, if I'd met you in a nonprofessional setting, my current goal would be to get you into bed with me."

Okay. No room for misinterpretation on that one. He wasn't giving her an easy out. No pretending allowed.

"So how do I know that when I'm lying on your

table and you've got your hands on me that you aren't fantasizing about me?"

"Because I give you my word that I'm not."

"You're a man, Jay. I assume you have normal male sexual instincts and drives. How do you expect me to believe that you can simply turn those off because you walk into a little room with a table in it?"

"It's not the room. It's the mind-set," Jay said without hesitation. And with conviction. "You're a counselor. You know that sexual drive, while a product of hormones, is also largely a product of thought process. Controlled by thought process. When I'm working, I'm not seeing male or female. Sexual parts don't exist on my table. I am fully focused on muscle placement, tightness, obstruction. On ligament and skeletal alignment, tension and elasticity, tissue depth. I communicate with my client the entire time, listening to what the client's body tells my hands so that I can best serve the body's muscular needs. I've never yet met an adult with completely healthy muscles. We all carry tension and toxins within us. My job is to find them and attempt to release them. Damaged muscles are not a turn-on."

"Then why is massage recommended to couples in sexual counseling?"

"Like I said, it's all in the focus. When you are lying naked with someone who is also naked, your mind tends to focus on the ultimate goal of sexual intimacy. Even if you aren't naked, but you know you're touching them for mutual pleasure, you tend to focus on the ultimate goal of mutual physical pleasure."

She was not only a certified counselor, she'd been through marital counseling with Aaron. And enough of her own counseling to write a textbook. What Jay said fit everything she'd been taught. It made logical sense.

There was nothing logical about Ellen's issues.

Sometimes the simplest touch was an invasion to her. A threat. A hug from her son felt as though she was being tied up. Bound. Robbed against her will.

To submit to touch from a man who admittedly wanted something from her body for his own gain—something that could be invasive and painful...

She'd be stupid to continue treatment with Jay. Setting herself up for failure.

Disappointment welled within her. She hadn't realized, until that moment, how much she'd been hoping Jay had been right in his assertion that he could help her heal. She'd actually been considering, in random passing thoughts, that she might be capable of enjoying sexual encounters someday.

Marry. Have a full family of her own. And become a normal part of Shelter Valley society, rather than the girl who stood out.

She couldn't stand to be that girl anymore. To face an incomplete life.

So what if she failed with Jay? Would she be any worse off than she was now?

And if he really was a miracle worker...

Minutes passed while Ellen contemplated, debated, and tied herself up in knots.

Jay didn't push. Didn't defend his case. Or try to talk her into anything.

"It's different." Her words cracked the silence loudly.

"What is?"

"Being around you. You don't seem to need me to see your position. My family, the town, it's as though if I don't do what they think is best, it will be bad for me. They need me to see things like they do. To agree with them."

"That's not normal. You know that, right?"

"They care, Jay. You didn't see me five years ago. They did. They know how fragile I was."

"You were injured, Ellen, not fragile. You recovered."

For the most part he was right.

"It goes deeper than that, though." She struggled to verbalize something she'd never expressed before. "I think guilt prompts a lot of my mom's actions. She feels like she let me down, that she wasn't a good enough parent, a good enough protector and that if she had done better, I wouldn't have been raped. She knows that I didn't call her for help because she was so overworked, trying to do the job of two parents. Any other time I would have called. And if I had—"

"Your mother didn't ask her husband to leave her for another woman. She was one person, doing the best she could."

"I know that. I don't blame her. But I think she blames herself. I think she promised herself that she won't let me down again. She won't miss one little thing that she might do or say that could keep me safe."

"You're an adult. It's no longer her job to keep you safe."

"I know. But it is my job to watch out for her. She's my mother and I care about her struggles. I want to be there for her. Which means that I have to understand when she gets too forceful with me. I just have to be careful not to give in to what she wants unless I believe it's the right thing to do. Which means that I'm always on alert when someone is asking me to make life-changing decisions. I appreciate that you give me the space to think things through on my own."

"I believe that each person is put on this earth to have his or her own experiences. His or her own learning curves. We have to make our own decisions if we are to get the most out of our lives. Only you know what's best for you. Because only you have your own perspective. Only you have to live with the ultimate consequences."

Consequences. It always came to that—and they were something no one knew for sure going in. The full consequences were clear only in hindsight, when it was too late to call an overworked mom for a ride.

"I don't fully trust myself to make the best decisions for me." She'd known this for a while.

Counseling had helped her to realize what was going on inside of her so she could control it rather than have it control her. But Ellen knew that, sometimes, knowing still didn't give you control.

"I don't think anyone does. How could we? If we knew ahead of time how things would turn out, there would be no decisions to make, would there? We'd simply move through life choosing our consequences. Let's see, I'll take this job that I might not like as well because I see right here in the consequences list that in two years there's going to be a product developed that will net me enough money to retire the next day."

Jay's tone suggested facetiousness, and Ellen grinned. But the truth of his words resonated deeply within her.

"You do what you think is best at the time," she said.

"Yep. And sometimes things turn out even better than you hoped. And sometimes they don't turn out the way you wanted. But in every case, you learn something and hopefully the lesson leads you on to a better outcome next time."

"I often think that if I ponder hard and long enough, I'll see the consequences before I make the decision."

"And if you don't, then what?"

"I keep pondering."

"And spend your whole life stuck in one place while opportunities pass you by?"

"Occasionally the answers are clear." Although not this time. And if she pondered indefinitely, she would most definitely lose this opportunity.

"But not this time."

"Nope, not this time."

He didn't say anything to that, didn't try to convince her one way or the other.

"I like you, Jay."

"You make that sound like a bad thing."

"I'm not sure it isn't. It would be very bad if I developed some kind of reliance on you. You're here and then gone."

"A good deterrent from becoming dependent on your therapist. If I were a counselor, I'd agree, you know. It's a good thing I'm not going to stick around long. That relationship is very different. But my job is to gain your trust only long enough to prepare you to trust others enough to accept physical attention from them."

"You're very different from anyone I've ever known."

"I know."

If she wanted others to trust her to be able to take care of herself, she had to trust herself to do it. Based on her own instincts. Her own thoughts.

"I want to continue therapy." The words weren't so hard to say. They were much more difficult to hear.

Striking fear deep within her, and yet, resounding with good judgment, too.

"Good." He met her gaze and it was as though he was absorbing her into him. They could talk all they wanted. They could say they were going to keep things on a professional level. But the words didn't break the invisible thread pulling them together.

She was exhausted. Not so much physically as mentally. "Do you ever get to the point where you wish you could turn off your brain just for a little while?" And then, before he could answer she said, "No, you probably don't. You simply move on, don't you?"

"I've never found a way to leave my thoughts behind. They tend to follow me wherever I go. But yes, I do get to the point where I wish I could quiet the cacophony. When I was younger I used drugs and alcohol for that. These days I've found a healthier vice. Finding forgetfulness is a hell of a lot more fun, and there's never a physical hangover."

She was curious. About everything Jay did. "What's the vice?"

"Casinos. You ever been to one?"

"No." David would have a fit if she ever thought about gambling. He didn't think it was right to throw away money when people were starving and homeless.

"There's one a few miles from here."

Her parents had been on a committee with Becca and Will to prevent the building of that casino when Ellen had been a kid. She and her siblings had been bored listening to the many invasion-of-the-casino conversations over dinner.

"I know."

"You want to go?"

"Now?"

"You look like a woman who could use some non-physical forgetfulness."

"I only have a twenty with me."

"That will be enough. We'll play pennies. And the rule is, when the money is gone, the game is over."

She was tempted. Jay's world seemed so much easier than hers, sometimes—no one to answer to, no rules to uphold. She had to admit, his life sounded exciting, too.

She'd never be happy away from Shelter Valley—that was a given. Shelter Valley wasn't only a place to her, or a home. It was a way of life that she loved. Wanted. Shelter Valley was a piece of heaven on earth.

But if she could find a way to have a little bit of excitement mixed in with the peace and the love and the support and giving, she'd like that, too.

She was young. And some days it felt as though she was living the life of a woman twice her age.

Still, throwing away twenty dollars...

"I'm not good about wasting money."

"Me, either. I don't see the money I spend at the casino as a waste. It's entertainment, like going to the theater or a football game. I'm paying for the mental relaxation. And it's cheaper than antidepressants as along as you play responsibly."

No worries there. Ellen did everything responsibly.

"But if you're uncomfortable, we won't go. Some people like it, some don't. I'm good either way. The place is open 24/7. I can get there anytime."

It was her choice.

Hers alone.
No guilt.
"Let's go."

CHAPTER SEVENTEEN

SPENDING TIME WITH ELLEN was good for Jay. But it wasn't easy. In some ways so refreshing, she was also so unconsciously guarded, so timid to trust, he knew that if he screwed up his association with her, if he betrayed the trust she was placing in him, the risk was great. She could lock herself up in a permanent emotional prison.

He'd never forgive himself.

As he drove toward the casino, Jay focused on not noticing the woman behind him. Those hands—now at his waist instead of on his shoulders, inching their way around—were no more than a safety belt.

Ellen's safety belt.

While instinctively he needed to relax, go with the ride—and the woman, let nature be nature—he could not do so.

The result was personally painful.

And completely right.

Just like that night twelve years ago when he'd made the call that had resulted in handcuffs chaffing his wrists, a booking photo, the admission that he had no one—then eighteen long months in jail. He'd done the right thing then, too.

And it had hurt him like hell.

Compared to that, helping Ellen should be a piece of cake. A walk in the park. And every other cliché that had ever been or had yet to be invented. He could do this.

Really, the fact that she was a client was saving him from himself where she was concerned. Her being a client was a safety net from the way she was affecting him—tugging on emotions he didn't use.

Or even want to use.

Her hands shifted and connected. With each other. Just above his waistline. Over his navel.

Ellen Moore was holding him.

Safety belt. It was only a safety belt.

The sky was blue. There were plants in the desert. Prickly looking plants. Mean plants. And a car ahead of him that was obviously running on cruise control. The guy was hogging the passing lane with no cars for a long distance in front of him. Jay was trapped behind him and the car on the right that cruise-ass should have been passing but wasn't.

There was a good, sound, logical reason for his level of frustration. Jerks who thought they owned the road. Ask any guy—he'd tell you that drivers like that pissed guys off. It was normal. Fine. Reasonable.

If he were alone on the bike, he'd rev his engine and speed between the two vehicles—a maneuver that was legal in Arizona.

He wasn't alone.

Hands were right there, an inch or two above his—

It was growing.

No matter how many times he told himself she was a client, he wanted to have sex with Ellen.

But he also wanted to help Ellen. So much that he wouldn't make himself stop seeing her.

And the prayer he'd recited every night in prison started in his mind.

Oh, God in heaven, if there is a heaven, if you exist, now would be a good time to help me....

SHE LOVED IT! GAZING around wide-eyed, Ellen couldn't take in all of the sights and colors and sounds. They'd entered the marble foyer and taken the four steps that led to the red-and-blue carpeted main floor.

Piped-in pop hits played in the background, though she could only hear the tunes intermittently. Bells rang, hums and buzzes and sirenlike melodies sang all at once, forming a cacophony of sound that produced excitement like Ellen had never known before. It ran through her veins, igniting her.

The machines were all so colorful, with glass-cased screens that animated like miniature movies—some actually played movies in bonus rounds.

They'd been there half an hour and Ellen still had her twenty dollars in her pocket. She was going to use it—there was no doubt about that—but she was having so much fun watching, she was content to wait for her own experience.

She was still learning the ropes.

"Watch this guy," she said to Jay as he came out of the men's restroom. She'd been waiting for him and watching a man in his sixties feeding a one-dollar slot machine. "He put in a hundred-dollar bill less than three minutes ago, and he's already down to thirty-three dollars. Look how fast he pushes that button—before he even knows what he got, he pushes again. I don't get it."

Standing next to her, close but not touching, Jay said,

"He's playing the odds, knowing that he has to invest in order to win. He's waiting for the machine to hit."

Ellen watched. In the midst of the wildness and noise around her, Jay's familiar warmth was nice. Really nice.

"Will it?"

"Probably, if he sits there long enough."

"But will it be worth it?"

"Will he make back what he invested, you mean?"

Still watching the reels spin, she nodded. And thought about Jay standing there next to her. With her.

And about the fact that she liked him with her.

"Maybe. He might break even. He might come out ahead. And he might not. That's why it's called gambling."

"Wow."

"The key is, does he invest more than he has to lose?" Jay said, leaning down so that she could hear him over all of the competing noises in the huge, rambling room. "If he does, he's got a problem. As long as you're paying for entertainment, within your entertainment budget, rather than gambling to win, you'll be okay."

"Doesn't everyone want to win?"

"Of course. But if you gamble only to win, that means you gamble until you win, which could mean that you spend all you have and then look for ways to get more, driven by the belief that the big win is coming up right around the corner."

"That's when it becomes a disease."

"Right."

Pulling out a twenty, he stepped up to a penny machine. He pulled her with him and Ellen stood close as she watched. He bet sixty cents, hit for sixty cents and the reels that had won evaporated and more cascaded down to fill in the blank spots. Her heart leaped. Something had lined up. He won another twenty cents, and the reels evaporated again, more fell into place. On the same bet he hit for another ten cents.

Ellen grinned. Watching the reels as Jay bet his sixty cents over and over again—coming up short sometimes, and ahead on others. He hit a bonus and the reels played by themselves, racking up fifteen dollars worth of pennies.

A woman screamed behind her and Ellen turned. The woman, about seventy, was sitting at a machine that had money spurting on the screen. A continuous geyser of animated gold coins. The words *Super Big Win* were in bold black letters at the top of the geyser.

"Look!" she said to Jay, grabbing his arm without thinking. She let go quickly, as soon as she realized what she'd done. But the sense of touching him lingered as he turned around.

"Good Lord!"

Black-suited gentlemen appeared by the woman.

"What?"

"She won 400,000 pennies."

"Four thousand dollars?"

"Yep."

"Well, good for her." The woman was on her cell phone. She was laughing. Her hand was shaking.

Ellen was ready to play.

After hanging together for about an hour, she was ready for Jay to give her a little independence. "You can go do your thing." She had bet twenty cents here and ten cents there, and still had ten dollars.

It kind of scared her how much she was enjoying having him by her side—part of the reason she'd needed him to go off on his own. If she was to start being aware of the opposite sex again, to enjoy male company, she needed to do so with someone who lived in Shelter Valley and intended to stay there.

Pushing those worries aside, she focused on having a blast. There was so much to see, to hear, so much excitement the adrenaline raced through her. She had no room for worries or decisions or issues. She'd been transported to a different world, one with no clocks, no outside. A world filled with the most wonderful opportunities and possibilities.

And all it cost her was twenty dollars—not even because she hadn't bet it all.

"I'm not leaving you alone in here," Jay said, sitting next to her as she played a fish machine she'd been sitting at for half an hour. Every once in a while a fish would swim around and there would be a bonus round. She'd hit ten of them and was about even for her time at the machine.

"I can move somewhere else if there's something you want to play."

"Are you kidding? I'm having fun watching you."

She hit the button again, playing her usual twenty cents. A fish came out again—telling her to pick a chest. Most times he blew into a balloon that grew with coins until it popped and she would win the number of coins it blew. She'd made five dollars on one blow.

"How do I pick it?" she asked, staring at the betting buttons in front of her.

"Touch the screen." His arm came close to hers as he pointed. But he didn't touch her. He hadn't touched her at all as they'd moved about the casino.

He simply stayed close. Comfortably close.

There were two rows of chests. Ellen chose the one in the upper left corner. It popped out a key, which jumped onto the screen and doubled her winnings, and told her to pick again. She did. Again and again and again. Her win had increased five times.

"Five times what?" she asked Jay.

"We don't know yet."

Pick again. She only had two chests left.

She picked and the number five hundred popped out of the chest.

"I won five hundred pennies?" Her heart pumped in anticipation.

"You won five times five hundred pennies." Jay grinned.

"No way. I won twenty-five dollars?"

"Yeah."

"I did not." He was teasing her. She'd only bet twenty cents. Then a big box appeared on the screen, confirming Jay's claim.

The machine shouted and so did Ellen. "Wahoo!" Jumping out of her seat, she turned and hugged the man who had brought her to this world. She threw her arms around his neck and held on.

And replayed the moment over and over again during the long hours of that night while she lay in her bed alone. She would have preferred to think about the win. About the twenty-five dollars.

Instead, she couldn't stop thinking about the feel of Jay's groin pressed into hers as he'd stood to catch her hug.

She was starting to feel again.

And, heaven help her, whether Jay was long for Shelter Valley or not, she didn't want those feelings to stop.

JAY HAD SUNDAY OFF. AND he took a long ride. Arizona might not have beaches, but the mountains had their own natural call—their ruggedness suited him. Riding his bike along the trails, pushing it and himself, around sharp turns and up steep inclines, he raced the demons that chased him.

He beat them, too, the way he always did—until he thought about heading back to Shelter Valley. The place, with all its adobe homes so close together, the adobe privacy fences that enclosed the yards, the people who walled in their town with their watchful eyes and caring interference were squeezing the breath out of him.

He couldn't find the bastard who had fathered him.

He was going to have to figure out what to do with the boy—Cole. He had to meet him. There seemed to be no doubts in him anymore about that. He had to be honest with the boy—about everything, his lifestyle, his past and even his doubts.

Beyond that, he had no idea.

But if the boy wanted to be with him, if Cole thought they could make a life together, if he even wanted to try, Jay would have to find a way.

He wasn't going to abandon his son.

And as for Ellen— For the first time in his life he wasn't sure he could do what he'd set out to do. She was responding to therapy. That wasn't the problem. The problem was that he was responding to her.

He'd promised her he could separate the man from the massage therapist. After last night's hug, he wasn't so sure. He'd woken up hard twice in the night—both times with dreams that involved her holding him.

Something in him, something bigger than mere sexual desire, pushed him toward making a move on her.

And because he didn't recognize himself around her these days, he couldn't trust this odd man who had surfaced within him to behave as Jay dictated.

They had an eight-o'clock appointment tomorrow and he'd be there. But it might be the last time he saw her. He was absolutely not risking setting her back in her recovery.

Stopping at a deserted scenic viewpoint somewhere halfway up a mountain, Jay checked his cell phone for service. Four bars. With the push of a couple of buttons, he'd retrieved his contacts and dialed Kelsey's number.

"Hello?"

"It's Jay Billingsley. Can you talk?"

"I'm outside at the pool. Alone. So, yes. Have you made arrangements to come get Cole?"

"I never said I was coming to get him."

"He's your son, Jay. I've handled him for twelve years. Now it's your turn."

"You'd hand over your own son? Just like that?" Either the kid was more of a terror than she'd admitted or Kelsey was less of a woman than he remembered—and his memories of her weren't all that complimentary.

"I've tried everything," she said. "Had him in every program, every sport—even paid for private batting instruction. He's been through three nannies. I'm at my wit's end. I don't know what else I can do."

"So what do you think I can do that you can't?"

"I don't know. I do know that your son is disrupting our home. He's always after James and John, making them cry. He's a bad influence on them and I'm not going to have him lead them down his wrong path."

James and John. Kelsey's four-year-old twins. She'd told Jay about them during that first call.

"Have you told Cole about me yet?"

"No."

"Don't you think you should? At least prepare the kid before you pack his bags and kick him out?"

"I think you should tell him."

As much as he disliked the idea, disliked the entire situation, Jay was beginning to agree with Kelsey on that one.

"Does he have any free time next week?" What in the hell was he doing? He wasn't ready to be a father to a troubled kid. He had no plan. No idea.

No home to give him.

"Thursday night, he's free after six. We've got him in a private hockey league and he has practice every day after school."

"Is he good at it?"

"Not really. But it keeps him out of the house and off the streets."

Curious, Jay asked, "Whose idea was it that he play?"

"McGuire and his dad came up with it." McGuire, Kelsey's husband and, once upon a time, Jay's friend. As he recalled, McGuire had played hockey as a kid.

"Has Cole ever expressed any interest in hockey?"

"The only thing your son ever expresses interest in is pot, that damned MP3 player of his and the computer."

His son. Wasn't Cole Kelsey's son, too?

Not that Jay had any illusions about her parenting. She and his own father had a lot in common—an ability to shove their kids off onto someone else to raise.

Whatever happened to unconditional love?

"I'll pick him up on Thursday at six," Jay said. "Tell him I'm an old college friend. I'll take care of the rest."

He didn't know how. Or what good it would do. He

wasn't going to ride off with the boy, no matter what Kelsey thought. Cole was her son. She didn't get to throw him away.

But Jay would have to see the boy sometime. Even if that meant regular visits to Arizona.

He had to keep looking for his father, as well. At one point the man had existed. Jay simply wasn't looking in the right places.

One thing was for certain. Jay couldn't wait around any longer. Greg Richards had paid him another visit that morning and Jay had half expected to be castrated for hugging Ellen. He couldn't move without someone in town watching him. He had to get moving before life in Shelter Valley strangled him to death.

CHAPTER EIGHTEEN

JAY WAS AT HOME, LOOKING for jewelers in the Tucson area that had been open for business thirty years before. Monday, after his appointments, he intended to visit every one of them to show a picture of his mother and ask if there were old records of wedding ring sales. Or someone who might remember...

It was the kind of investigating paid detectives didn't have time for. A long shot.

He'd had longer ones pay off.

The phone rang as he finished with the fourth entry on his list. A glance at the caller ID showed Ellen's name.

Was she calling to cancel?

If so, he wouldn't try to talk her out of it. This was her choice, her journey.

"Hello?"

"It's Ellen, am I bothering you?"

Hell, yes, she was bothering him. Every second of the day. And it wasn't all sexual, either. That he could handle. Maybe.

"I'm going over files," he told her.

"That's what I'm calling about. David found some old church records and he has something he wants to show you. Can you come over?"

"Are you at your mother's?"

"Yeah. "

"I'm on my way."

The sooner he found his bastard of a father, the sooner he could be out of this town. And if he couldn't get his impulses about Ellen under control, he might be on his way even without finding the man.

ELLEN HADN'T TOLD HER mother and David about the casino trip. She figured what they didn't know wouldn't eat away at them. She was a grown woman. An adult who had to trust the validity of her own mind—starting with the ability to keep her own counsel where her parents were concerned.

No doubt about it, this was awkward, having Jay in her parents' house when they so clearly didn't want him there. She felt like a recalcitrant kid as she sat in her mother's living room, on the same couch she and Aaron had made out on. The same couch she'd lain on as a teenager with cramps, as an abandoned daughter, as a rape victim, as a young mother grieving her failed marriage. So many ups and downs.

She wasn't a kid. And she'd done nothing wrong.

Jay sat across the room from Ellen. And far away from the folder her stepfather had left on the coffee table. The manila piece of cardboard was not far from where Ellen sat. On purpose.

"I took the liberty of requesting church records from our archives this past week when Ellen told us why you're in town," David said.

Ellen loved her stepfather—more than she loved her biological one. Even now, while she knew he wanted Jay in another country, David was calm, kind, hospitable as he faced the man. He was still willing to help. And not only to speed Jay's exit from town.

"I spent a couple of hours going through records," David said. "We have some birth records as well as records of any marriage that was performed within the church grounds, whether by the officiating pastor or not."

Sitting forward, his elbows on his knees, hands clasped between, Jay looked between David and the file he now held.

"I didn't realize Jay was already here." Martha walked in. "You'd think with all of the kids out and the house quiet, I would have heard the voices."

Her mother was babbling. Which meant she was uptight. Ellen smiled. Patted the couch beside her.

Waiting until Martha was seated, David said, "I'm not sure this will amount to anything, but I think it might." He handed the folder to Jay.

Ellen waited while he looked over the contents David had shown her earlier—a brief record regarding the arrangements for a small private wedding that never took place. And the photo that accompanied it.

"It's her." Jay's voice was flat. He didn't look up so Ellen couldn't see his expression. "I have a copy of this photo. It was her high school senior picture."

"I thought she was the same woman in the photo Ellen showed us." David spoke softly, as well. Reverently. Compassionately.

Because that's how the people of Shelter Valley were. They genuinely cared. Not only about their own, but about anyone who needed help.

"It says that the groom was a no-show."

"Yes."

"And the name...this...Jay Donnelly?"

"I'm guessing he's your father," David said. "Have you ever heard anyone use the name Donnelly?"

"No one in any way related to me," Jay said. He glanced up, and his eyes, when they met Ellen's, were glinting.

With anger?

Pain?

She couldn't be sure. She only knew they called to her.

"Let's look through your files again," she said, standing. "See if we can find any reference to a Donnelly. Maybe on the U of A tennis team. Or on Montford's. Or in an article."

Jay nodded as he rose.

David stood, too. "I'll ask around to see if any of our parishioners remember your mother. She must have had some association with the church if she intended to marry there. There are a lot of folks who worship with us on Sundays who have been doing so for more than thirty years. Someone is bound to remember something."

With the folder still in his hand Jay turned toward David, offered his hand. "Thank you, sir."

"You're welcome. I hope this helps you with your search."

Martha was beside David then. Ellen hadn't even been aware that her mother had left her seat on the couch.

"You went to the University of Arizona, didn't you?" she said to Jay. A stalling tactic. Ellen saw it for what it was. Her mother's mind was spinning, searching desperately for a way to keep Ellen from going to Jay's house with him.

Ellen wasn't going to let her mother stop her. She was a grown woman. Not a child. She had to demand ownership of her life or lose it forever.

"Yes," Jay said.

"Until you were arrested."

"That's right."

"You only had a year left."

The muscles in Jay's upper shoulders tightened—a reaction made more noticeable by the sleeveless shirt he'd chosen to wear. "Yes, ma'am." He didn't disrespect her mother by moving away or heading to the door. He withstood her inquisition.

Because that was the kind of man Jay was.

"Did you go back when you got out? Did you finish? Get your degree?"

"No, ma'am, I did not."

Ellen hadn't asked. She'd assumed, with Jay's credentials, a college degree had been involved.

"I went to a technical school to train for my trade."

"With only one year left on a degree?"

"Yes, ma'am."

Ellen tensed, wishing she could get him out of here. She knew what was coming.

Next to protecting their people, the most sacred thing in Shelter Valley was education—*college* education. Montford University not only supported the town, it also trained people who helped change the world. Ellen knew the rhetoric. She'd grown up with it.

And she believed in it, too.

"Well," Martha said, sending Ellen a pointed glance, "I guess you can always return when you're ready."

"I have no intention of going back," Jay said, his voice soft, kind and firm, too. "Formal education is highly overrated as far as I'm concerned. Most parents struggle to cover the thousands of dollars of tuition, books and living expenses. All for classes that a large percentage of the attending students remember nothing about by the time they graduate, let alone once they're out in the world."

"I don't agree," Martha said while David gave Ellen a sideways glance that said, *uh-oh*. He knew how adamant her mother was about education.

Because Martha was the only one of the Shelter Valley heroines who didn't have a college degree. She'd married and had children before she'd graduated. In the end, her mother had paid a steep price for that lack of education when she'd been forced to support four children on her own.

"I took a class in Russian history," Jay said. "I studied—got an A. And I can't tell you one thing about Russian history."

"It's not necessarily retaining the facts from particular classes that mean so much," Martha said. "It's the security the degree offers."

"Which is why so many white-collared people are having their homes foreclosed on while truck drivers are in demand." Somehow Jay made the statement sound like a lament, rather than a challenge.

"I can see this conversation lasting all night," David interjected lightly, his hand on his wife's elbow as he led the way to the door.

"Ellen, I just remembered, I brought home a film from the studio that I need you to look at—it's set to air tomorrow. A piece that the students put together that deals with a family discovering their teenage son is gay. I'd really like your opinion before I show it—"

"Tomorrow's Monday, Mom. It's fine arts day."

"Oh, right." Martha grimaced. "The film doesn't air until Tuesday."

"I'll be by to look at it tomorrow after work. I'm sure you've seen it and know it's fine. I'll be okay at Jay's house, Mom. He's not a rapist."

Martha's grin almost broke Ellen's heart. Her vivacious, energetic and solid-as-a-rock mother was struggling. "I was pretty obvious, huh?"

"Yep."

"I'm sorry. Go with Jay. You're good at research— you catch all the little details. You always did."

"I won't hurt your daughter, ma'am." Jay could have left through the door David was holding open. He didn't. He stood directly in front of Martha.

"I hope not. She's been hurt too much."

"I know. I give you my word, I will do all I can to help her then be on my way."

Martha nodded. It was obviously the best she could do.

For Ellen, it was enough.

"I THINK IT'S BEST IF you don't come with me," Jay said as soon as they were outside the Markses' home.

Mouth open, Ellen stopped in her tracks. She looked... hurt.

"I— The hug last night... I want you, Ellen." He shrugged. "I promised your mother I wouldn't hurt you. So I don't think it's a good idea for us to be alone together at my house."

"You're not a rapist, Jay."

"I know that."

"If anything were ever to happen between us, which it won't, I would have to agree to it, wouldn't I? And if I agreed, where's the problem?"

"I won't physically hurt you, but that's not what your mother's worried about."

"So, you're going to hurt me—what?—emotionally? How are you going to do that? If I cared about you enough to be emotionally hurt by you, how would you stop that?"

"You're not the type to have casual sex, Ellen. And if something happened..." This was not going well. At all. To make matters worse, he'd seen a twitch at the front curtains. Someone inside was watching them.

"Now you're like my mother and the rest of Shelter Valley, thinking you need to protect me from myself? I will get hurt again in my life, Jay. God, I'm hurting right now with my son away with his father and me here alone. But at least I'm living. Feeling alive."

"If we had sex, I couldn't treat you anymore."

"And if anything ever happened between us, I wouldn't really need your treatment anymore, would I?"

Feeling as though he'd been involved in some kind of bizarre foreplay, Jay gave in and let her join him. He would have liked to believe that he was doing so because she was a good researcher and he didn't want to hurt her feelings, but feared he'd allowed her to come home with him simply because he wanted her there.

After a thorough examination of the documents, they found nothing that showed a connection between anyone named Donnelly and Tammy Walton or Tammy Billingsley. Jay was beginning to doubt that his mother's name had ever been Billingsley. She'd been born Tammy Walton. His aunt had buried her as Tammy Walton. His mother had never been married. That was pretty clear.

The research session a bust, Ellen left without so much as a handshake.

Jay took a dip in the pool, although it did nothing to cool him down.

JAY DROVE TO TUCSON ON Monday afternoon, where he canvassed jewelry stores and turned up nothing. After his visit with Ellen's stepfather the night before, he'd expanded his search of jewelry stores in business thirty years ago to any stores within a hundred miles of Shelter Valley, and that had also netted him a big fat nothing.

So far he hadn't found any connection between his mother and Shelter Valley, other than the picture from the tennis match and arrangements for a wedding. So he'd keep looking. She'd been there. Chances were, she'd left a trace someplace.

Or maybe the man who had gotten her pregnant had.

Had his paternal gene pool been from Shelter Valley and not Tucson as his aunt had claimed? Was that why she'd been so insistent he not attend Montford?

So who was this loser who had impregnated his mother then cut out right after Jay was born, giving up all rights to him? Who was the fiend who had left his mother so destitute that she had been forced to live in lower-income housing, placing her at risk to the sick asshole who had broken in one afternoon, raped and murdered her? Where was Jay's father when his mother had needed protection?

Not being a man, that much Jay knew.

And what about him? Was he really any better than

the man whose blood ran through his veins? Had he ever stayed in one place or committed to one person in his adult life—other than the eighteen months he'd been incarcerated and had had no choice but to stay put?

He had known about his own son's existence for more than a month and he hadn't even gone to meet the boy.

He woke up in cold sweats even contemplating having the kid live with him.

But there was one major difference between him and his old man—Jay was going to do what it took to be there for his kid. Somehow. He was a wanderer. Not a deserter.

And if that meant Cole had to go on the road with him, so be it.

Jay focused on muscles and Cole, keeping his thoughts away from Ellen. He saw her Monday, Tuesday and Wednesday mornings, like clockwork. Eight o'clock in. Work her muscles. Eight-thirty out. Muscles. Cole. Not woman. Not Ellen.

He was going to keep his word to her. To her mother. And to himself. He was going to treat her issue. Help her heal. He was not going to hurt her.

"Have I done something to anger you?" she asked after their session on Wednesday.

"No, of course not."

She looked at him. "You're sure?"

Meeting her gaze wasn't easy. Especially with the feel of the back of her thighs still so fresh against his fingers. "Of course."

"Then what's the problem?"

"We have no problem that I know of."

"You're acting like you don't know me."

"I don't, really." And he wouldn't. He would help her. He would not betray her trust with lustful indiscretions. He would not play with her heart, knowing full well that he wouldn't be around for long.

"Yes, you do." Her unwavering stare was not as hard to take as it should have been. He admired her guts. "Now tell me what's going on."

He could lie to her. Of course, that would be a betrayal of trust, too.

"I made a promise."

"To who?"

"You. Your mother. Myself."

She blinked. "Oh."

Ellen turned toward the waiting room. "Same time tomorrow?" she asked over her shoulder.

Jay nodded.

He didn't walk her out.

CHAPTER NINETEEN

ON WEDNESDAY AFTERNOON, in between a plastic canvas class, which she taught, and water aerobics, which she merely sat in on, Ellen listened to her sister Shelley lament, via cell phone, about a conductor she was working with in Phoenix. Shelley had auditioned for, and won, a solo soprano role in a cantata being performed with the Phoenix symphony in the fall and the conductor rode her mercilessly, if you believed how Shelley told it.

Ellen, who was used to her dramatics, suspected that her sister had a crush on the handsome young artist.

She hoped so. After Shelley's trouble in high school—a time when her sister had turned to the wrong kind of guy for the love and protection her father had taken away—she hadn't shown much interest in men.

After work, she stopped by the Stricklands' house to turn on the air conditioner and cool the place since they were returning from vacation later tonight. Then she went to Rebecca's apartment near the university to help her youngest sister with the lasagna she wanted to make for her husband. Finally, she headed home to finish the caboose on the train she'd painted on her son's wall. On a whim, she added a puppy in the window since Josh wanted a dog.

Maybe it was time to get him one. She could tell

him about it the next time she talked to him. Maybe she could even have it waiting here for him when he got back. Hard to believe she still had almost two weeks left without him. What kind of puppy would he like? What kind would be best for them to have?

What was she doing? Trying to buy her son's affection with a puppy? She'd told him they would get a dog when he was old enough to take care of it. To train it. Five was still a little young for that.

Really, what she was doing was trying not to think about Jay. In a couple of short weeks she had become addicted to the feel of his hands on her body.

For the past four days, she'd been thinking about those hands doing other things to her, too. Sliding her clothes off, stroking her sides, brushing the sides of her breasts.

The heroines of Shelter Valley stripped to their panties for their massages. A tidbit she'd learned from one of the millions of discussions between her mother and her friends that Ellen had been privy to.

What would Jay do if she stripped down to her panties before pulling the sheet up? She imagined herself lying in wait in the near nude, with the soft lighting and her garden music playing. Thought about him opening the door. Coming inside.

He'd reach for her, start to stroke. And find her skin waiting for him.

Sitting alone in a hot bubble bath that night, Ellen thought of Jay's fingers. And her nipples puckered.

He'd said he wanted her. That's what had started all of this fantasizing.

Hadn't it?

Or had it begun before that?

A vision of him, Black Leather, roaring into town on that powerful machine of his, came to mind. And her lower belly got *that* feeling.

Sitting straight up, Ellen splashed water all over the floor. "Oh, my God," she said aloud. Her voice didn't quell the buzzing. She thought of Jay's jeans—his zipper. Imagined that zipper opening. Imagined his hard penis coming toward her.

She put her hand between her legs, applying pressure in an attempt to hold off the buzzing. She was turned on. The thought of Jay's penis didn't shut her down. It revved her up.

She pictured it again. Applied more pressure.

Oh, my.

By THURSDAY MORNING, Ellen was a charged conglomeration of excitement, practical justification and fear, trying to focus on holding herself together.

She went to her appointment because that was what she'd agreed to do. Her sessions with Jay had become routine. Though she thought about undressing, she didn't, of course. There was a huge gap between thought and action—a gap Ellen wouldn't really cross.

She covered herself with the sheet, placed her head on the support and waited.

She wanted to have sex. For the first time since she'd been raped, her body pulsed with need. She could have taken care of the need herself—self-pleasuring had been suggested in counseling. But that had never been a goal. Being alone, period, wasn't her goal.

She didn't want just an orgasm. She wanted to have one with a man. Because of a man.

Jay was there to facilitate her ability to welcome

physical touch. He'd said that he'd do what it took to help her heal.

He'd said he was sexually attracted to her.

He'd said—

The door opened. Ellen closed her eyes. Waited for the pressure of his hands. And let her mind take her wherever it wanted to go.

JAY WAITED FOR ELLEN in the hall. He'd managed to get through the half hour without having a single errant thought regarding her body or person—managed more easily than he had all week, due to his level of stress.

He was meeting Cole this afternoon. Jay was no clearer about what to do, or say, than he'd been before he found out the kid existed.

"Has David been able to find out anything more about my mother?" he asked when Ellen joined him.

"Not that I've heard. He's been asking around all week. He had a dinner with the senior classics last night and I know there were a few folks there he was eager to speak with. How are you coming with your research?"

"Nothing yet."

The kind of tedious reading, rereading and cross-reference reading he was doing could take months. Years.

He'd expanded his search from wedding dress ads and jewelers to any articles written on the subject of tennis in Arizona over a three-year span.

This morning he'd called his landlord about sub-leasing the place. His first month was almost up and he was ready to move on.

Had to move on.

"I'm free tonight. I'd be happy to read for a while,"

Ellen offered. That smile of hers, as though his quest meant something to her, nicked at him.

"I'm busy."

"Oh." The smile on her face became forced. He hadn't meant to be so abrupt. He had to stay away from Ellen, not be cruel to her.

"I'm going to meet Cole tonight."

"Wow." Eyes widening, she stared at him. "Does he know about you, yet?"

"Nope. It's been left up to me to tell him."

Opening the door to his room, Ellen reentered. Curiosity dragged Jay in behind her.

"Do you have any idea what you're going to say?" Ellen's arms hugged her midsection, almost as though it was hurting.

"Nope." He'd never been one for planned speeches. Not even when he'd taken a speech class his freshman year of college.

"What are you guys going to do?"

"I have no idea."

"You're going to show up and wing the whole thing?"

"Pretty much."

"Jay, this is a huge deal. It could affect the rest of that boy's life."

Chin jutted and lips pursed, Jay nodded. He fully understood the ramifications. But he couldn't figure a way out of watching the train wreck.

"You know that already," she said, dropping onto the chair. "Is there anything I can do to help?"

He wanted her help. That was no good. Jay had a problem and his instinct was to run to Ellen.

The same as everyone else around here.

What was with him? Was this sudden need for a

confidant because of Ellen? Because she exuded something that drew people to seek out her particular brand of nurturing?

Or was there something wrong with him? Had this town done something to him? Was being enmeshed in an atmosphere of goodwill messing him up? Either way, his malady would be cured by getting out of town.

"I don't practice family counseling, but I did a six-month internship as part of my senior year at Montford. And I'm certified as a family counselor."

Her brown eyes were so wide and warm and welcoming, as though, if he lowered his defenses, she'd suck him in like some kind of creature in a science fiction horror show.

"I could go with you. Sometimes it helps the child to have an advocate there—someone he can vent with. Cole might be angry. Really angry."

"If he needs to vent, he can vent on me. I can take it." He'd faced down violence in prison and won. He could handle a twelve-year-old kid. "The boy deserves time alone with me, to react without judgment or assessment."

"I was thinking about you, too." Ellen's soft words brushed by him. But returned to linger, to tease him with a softness that wasn't a part of his life. "He's your son. You've been rejected by your father. It's not going to be easy for you if the meeting goes bad."

"I'm a big boy. I can handle it."

Nodding, she stood. "Can I tell you what I think?"

"Of course."

"Will you listen?"

He wasn't sure, but he had an idea Ellen had his

number. He was scared shitless. But he had to do this on his own.

"I'd appreciate hearing anything you've got to tell me," he finally said. Because this wasn't only about him. This was about a boy who would soon find out that he'd been lied to his entire life.

"You're coming in from behind on three fronts. Cole has been lied to, you're the bearer of the bad news *and* you're the other half of the lie. He might not believe that you didn't know about him until recently. Initially, he might reject everything you tell him. I'd talk to him a bit before telling him you're his father. Let him get a feel for you before he has to deal with you in a personal way. Take him for a ride on the bike. It'll help if he thinks something about you is cool. And trust your instincts. If you don't feel tonight's a good night to tell him, don't."

"No night is a good time to find out your life is a lie."

Ellen didn't say anything. At least not with words. But the way she looked at him…she could have been cradling him in her arms.

"What?" he asked. "You think I'm not that much different from Cole. I'm finding out that my life was a lie, too."

"I didn't say that."

"But you were thinking it." He wasn't accusing, simply stating.

Even her shrug was sweet. "It's the truth."

His truth. He'd deal with it. Had dealt with worse.

"If I don't tell him tonight, I become party to the lie his mother has been feeding him all these years."

"There's a chance he'd see it that way regardless."

Hands in his pockets—mostly to keep them to himself—he nodded. "Any other words of wisdom?"

"Be yourself. And no matter what he says, don't abandon him. Not in word or in action. Stick with him like glue. You've got twelve years of insecurity to overcome. He needs to know that, no matter what, you aren't going to abandon him again."

"I didn't abandon him the first time."

"Yes, you did, Jay. Not on purpose, not knowingly, but the boy grew up without his real father. In that light, your innocence in the deception might not matter to him at first. Eventually it will, but tonight, his biggest crisis will be learning the truth and dealing with it. There probably won't be a whole lot of room for understanding. Remember, he's only twelve."

Jay tried to remember being twelve. And came up blank.

CHAPTER TWENTY

ELLEN FINISHED WORK EARLY Thursday since it was doctor visit day and residents were occupied with their checkups. More family members than usual visited, hoping to catch the doctors on their rounds. The staff was distracted. Not much call for a social director and, unless the doctor had news that precipitated a major decision, she wasn't usually needed as a counselor, either.

During the day she had read to Gladys Cottrill, a woman she'd known since kindergarten. Gladys, old even then, used to volunteer at the elementary school, reading to the kids during story time. She talked with family members about concerns a couple of residents had. She helped the nursing staff find charts and run errands for doctors as best as she could. She comforted residents who thought they were going to be forgotten or who were stressed by what they might hear.

Eventually, she got out of the way. She'd promised the canning ladies that she'd be there by noon, and she was fifteen minutes early. She spent four solid hours with them boiling lids and various other beginner jobs as she watched and learned the art of canning. And before she left she begged a case of tomatoes and beans for Joe to deliver on her next visit up the mountain.

Jogging was next on her agenda. Being on the streets

of Shelter Valley, soaking up the hot August afternoon sun, rejuvenated her. She loved the mountains
that protected the town, the desert that set it apart,
the natural beauty that surrounded it, reminding its
inhabitants that there were strong powers that watched
over them.

And could take care of them.

She couldn't imagine feeling this safe by herself
on the streets anywhere else. The self-defense classes
she'd taken in Phoenix had stressed that women should
always use the buddy system for outdoor activities.

Not being able to jog alone would trap her in a life
she didn't want. She got claustrophobic just thinking
about it.

Thoughts of other places reminded her of Jay. He
would be on his way to see his son. He'd probably been
right to go alone. But she wished she could be with him.
He'd had to face too much of life alone already.

She didn't doubt his capability—certainly Jay could
handle what life gave him. But did there come a point
when someone had been disappointed so many times
that he lost his ability to be open to sharing? And caring?

She missed seeing the sewer grate in her path and
stumbled, then righted herself. Why did the thought of
Jay being alone bring tears to her eyes?

Randi Foster, baby sister to Will Parsons, was in her
front yard with another new puppy. She waved as Ellen
passed. Ellen returned the gesture. Randi, the women's
athletic director at Montford, was also advisor to the
university's pet therapy club.

Had Jay ever had a pet? Would his son want one?
And why did the man's personal situation matter to her?

When thoughts about her bath the night before sprang to mind, Ellen turned toward home, got in her car and drove to the Sheffields'. She needed a dose of reality and who better to get that from than the twin children of a psychologist?

"Ellen!" Calvin and Clarissa, nine now, met her at the door with hugs. "Mom! Ellen's here."

"Shh," she said, hugging them both. "How does ice cream sound?"

She'd been watching these two since their birth. Had been sickened when two-year-old Calvin had been abducted by his father's former student. They'd all been in Phoenix to support Phyllis during the trial.

"Hey, stranger, how you doing?" Phyllis approached, wiping her hands on a paper towel.

"Good. Can I take them for ice cream?"

It was after six and the twins ate at five. Phyllis was a stickler with their schedules.

"Of course," she said with a penetrating gaze. "Maybe when you get back we can talk."

Phyllis had been there for Ellen many times after the rape. Always the voice of solid reason and compassion.

"Maybe," she said now. Phyllis was also one of her mother's closest friends. And there was no way in hell she wanted her mother to know the kinds of things that had been plaguing Ellen's mind all week.

"Guys, go get your flip-flops," Phyllis said to the kids.

As soon as they were racing each other up the stairs, Phyllis said, "Your mom tells me you're in therapy with the biker guy in town."

"Yeah." Of course, considering Phyllis's profession,

Martha would have run to her. Made sense. Friends or no.

"Well, I told her I think it's a good idea. Thought you should know that."

Heart beating a tattoo against her chest bone, Ellen stared at the other woman. "You do?"

"I do. I did some checking. He's reputable. And his theories are sound. It's been seven years, El. You've tried all of the traditional counseling. Trying something different might work. If you don't attempt it, you'll be consigning yourself to less than the life you want."

The air left Ellen's lungs. She sucked more in and grinned as big as she had when she'd passed her state certification. "I can imagine what Mom had to say about that."

Flopping rubber descended, but Ellen didn't miss Phyllis's sardonic words. "Yeah, well, I'm tough. I can take it. You can't live your life for your mother, El."

Ellen knew that. But it still felt good to have validation from someone who loved her mother almost as much as Ellen did.

COLE WASN'T THAT BAD. His hair was clean. Cut. He didn't have any obvious tattoos. His shorts didn't hang below his butt. And he didn't walk like a punk.

"That ponytail makes you look like a girl."

Jay had hooked up Cole to the earbud system in preparation for a trip to somewhere from the ice rink so the words were delivered clearly.

"You hungry, kid?" he asked. Cole had been told Jay was a friend of his dad's from college—completely true as long as the term *friend* was used loosely. He was in town visiting and picking Cole up because his parents had a business dinner that they couldn't miss.

"Yeah, I'm hungry," Cole said. "What's for dinner?"

How the hell did Jay know? Pizza and beer was out. At least the beer part.

"Hamburgers and French fries," he said, settling himself on the bike, getting a feel for the weight behind him.

The kid was skinny. And he wore glasses. Kelsey hadn't mentioned that part. He looked more like a book-worm nerd than a troublemaker.

He was the spitting image of Jay at that age. Of course, these days, Jay wore contacts.

"Cool." Cole named a popular fast-food joint where he wanted to eat.

Jay made it a point to never eat fast food. But if that's what Cole wanted...

"Move with me when I move," Jay said into the mic attached to his earbuds. "No sudden jerks, and for God's sake, hold on."

The hands that touched his shoulders were too small to have been in jail.

"No, kid, really hold on."

"I'm not holding a guy who looks like a woman."

"You hold on, hands around my waist, or you don't go." It was that simple.

Cole's hands slid around his waist.

Childish hands. His son's hands.

That bothered Jay.

JAY DROVE BY HALF A DOZEN hamburger joints. Cole didn't bother pointing out the fact that he'd missed them.

Based on the whoop, and the laughter coming through the headset, he'd guess that Cole was having a blast.

"You ever been on a bike before?" Jay asked when he could trust himself to speak without sounding like the girl his son had called him. He should have asked before. Would have. If he'd had a clear thought.

"No, man, this is cool. You gotta talk my dad into getting one of these."

No need. Cole's dad already owned a bike.

Jay had a son. A small him.

A little guy who was all bravado—probably to cover how scared he was of all the shit life threw at him. Or maybe it was a way to deflect the mocking from his classmates.

He could have helped Cole with that one.

"How long you staying with us?" Cole asked. "Can we go out again tomorrow after school? I don't have practice on Fridays."

"I'll talk to your mom," Jay said. He wasn't going to lie to the boy. Not ever.

He'd lost twelve years of protecting this child. Twelve years of his son's life.

Jay's eyes were watering, which made no sense. Dust wasn't particularly high in Phoenix today—monsoons had swept through during the night. He didn't have allergies. And he hadn't cried since he was Cole's age.

ELLEN ATE ICE CREAM WITH the kids. Plain, old-fashioned hot-fudge sundaes for her and Clarissa. Calvin had hot fudge, too, but with bubble gum ice cream.

Her dinner, their dessert.

Phyllis was on the phone when she dropped them

back at home. Waving at Matt, who was on his computer, Ellen made her escape.

There were no lights on at Jay's place so he probably wasn't back yet. Instead, she stopped by Shelley's rehearsal room at Montford, where her sister would be practicing the piano.

"What do you think?" Shelley asked after finishing a particularly difficult classical piece, her expression apprehensive.

"You're gifted, Shel, you know that."

"I have to get it right," Shelley said. "I missed the B-flat crescendo."

If she said she did, she might have, but Ellen certainly couldn't tell.

"You're frowning," Shelley said. "I screwed up bad, didn't I?"

"No, you did not screw up. I swear, I didn't hear a single mistake. I'd tell you if I did. You know that."

Nodding, Shelley's brow cleared. "So what was the frown about?"

"I want to have sex with him."

"With that biker dude who's driving Mom crazy?"

"Yeah."

"Don't you think I should meet him first?"

"No."

"Oh." Shelley frowned again. "I wouldn't approve?"

"It doesn't matter if you do or not. I'm not going to have a relationship with him."

"Wait." Leaving the bench, Shelley approached the love seat that was the only other piece of furniture in the tiny room. Sitting next to Ellen, she took Ellen's hand and leaned forward, looking her straight in the eye.

After the rape, Shelley hadn't been able to look at

Ellen. Her younger sister had blamed herself for the attack on Ellen. If she hadn't been so wild, giving her mother so much trouble, if she'd done her share around the house and with the younger kids, Ellen wouldn't have been so reluctant to call for help. If Shelley had picked the kids up from school once or twice, maybe Ellen wouldn't have been out of gas.

It had taken Shelley a couple of years before she'd been able to tell Ellen how sorry she was for letting her down. Unfortunately, not the confession or the apology, or Ellen's repeated assurances that the rape had in no way been Shelley's fault, had seemed to ease the guilt Shelley bore.

"Think about what you're saying, El. This is you. Miss 'I believe in love ever after, riding off into the sunset, making love is sacred,' you."

At least Shelley had listened to the repeated lectures her older sister had doled out.

"You can't have sex without caring about a guy."

"I didn't say I didn't care about him. Only that I'm not going to have a relationship with him. Jay's...Jay," Ellen said. She was smiling like a goggle-eyed schoolgirl. But she couldn't help herself. If anyone would understand, Shelley would.

And Phyllis had said it—Ellen had already tried all of the traditional counseling routes. It was better to give an unusual solution a chance than living her whole life being less than she wanted to be.

"He hates Shelter Valley. And has no use for higher education, either," she said. "He's thirty-two years old and has never had a committed relationship in his life. His idea of home is wherever his motorcycle takes him. The thought of settling down gives him hives."

"And you want to sleep with him…why?"

"He turns me on, Shel." It was something you could only tell a sister who had gone through puberty with you, who had held your hand when you gave birth, and who had cried with you when your marriage broke up because you hated sex.

"Seriously, El? As in…what?"

"All of it. Everything."

Grinning, Shelley sat back. "It's a miracle. Oh, my God, El." Her voice broke. "I thought…if what I'd done…if you'd been robbed of the most intense, beautiful…you have no idea how much I've worried. And prayed." Throwing her arms around Ellen, she held her tightly. And when she pulled back, she studied Ellen intently. "You're sure?"

"Completely sure. It's driving me crazy."

"And you think you're okay, with…you know, doing it…without happily ever after attached?"

"I think it's the only way I can be sure I'm really capable of following through with it," Ellen said. "If I were in a relationship, if the future of the relationship or the guy's feelings were attached to the act, then I'd be all tied up and afraid of failing him. It would be worse, if the feeling went away, and I had followed through anyway because I loved him."

"Like you did with Aaron."

"Right. This way, it's part of my therapy. Unusual, to say the least, but safe, protected and completely without commitment. No conditions attached, except that if I decide, at any time that I want to stop, we stop. No hard feelings."

She withstood Shelley's perusal. And still felt pretty confident that she was making the right choice.

"There's one problem," Shelley finally said.

"I'm on the Pill," Ellen reminded her.

"No, him. I mean, how can you be so sure he'll go along with this? Not that you aren't the hottest thing in Shelter Valley, you are, but—"

"I'm not hot." Ellen laughed. "And I'm okay with that. I don't want to be. And I'm pretty sure he'll go along with it because—" She stopped. Jay's confession to her had been private. Sacred.

"Just because," she finished. "And if he doesn't want to help me, then I won't be having sex with him."

"Wow." Shelley held both of her hands. Swinging them lightly. "I can't believe this."

"You don't think I'm crazy?"

"I don't care if you're crazy. I'm thrilled that you can feel again. If this works, El, you could start dating. Get married to a guy who's worthy of you. Have more kids…"

Shelley teared up, and so did Ellen. The life her sister described was exactly what Ellen wanted, what she'd almost given up hope of ever having. All she had ever wanted was to marry, have children. Be a wife and a mother and raise her family in Shelter Valley.

If Jay could give her that chance again, she'd be forever indebted to him.

And so would her future husband be. They could name their first child after him.

The idea didn't hold as much appeal as the thought of having sex with Jay.

CHAPTER TWENTY-ONE

"COLE, THERE'S SOMETHING I have to tell you." Sitting in a booth in the deserted playroom of the restaurant Jay had eventually stopped at, he popped a French fry into his mouth. Watched while his son chewed and swallowed the last bite of his burger. After driving around for an hour, he'd gotten used to the idea of having a son.

If Cole was like him, he'd be fine with the idea, too. He and Cole would ride around the country on the back of the Harley. Until his son turned sixteen and had a bike of his own. Then they would ride side by side. Two guys on the road. Needing no one.

"What? You can't take me out tomorrow after school? Don't worry about it. Mom probably wouldn't have let me go anyway. She doesn't like me to have fun. She doesn't think I deserve it."

"That's not true. Your mother wants you to have fun."

"No, she really doesn't." The boy slurped to finish his drink. "She says a bad kid like me doesn't deserve good stuff."

"You think you're a bad kid?"

"She does."

"Do you?"

"Hell, I don't know. Maybe. Anyway, what was it you had to tell me?"

You're my son. Jay heard the words in his head. His frozen throat prevented them from sounding out loud.

"Let me ask you something, first." He tried a different tact.

"What?"

"How would you feel about spending time on the road with me?"

"On the motorcycle?" The boy's eyes were huge.

"Yeah."

"I'd say, let's go."

"Could you see yourself ever living at the beach?" Part-time only. Kelsey still needed her son. And even if she didn't, Cole needed his mother. But for summers, weekends and school holidays, Jay could have his chance.

"Hell, yeah." Then the boy frowned. "Wait, what is this? You some kind of cop or something? Am I under arrest?"

"No. What makes you think that?"

"There was this kid at school, kind of a friend of mine. Some guy came and took him off to a place where he's locked up. They called it a school, but it ain't like no school I've ever heard of. He doesn't even get to come home for Christmas."

"I'm no cop," Jay said. "Though I am a licensed private investigator."

Cole held up both hands, palms out. "Hey, I haven't done nothing, man. No matter what Mom has told you. I'm clean. I swear."

"Cole, I'm not out to get you."

The boy sat back, his arms folded across his chest. "Then what is this? You aren't staying with us, are you? You aren't a friend of my dad's."

"I'm not staying with your parents, but, yes, I was a friend of your father's in college. I was a friend of your mom's, too, and that's why I'm here."

"Because you're investigating them? You're using me to find out stuff about them?"

"No."

"What then? Who are you?"

"I'm your father." The words, the truth, slid right out. Almost naturally. Jay took his first easy breath since pulling into Phoenix. It hadn't been that bad.

Cole jumped up with such force, he knocked their tray off the table, spilling Jay's fries all over the floor.

"You're *lying!* You bastard. Take me home. I want to go home. *Now!* You can't keep me here. I'll call the cops. Say I've been kidnapped… I probably have been kidnapped. I know how this goes. You tell me you're my long-last dad, I believe you and then you take me away and do sick things to me. Well, I'm not falling for it…."

The boy's voice rose enough that people in the dining room on the other side of the wall were staring at them.

"Here." Pulling his phone out of the case at his waist, he handed it to Cole.

"What?"

"Call your mom. You dial. You know the number and her voice. Call her."

Cole stared for a solid minute. At the phone. At Jay.

"Everything okay in here?" A manager-type came into the enclosure.

Jay looked at Cole. Head bowed he sat.

"Everything's fine," Jay said.

"Son?" The manager came closer.

"Yeah. I just need to call my mom," Cole muttered.

Seeing the cell phone in the boy's hand, the man gave Jay another look, as if to warn him that if he tried anything funny he'd find himself on the wrong end of a pair of handcuffs, and left them alone.

He'd be watching them, though.

"Call her," Jay said. He'd thought about telling the manager that he was Cole's father, but with the reaction that news had received, he'd figured it was best to hold his tongue on that one.

Turning his back on Jay, Cole dialed. The wait seemed interminable then Jay heard Cole say, "Mom?"

The boy sounded as though he was crying.

"Jay says he's my dad." Another pause. "No, he's not. Dad is. You're lying to me because you guys don't want me."

The wait was longer this time. "Whatever." Almost immediately he repeated that word. Then again. "No, you don't." He paused before finally muttering, "Bye."

Slumped in the seat, Cole handed over the phone. Jay waited. Nothing was forthcoming.

The manager's curious stare through the window was becoming annoying. "You ready to go?"

"Sure," Cole said, stepping on the fries he'd spilled, crushing them into the tile. Jay had forgotten all about them.

With a silent apology to whoever would have to clean up his son's mess, Jay followed him to the bike.

Cole pulled on his helmet, adjusted the sound level, then climbed on. He slid his arms around Jay's waist without being told to. He didn't say a word the whole trip back, not even when Jay pulled up to the security booth of the gated community and typed in the code that swung open the gates.

"You want me to come in?" he asked as Cole jumped

off the bike almost before it had stopped in front of his house.

"No," Cole said. "And I don't want you, either. I don't care what any of you say. You aren't my dad. If you were, where have you been all my life?" Without waiting for an answer, he headed toward the house.

As if on cue the front door opened, and Kelsey stood there. An older Kelsey. She'd put on a few pounds, but not many. Her hair was still blond, long and silky-looking. But the lines on her face were all new since Jay had seen her last.

Putting an arm around her son's shoulders, she pulled him inside and, with a dismissive wave in Jay's direction, shut the door.

Both times Jay stopped on the way to Shelter Valley to call Kelsey's cell phone, she didn't pick up.

There was a message from her, though, when he arrived at his rental home.

"Jay, I'm really sorry to have dragged you into all of this. Meeting you was the catalyst Cole needed to see how much we mean to him, how much living at home means to him. It's been a wake-up call for all of us. He's promised to listen to us from now on. He understands that we have rules because we love him and that he has to do as we ask. And we have you to thank for that. I'm sorry to have bothered you, but you can rest assured that your son is loved and well cared for. We'll call you if we need you. Thanks again. Bye."

What the hell?

IT WAS AFTER NINE O'CLOCK when Ellen finally saw lights on at Jay's. He'd been gone over five hours. Did that mean things had gone all right with Cole?

Or that they hadn't?

Sitting outside his house in her car, she thought about calling him. But was afraid he wouldn't pick up. From what she'd seen, Jay had a way of closing in on himself when he had wounds to lick.

Apparently, life had required that of him.

He didn't need to do that tonight.

And if he was fine and didn't need company? She'd say good-night and be on her way home.

Maybe to take another hot bath. A dip in the pool would be nice, too—it had reached over one hundred and ten degrees today. She could stop by her mom's— provided she didn't mind answering questions about where she'd been and why she was out so late. But it would be nice to talk to David, find out if he'd heard anything.

And if Shelley was home, maybe the two of them could watch a movie. For that matter, she should have asked her sister to spend the night with her. Shelley didn't have class in the morning.

She was at Jay's front door. Lifted her hand. Knocked. She almost jumped back when he pulled open the door.

"Hi," he said, as though he'd been expecting her.

"Hi. You want some company?"

"Sure." He stepped away. Once she was in the house, she noticed that he was wearing cutoffs. And his hair was wet.

"I just came in from the pool to get a drink when I heard your knock."

She would have missed him if she'd been a few minutes earlier. Or later.

"I'm having beer. You want something?"

She hadn't had a beer in years. During her first

year of college, she'd consumed more beer than water. "Sure."

Following him through to the kitchen, Ellen waited for him to lead her outside.

He came to the table instead.

"You said you were out at the pool."

"I was."

"Then let's go back out. I miss having a pool of my own. When I lived at home, I used to sit outside on hot summer nights and feel like I was the luckiest girl alive."

She still felt pretty lucky. Most days. One particular day aside.

"I can be done for now."

"Really, I don't mind," Ellen said. "Don't cut your swim short because of me."

He was different. Too subdued. As if he'd been socked in the solar plexus.

Shock, she figured. He'd had a traumatic night and was here all alone. She was glad she'd stopped by.

"I swim in the nude."

"Oh. Well…" She wouldn't mind. "Don't you have a suit you can put on?"

"Yeah. If I wanted to bother. I don't."

This Jay was different. She didn't quite know what to do with him. She wasn't afraid, or even uncomfortable. She simply wasn't sure how to help him.

"Can we sit outside?" she asked. He'd said once that the pool and backyard were the best part of the house.

"Sure."

Taking the beer he'd handed her, she settled into one of two lounge chairs and waited while he dropped to the one next to her. With his feet up in front of him, Jay leaned back.

"So how did it go?"

He stared at the pool. Then at the stars in the dark sky. The cacti and bougainvillea lining the stucco wall around his yard were mostly shadows, but visible in small patches from the landscape lighting.

The light in the pool was on, too.

"Good." Jay's answer was a long time coming. And sounded...weary.

Nothing like the man she'd come to know.

"Did you tell him?"

"Yeah."

"And he took it well?"

"No. He cussed like a sailor and almost got me arrested for kidnapping and child molestation, I think."

"What?" Ellen sat forward, studying what she could make out of his expression. "What happened?"

She listened while he told her about Cole's call with his mother, and the message she'd left for Jay.

"They used you?"

He shrugged. "I don't know if it was that calculated, but maybe. It wouldn't be the first time."

Angrier than she'd been in a long time, she could barely stay seated. "They can't do that to you. It's wrong."

"They can do it. They did."

"Did she lie to you about being Cole's father?"

"No, that part is true. Looking at that kid was almost like looking at myself in the mirror twenty years ago."

"Then you have rights, Jay. No matter who they are or how much money they have."

"Leave it alone, Ellen. It's okay, really. For the best."

"*For the best?* It's not for the best. How could it possibly be for the best to tell a man he has a son, to tell a boy he has a father he's never known, then expect both to forget they met each other?"

"McGuire's the only father Cole's ever known. More importantly, he's the only father Cole wants. I don't blame him. I'm sure as hell not going to disrupt his life with my rights and demands. It looks like things are going to settle down for him. Like he's going to get on the right road and stay there. That's all that matters."

"Is it?"

He took a long swig of beer. "How the hell do I know?" He set down a nearly empty bottle. He'd just opened the thing. She wondered how many he'd had.

Not that she blamed him. A few beers at home by the pool seemed tame. He'd had a bad night by anyone's standards.

"You can stay in touch with Kelsey," she said. "Maybe work something out for occasional visits."

Jay shook his head. "Not if it's going to disrupt the family life he's got. And needs. He's at a critical age and I'm not going to cause him confusion."

"He knows about you now. It's not like he's going to forget meeting you."

"No, but his parents can help him deal with that— tell him I was in prison and didn't know about him. Or tell him that I was in prison and did know about him. As long as the kid's okay, it doesn't really matter."

"You don't really believe that."

"I don't know what I believe."

The truth of his words was so stark, so real, Ellen felt tears in the back of her eyes.

"They might not tell him you were in prison at all."

"McGuire and Kelsey? Sure they will. If nothing else, to scare him straight. To make sure he doesn't turn out like his old man."

"If he did, he'd be one lucky guy." She hadn't meant to say the words, yet, once out, they felt right.

"I took the fall for all them," Jay said in a conversational tone, as though discussing how much chlorine he'd put in the pool. "I was the bad apple, the one who brought the drugs. The rest of them had no idea. They all came out smelling like roses."

"Who really brought the drugs to the party?"

"McGuire brought the cocaine. I have no idea who had the ecstasy."

"Did you do any of it?"

"The ecstasy? No."

"The cocaine?"

"Yeah. We all did."

She wished he hadn't. "What was it like?"

He turned toward her. "Seriously?"

"Yeah."

"Like the anticipation of Christmas morning."

"That good, huh?"

"Yeah. And that bad, too. Coming down is worse than finding out that the only packages under the tree for you are socks you don't need."

Ellen chuckled. "I hate that I took you away from your swim."

"The pool's not going anywhere."

She didn't want to go anywhere, either. But she had no idea how to wrangle an invitation to stay. Shelley would know.

Ellen finished her beer. Put the bottle down. "We could swim together."

"You don't have a suit."

"You said you don't wear one."

He froze. If she didn't know better, she would say the blood stopped flowing through his veins he was so still.

"Do you want me to go?" she finally asked.

"What I want is for you to explain that last remark."

"I want to…take off my clothes…and get in the pool. With you." The words heated her skin. And everything inside it, too.

"What's going on here?"

"I…"

"Because if this is some kind of Ellen to the rescue, make Jay feel better thing, I'd appreciate it if you left and we both pretended you never stopped by."

If she'd been at her best, she would have seen that one coming.

"What if it's a Jay to the rescue, make Ellen feel better thing?" She was so far out of her element, she wasn't sure she was on the same planet. The darkness helped. But would she have stopped herself in the broad daylight? If Jay was the light at the end of her tunnel, she would be a fool not to walk toward him.

"You'll need to explain that one."

She'd been afraid of that. And yet, knew he was right. They had to do this together, fully agreeing on what they were doing and why, or it couldn't happen.

"I guess, in a way, I'm no different from Kelsey and her husband," she said, choosing her words. "I'd like to use you for my own gain."

"Use me how?"

"I want to have sex with you."

"You do."

He'd taken that calmly. "Uh-huh."

"Can I ask why?"

"I'm not sure why. I mean, you're drop-dead gorgeous. And unlike anyone I've ever known. But this is me we're talking about."

She waited for him to say something. To rescue her. He didn't.

If Mom could see me now. The random thought did nothing to quell the desire coursing through her.

She knew what to do. It was bold. Forward and promiscuous and probably deviant, too. The realizations didn't diminish the sense of rightness.

She rose to stand beside Jay and undid the button on her pants. He watched her hands.

Taking his silence as an invitation to continue she slid down the zipper.

"Can I have your hand?"

He held it up to her as she'd somehow known he would. Jay wasn't going to deny her.

There was something to be said for Ellen's habit of wearing loose clothes. They left room for her to slide Jay's hand down the front of her pants, guiding his fingers until they were between her legs. Only her panties separated him from her.

But it was her panties she wanted him to feel.

"You're soaked."

"I know."

"Because of me?"

"Uh-huh. Since we talked on Saturday. And in full force since last night. I want to have sex, Jay. I mean, I really, really want to have sex."

She released his hand, but he did not remove it.

"Just sex," he said, his gaze locked on hers.

"Just sex. I know it sounds crazy and like I don't know what I'm doing. And maybe I don't. But do you have any idea how miraculous it is to me to have my body working again? To be able to feel this way?"

"I can imagine."

"I know you aren't the staying kind, Jay. I'm not under any illusions here. This might be the only way for me to move on because there are no strings attached. If I freeze, I don't have to worry about the death of a relationship, or about hurting your feelings. You have no expectations, so you won't be disappointed."

"And you owe me nothing."

"Right."

His fingers hadn't moved. Not on her. But not away from her, either. "Should I expect your mother or stepfather, or the sheriff or anyone else at my door with a shotgun in the next few minutes?"

"No." She wanted to grin. To lighten the moment. But she couldn't. The pleasure-pain he created within her was too beautifully excruciating. "My sister knows the plan. She'll run interference for us."

"You told your sister you were going to have sex with me?"

Ellen nodded, wanting him to know she'd thought this through.

"If I do this, it's not going to be as your therapist. It will be as a man."

His words made her crazier for his touch on her body. Everything about him turned her on. From the ponytail to the way he handled this conversation.

"I understand."

"I'm going to enjoy it."

"Okay."

"Fully." And she understood what he was saying to her. He was willing to be used, but not to be sacrificed.

"You're going to come."

"That's right."

If he didn't soon put her out of this misery she was going to jump in his pool and drown herself.

"Okay."

"You're sure."

His hand between her legs was about to drive her mad.

"Completely."

"I have no STDs. Never have had, and never intend to have, either."

"Me, either."

"So, you want to go swimming?" He moved one finger. Only slightly. She almost came unglued.

"Yeah." Did that wanton croak belong to her?

"May I undress you?" Another clever wiggle of one finger.

"Yes."

Ellen stood completely still as Jay gently eased his fingers out of her pants and took hold of the bottom of her shirt. He started to pull it upward, exposing her stomach. And her ribs. Her breasts would be next.

He paused. Giving her a chance to change her mind before they crossed a line they couldn't uncross. Once he saw her naked he could no longer be only her therapist. She understood that.

And when his searching gaze found hers, she nodded anyway.

CHAPTER TWENTY-TWO

JAY WASN'T UPTIGHT WHEN it came to sex. He'd had women in unusual positions and unusual places. In his stupid days, he'd even had sex with two women at the same time. If there was a fantasy that didn't involve sadism, masochism, foreign objects or same-sex encounters, he'd probably at least tried it.

None of it compared to standing in his backyard undressing Ellen. The encounter was different, bigger than sex, larger than him. His hands shook as he lifted her shirt over her head. She looked up at him, her gaze smoky with desire, and trusting at the same time. Emotions he wasn't sure he recognized assailed his senses.

Her bra was white. Ordinary. Sensible. And incredibly sexy. With one click he loosened it.

"You okay?"

"Yeah." Her voice broke.

"If you need me to stop, say so."

"I will."

"I mean it, sweetie. We'll do more harm if this goes bad and we continue."

"I know." She licked her lips and he fought his immediate instinct to bend and kiss them. He wasn't going to close off an air passage. She needed freedom to breathe. Space to breathe.

With gentle strokes he worked his hands up her naked back and down again. Then over and up again until he was at her sides. His thumbs brushed the edges of her breasts.

"I want to touch them."

"Okay."

"You can touch me, too, you know."

As her fingers slid under his T-shirt, he wished he hadn't invited the invasion. This was about her. And he was having trouble concentrating. On keeping his mind—and body—in check.

He cupped her breasts and her eyes closed.

"Let's get in the water."

If he didn't cool down, he was going to disappoint her. Fail her. And himself, too.

He kept his clothes on as he led her to the steps then down into the water. Without a word, Ellen stepped in, the light cotton of her unbuttoned pants clinging to her skin.

She looked him in the eye, though. And smiled.

"Okay?"

"Oh, yeah."

So was he. And hard and ready, too, in spite of the cool water.

She leaned forward, let the water propel her to his body. He thought she was going to put her arms around him, hold on to him. Instead, she stripped him of his shirt and buried her face in the hair on his chest.

He'd gone to heaven without dying.

With the water lapping gently against his skin, he didn't immediately realize that she wasn't simply rubbing her face against him, that her tongue was darting out, tasting him.

Teasing her nipples with his thumbs, Jay tried to concentrate on her pleasure, to ignore his own need. Her touch and his penis worked in concert to make that goal impossible.

And when her hands reached around him, sliding down to touch his butt through his shorts, he gave up the fight.

It only took a second to rid Ellen of her pants. And panties. Then lose his shorts. He lifted her to the side of the pool, spread her legs, and did all of the things he'd refused to let himself fantasize about doing with this woman. Where she'd been hurt, he was most reverent, insuring that she felt nothing but pleasure with him.

With her hands on the deck behind her, and her head thrown back, she sat there, legs spread and came for him. Jay almost came, too, saving himself only at the last second with the reminder that Ellen wasn't going to be confident of her ability to enjoy sex until he'd been inside her.

He eased away from her gently in the water then climbed out of the pool. His penis was engorged, right out there in front of him. He wanted her to see it. To know what was coming.

To give her ample opportunity to change her mind.

Instead, she took his hand, pulled him to the lounge chair, lay back and pulled him down with her.

"Oh, Jay, it's never been like this. Not ever."

Not for him, either, but this wasn't about him.

"You're an amazing woman, Ellen," he said. "I'm going to climb on top of you now. Are you ready?"

"Yes," she said, smiling a lazy smile. "You want to feel?" She brought his hand between her legs again. She was wet. And a little tight, too. Jay played with her a bit, tantalizing her until her hips were reaching toward him. Then he moved, positioning himself at her opening.

He didn't push. He held himself there, and watched her face. She was watching him, too, and her eyes were filled with fear.

"Is it time to stop?" It wouldn't be easy, but he'd do it.

"I don't think so. I want to feel you inside me. I want to come on you. I'm just afraid it's going to stop and I don't want it to."

"If it does, we'll start it up again." He had no idea where the words came from.

"We will?"

"As many times as it takes, sweetie."

Then she grinned. "So maybe I should tell you to stop so we get to start over again. A lot."

Taking his cue from the hunger in her eyes, Jay pushed in a little and said, "Or maybe we don't stop and do it again later because we like it so much."

"So it's okay with you if we do it again?"

He pushed again and was fully inside her. "Oh, yeah."

"Oh, my word. Oh, Jay."

He pulled back, and pushed in again.

"That feels so damned good. You have no idea how good."

Maybe not, but he had a feeling he was pretty close to meeting her there. On the next push he felt her convulsing around him and had no choice but to spill himself inside of her.

She cradled him, with her body, with her arms, and with something else, too. Something he didn't recognize. Something that was purely Ellen.

The experience had been about her—for her. But for the first time in his entire life, Jay felt, for a second, as though he'd come home.

ELLEN HAD TO LEAVE. HER car was parked outside Jay's house. She'd left a light on in her living room. Both things people would notice.

But she had to leave for another, more serious reason. She had to leave because she so badly wanted to stay.

Possibly forever.

She moved and Jay extricated himself from on top of her and was barely on his feet before she was retrieving her wet clothes.

"Let me get you something dry to put on." He didn't seem the least bit conscious of his own nudity.

She was going to remember him that way forever— her wild, long-haired savior, standing above her like some kind of Greek god, ready to be worshipped.

He'd given her back her life.

"Thank you," she said, taking the dark green terry robe he handed her and slipping her arms through the sleeves. The old Ellen would have put on her wet clothes. A robe would be much harder to explain if she ran into anyone between Jay's front door and her own.

But she wanted something of him to take home with her tonight. Something to hold while she lay in her bed alone.

Rolling up her wet clothes, she tucked them under one arm. He walked with her through the mostly dark house, their way illuminated by the light over the kitchen sink he'd left on.

"Are you coming to therapy in the morning?"

Ellen's insides started up again. She could hardly

believe she was living in the same body that had been hers all of her life.

"Do you think I need to?"

"I think I want to give you a real, full-body massage."

The images his words conjured up...

"Okay."

And after that she was going to have to give him what he most needed in the world—his freedom to leave.

"Hey, Jay?" She turned before crossing the threshold.

"Yeah?"

"Thank you."

"Sweetie, believe me, I'm the one offering thanks at the moment."

He'd liked it that much? Her goal had been to get through the experience with normal reactions. She'd never considered that she might actually be good at it.

"Did you mean it when you said that we could have another go at it?"

Rather than giving her a verbal answer, Jay motioned downward with both hands, showing her exactly how ready he was.

She called him from her cell phone during the short drive to her house.

"You okay?" she asked, thinking of him alone in a rental house in a strange town that hadn't been all that welcoming to him.

"Yeah."

"I'm sorry about Cole."

"It wasn't like I knew how to be a dad, anyway. I would have sucked at it."

"No, you wouldn't have." Turning into her drive, Ellen pulled into the garage and closed the automatic door behind her. "No one knows how to be a parent when they first have a child," she said. "It's something you learn as you go, taking from what life has taught you and trusting your instincts the rest of the time."

"Some folks aren't meant to be parents."

Maybe. "You cared."

She hurt for him during the long silence. And even more when she heard his softly spoken, "Yeah."

"Don't give up on him, Jay. He'll call you at some point. He'll want your side of the story."

"If he does, he does."

"What about your father? You still going to try to find him?"

"My need isn't quite so urgent, but yeah. We stirred up too many unanswered questions. I need to know the truth."

"So...you going to hang around a bit longer then?" Dammit. She'd promised herself she wouldn't ask. That she wouldn't even think that way. She'd promised him—

"I've already given my notice on the house. I leave at the end of the month."

One day before Josh returned. The timing was perfect.

"That gives us almost a week." To find his father. To make delicious love.

No.

Scratch that.

There was no love between her and Jay. Great sex, yes. But no love. They hadn't known each other long enough.

He'd never even met Josh.

Her family hated him—except maybe for Shelley, who'd never met him.

He hated Shelter Valley.

She couldn't live anywhere else.

They were from different universes. He didn't believe in formal education. She valued it second only to family.

He was Black Leather. She was small-town gingham.

"Are you having regrets?" His question stole quietly into her thoughts.

"No." She spoke honestly, without thinking. "Are you?"

"Only if we've made things more difficult for you."

Because having casual sex wasn't usual for her? But was old hat to him?

"I've discovered that I'm not dead, Jay. My world has possibilities again."

"I've never met anyone like you."

"Me, either. About you, I mean."

"Sleep well, angel."

"You, too."

Hanging up, Ellen went in the house, thinking that *sleep well* was as close to *I love you* as she and Jay were ever going to get.

Maybe that was one tiny regret.

CHAPTER TWENTY-THREE

JAY'S PHONE RANG AT seven-thirty the next morning. Ellen canceling was his guess. He'd been expecting the call. To verify his assumption, he glanced at the caller ID on his screen. It was a local exchange, but he didn't recognize the number.

"Jay Billingsley." His voice was pleasant. Even. Could be a client call.

"David Marks, here."

"Yes, sir," he said, as though he hadn't had sex with this man's stepdaughter the night before. He didn't regret what he'd done—not if Ellen was still okay this morning.

His skin grew cold. Was she there at her mother's? Had something happened to her? Because of him?

"I had a call from a woman I've been trying to reach all week. She lives in Phoenix with her daughter and grandkids, but thirty years ago, she volunteered in the church office."

Daughter. Grandkids. Not Ellen.

"She remembers your mother," David said. "She knows something about your father. She's willing to meet with you this morning, if you're free."

"What time?"

"She can be in Shelter Valley by ten."

If David knew that Jay had an eight-o'clock appointment and who it was with, would he still be so willing to help?

Probably, was Jay's instant answer. People in Shelter Valley were unlike any people he'd ever known. When they wanted a guy out of town they didn't use force or target him with rotten tomatoes. They helped him. Gave him what he needed so he'd move on.

Everyone won that way.

After agreeing to meet the woman at David's church, and thanking the man for his facilitation, Jay hung up.

Answers. The final snip in the ties that bound him here. Cole didn't need him. And once Jay had answers about his own life, he didn't need Shelter Valley. He could be free by nightfall.

As long as Ellen wasn't experiencing any repercussions.

He was thinking about the Shelter Valley way a short time later as he waited outside his treatment room door while Ellen undressed and prepared for their session.

This would most likely be their final treatment. If she could withstand a full-body massage, she was well on her way to the life she wanted.

There could be setbacks. He knew that. She did, too. But for her to know, to believe, that she was capable of normal responses to touch was most of the battle won.

With one thought in mind, Jay walked into the room.

"Your stepfather called."

Jay practically blurted the words when Ellen, fully dressed, joined him in the hallway an hour later. He was sweating like a pig. Had untucked his T-shirt from his pants, to cover the bulge beneath his zipper.

He needed a good long ride on his bike. Space. Air to breathe. Open road.

But he'd made it through the session, seeing muscle and bone, not a gorgeous female body.

"He did?" Her face was red, as though she'd been jogging instead of lying on his table.

Jay told her about the call. And stared at her lips. In the past hour he'd touched every inch of her body— minus the intimate parts. Those he'd relished the night before. His body had been inside hers.

Yet he hadn't kissed those lips.

"Oh, my gosh, Jay." Her entire expression lit up. "You're going to find your father."

"We don't know that." He'd been in the investigative business a long time—long enough to know that most promising leads led to dead ends.

"But you'll learn something. I wish I could be there with you, but I have an appointment."

Jay didn't need her. Or anyone.

"David will be around." Any disappointment that Ellen wouldn't be with him had no place in this day.

"I'll call you as soon as I'm free." Her gaze was so warm, so…personal, he could feel her touching him and she was standing a good foot and a half away from him.

Her call wasn't necessary. They'd catch up at some point. He nodded anyway.

"Okay then, I'll talk to you in a little bit." She started down the hallway and turned back. Walking right up to him, she put her hands on his shoulders, leaned forward and kissed him. A real kiss, not a peck. A lingering kiss. Full on the lips.

"That's for luck."

THAT WAS PLAIN STUPID, Ellen lamented as, car loaded with groceries and new assignments from Phyllis, she headed out of town toward Joe's mountain.

Why in the hell had she kissed Jay? As though there was some kind of close affection between them.

Granted, they had had sex together, but that had been different. A favor. Therapy. Healing ground.

It hadn't been personal, which was what she told Shelley when her sister called five minutes into the drive.

"Get serious, El." Shelley snorted. "Of course it was personal. You got naked and slept with the guy."

"No, I didn't. I went home before I fell asleep."

"You know what I mean."

Blue sky, sunshine, the mountains, she took them all in. Allowed them to center her, to suck the nervous edge out of her veins. "Yeah, I know."

"So how are you? Really?"

Really? She couldn't look that close right now. "I'm not sorry."

"Even if you felt that way because he's your therapist? What if it was some kind of hero-worship stuff? Transference?"

"He turned me on, Shel. I'm physically and emotionally capable of sexual response. That's what matters to me."

"But what if it was a therapy transference thing? What if you don't ever feel that way again?"

"If I don't ever feel that way again, it'll be because I don't ever meet a man who attracts me like Jay does. You know as well as I do that the attraction thing is part personality, part circumstance and part pheromones.

My person reacts to Jay's person. I'm assuming it will also react to the man I'm meant to marry and spend the rest of my life with. But if it doesn't ever happen again, it's not because of the rape. It's because Jay was the one."

Slamming on the brakes, Ellen pulled over to the side of the road. She was hyperventilating. She put her head on the steering wheel.

Oh, God. Oh, my God. Jay was the one. Her lack of sexual response hadn't been only the result of the rape—though certainly her reticence had been more acute because of it. But it had been as Jay had said—she wasn't a woman who could have casual sex. She'd needed the right man.

And a bit of touch therapy, too.

As she sat there, hot and cold, sweating, she focused on breathing normally.

There had to be more than one right man for her. There would be. Her body was attracted to Jay so he could help her.

Her heart wasn't involved. He wasn't the only one who would bring her these feelings.

Yeah, that was it.

"El?" She heard the call from far away. "Ellen!" It came more sharply. "Ellen, talk to me dammit, or I'm calling Greg. *Ellen.*"

Shelley's panicked shriek got through. Lifting the phone to her ear, Ellen half whispered, "Yeah, Shel, it's okay. I'm here."

She took a deep breath. And another. She was fine.

"What's going on? Where are you? I thought you were on your way to the hermit's place."

"His name is Joe." She managed to sound like a normal woman. The sky was still blue. The sun was still shining. Watching for traffic behind her, she pulled out onto the road. "And I am on my way to his place."

"What happened?"

"I dropped the phone." It was true.

"You're sure?"

"Yep."

"So tell me the truth, big sister. You fell for him, didn't you? You're in love with this biker dude."

No, she had not. No, she was not.

"The truth, little sister, is that I'm fine. Jay's fine. Life is fine. And I need to get to Joe's before his milk turns sour."

"Uh-huh."

With Shelley's skepticism ringing in her ears, Ellen hung up. She had something far more important than her sex life to think about.

Joe. And his life.

Jay had given her back her life. Could she do the same for Joe? If it turned out that his wife had been murdered by the same man who had killed Jay's mother, would knowing help the older man?

If she brought up his past and it turned out she was wrong and there were no mementoes from Joe's wife in Jay's box, would she be sending the older man further into his personal hell?

In the end, as she drove up the track to Joe's shack, all conflicting emotion faded away. Her decision had already been made.

If she didn't at least try, there was no hope. And hope was a far better choice than safety that came with emptiness attached.

"YES, I KNEW THIS WOMAN. Tammy Walton. I remember because her last name reminded me of that old TV show *The Waltons*. You remember it?"

The eighty-year-old woman sat in one of the two chairs in front of David's massive oak desk. Jay sat beside her, elbows on the chair arms, his hands clasped in front of his face as he twiddled his thumbs.

Claudia's daughter, who had grown up in Shelter Valley and had driven her mother to town for this meeting, had taken her teenaged children to look at Montford's campus.

"I remember the show," David said from behind his desk. Wearing denim shorts, a T-shirt that advertised Acapulco Beach and sandals, the man didn't look like any preacher Jay had ever known. "The family lived up on a mountain."

"Right, and John Boy was a writer," Claudia said, her voice cracking with age. "Tammy was a writer, too. That's why I remember. Two Waltons. Two writers."

Jay stopped twiddling. "A writer?"

The faded blue eyes still had a sharp gaze—as Jay discovered when the old woman's attention turned to him. "Well, she wanted to be. She used to come to town to watch sports matches—said she did write-ups for a school newspaper."

"What school?"

"I'm not sure. If she said, I can't remember."

"Was it the University of Arizona?"

"No. A college maybe, though. One of those community things."

He sat forward, forcing himself to remain calm while adrenaline shot through him.

"Did you ever see her with anyone?"

"No. I only met her a couple of times. She came in to talk to Pastor Winslow. He was the preacher back then. A really nice man. Passed away ten years ago from kidney failure."

"Do you know why she needed to see Pastor Winslow?" David asked quietly.

"Of course I do. Back then, the church secretary was as much a pastor to the people as the pastor was. Especially with the women. She was pregnant. She and the young man were very much in love." Claudia smiled as she glanced over at Jay. He had no idea if the woman had caught all of David's explanation. If she knew that Tammy Walton was Jay's mother. "You've never seen a girl so in love as that one."

And the bastard had broken her heart, left her alone with a baby to support, which made her prey for—

"And the boy, too. I talked to him on the phone a couple of times. He loved that girl so much."

Jay gritted his teeth. If the woman only knew.

But why should she? Why would she need to?

"That girl, Tammy, she was so sweet. And so conflicted, poor dear. Her and her sister both."

"You know my aunt? Olivia Walton?"

"Olivia, yes, that was her name. Tammy called her Livvie. They were both trying so hard to live happy lives, and couldn't seem to see that they were the ones most preventing it. Especially Livvie. She'd had it bad. Protected Tammy from the worst of the abuse."

Jay shifted in his chair. The damned thing had to be the most uncomfortable—

"Abuse?" David asked.

"Their dad was a brute. Beat their mom until the day she died, then Livvie took the worst of it. But what hurt those girls most was their mom always telling them to never get married. She said their dad was a wonderful man, loving and kind, until they got married and had kids. She swore that men changed after they married and were never the same again. On her deathbed, she made both girls promise they'd never get married. That way she knew they would be safe, they'd never have to suffer like she had."

He couldn't be hearing right.

"That's why Tammy came to talk to us. She was pregnant and so in love with her young man, but couldn't bring herself to marry him. She didn't want to go anyplace in Tucson in case her sister found out. Truth was, I think she was almost as afraid of letting her sister down as she was of breaking a deathbed promise or having love turn sour on her."

"She had three strikes against her." David's tone compelled Jay to look up. And to hold on to the steadiness of that gaze.

"You said you talked to the father of her child on the phone a couple of times."

"That's right. He wanted to know what he could do to help Tammy feel better about getting married. See, after she first met with the pastor, she told the boy she'd marry him, quietly, here in Shelter Valley. They could keep the wedding a secret from her sister if she liked, for as long as she needed. The girl seemed okay with that. They set a date—that's the paper you got there."

The older woman stopped, took a few breaths. "But the girl got scared. She called off the wedding. Then the boy called again, a long time later. After the child was born. A boy, I think it was."

Jay and David exchanged glances but neither interrupted the story with information that didn't matter at the moment.

"Anyway, the young man—I wish I could remember his name—said that Tammy had changed her mind. She'd agreed to marry him. So I called her and sure enough, she had. We set everything up and she was going through with it this time. I was sure of it. She'd changed. She was actually excited about marrying the boy she loved so much."

"So they got married," Jay said.

"No." Claudia shook her head, her shoulders slumped and her eyes teared. "The poor thing was killed a few days before the wedding. I moved shortly after that and don't know whatever happened to the boy. Or if they found Tammy's killer. I only know that it seemed to me that God had forgotten that poor girl. It was many years before I ever went back to church. Sorry, Pastor."

David smiled. "It's okay, Claudia, I understand. Went through a rough patch myself a while back. It's easy to blame God, and hard to trust Him when things out of our control change our lives so drastically."

David spoke to Claudia, but looked straight at Jay.

"You're saying that the man was still with her the week she was killed?"

"He would have to be, wouldn't he? Since they were getting married in a few days."

"But you don't know for sure."

"No." Frowning, Claudia pursed her lips. "I don't think I ever heard of him after that last call, and that was about, oh, maybe a month before the wedding."

Which was about the time Aunt Olivia had said that his father had left his mother. Obviously, once she had really wanted to get married, once she'd been excited about the idea, he'd gotten cold feet. He probably hadn't wanted to marry her at all.

Jay swallowed the lump in his throat. His mother had had an abusive father. She'd been afraid to believe in love. When she'd fallen in love, she'd been afraid to marry. And right when she'd decided to take a risk, to follow her heart and live life to its fullest, she'd been deserted by the man she loved then brutally raped and murdered.

Jay stared at the desktop. At the floor. Trying not to blink. He was getting far too weepy in his old age.

Time to get out of this town before it ruined him completely.

CHAPTER TWENTY-FOUR

ELLEN SAT ON THE BENCH outside Joe's window, waiting for him to collect the materials he had for her to give to Phyllis.

Rubbing first one thumb along her palm then the other, she tried to work out what she would say. And to find a way to talk herself out of saying anything at all.

Who was she to disrupt Joe's life? Maybe he was as happy as he could be living up on his mountain. Maybe this was exactly the kind of life he wanted. Maybe bringing up the past would hurt him for no good reason.

"I think that's all of it," the slightly gruff voice said before Ellen heard a thump behind her.

She turned to pick up the folder and stared instead. There wasn't only one folder. There were at least a dozen of them.

Her pulse rate sped up. She'd been right to talk Joe into taking Phyllis's class. The man needed more than life alone on the mountain was giving him.

She asked him if he needed anything else—asked him how his week had been. He needed nothing and he was fine. The rote answers.

"What about that therapy of yours?"

"I think it's working."

"Enough for you to go on a date?"

"I think so. If someone I like asks me. Too bad you aren't in the market for dinner and a movie."

"I'm way too old for you girl. And too stupid, too. Besides, I gave my heart a long time ago. You need someone with a heart to give."

"You've still got life to live, Joe."

He didn't say a word. So Ellen did.

"Can I ask you something?"

"Doesn't mean I'll answer."

"It's about the past. Your past."

"Go on."

"When your…it happened…did you notice anything missing from your house? Anything your wife would have thought was special?"

Deathly silence hung between them.

"Joe?"

No answer.

Had her question sent him into cardiac arrest? She couldn't get to him to find out. He had the door bolted.

"Joe? Answer me or I'm coming in the window."

"Wh—who…"

"Who what? Joe, are you okay? Do we need help?" He might want to die up here, but she wasn't going to let him. Not on her watch.

She shouldn't have said anything. Should have left well enough alone. Joe's life was his own. She was like her mother, trying to run someone else's life.

"Joe, answer me, I mean it." She stood.

"Stay there…I'm fine." He was there, in the window. She could see his outline at the side of the seed bag he'd hung as a curtain.

"You scared me."

"Sorry."

"It's okay, Joe, but what's going on? I'm sorry if I upset you. I won't mention the past again—"

"Why did you ask?"

"Well, because...I care and—"

"No." He spoke louder than usual. And the sun was baking Ellen's skin—more of a burning sensation than a comfort this morning. "Why that question in particular?"

Dare she risk the truth?

"I wondered—"

"You don't wonder about a missing item of no monetary value."

"I didn't say it was of no monetary value."

He was still there.

"Joe? Was something missing?"

"Tell me who's asking."

"I am."

"Why?"

"Because I think I might know who raped and killed her."

The form behind the window sank slowly and Ellen didn't give any warning, or heed any from the past. With every ounce of her strength, she pushed against the rudimentary window block, until she'd moved the piece enough to slide through—which she did, headfirst.

She caught herself with her hands on a bench—identical to hers—on the other side of the window. Beyond that, she couldn't make out much in the room. Her eyes hadn't adjusted to the dim interior. And she cared only about the hump, heaving on the floor.

"Joe?" Lowering herself beside the man who was curled in a ball, Ellen realized he wasn't convulsing as she'd feared. He was sobbing.

"Get out. You have to get out."

"No." She slid an arm around his waist, holding on to him. "I have to stay, Joe. Talk to me."

"She...was...so...beautiful—" The words broke off into another bout of uncontrollable sobs. Fifteen minutes passed before Joe spoke again. "What he did to her...the way he...my sweet, sweet girl..."

"If something of hers was missing— There was this series of rapes and murders. It sounds like maybe...I don't know, but it could be the same guy. He broke into homes, told the women he was only hiding out. He let them get their most prized possession, to hold it so they wouldn't be afraid. Then he raped and murdered them and stole the item as a keepsake." She told the story quickly. As though she could reduce the pain attached to her words.

"The handkerchief," Joe said. "I looked all over for it later, after they'd taken her away and everyone was gone. I was all alone in that house, with our things, and I looked all over for the handkerchief. It was my wedding present to her. White, with lace edges..."

This time it was Ellen's blood that ran cold.

"I'M NOT GOIN'."

"I'm not leaving you here alone. Not like this."

Ellen had coaxed Joe to the bench and sat beside him, holding his hand. He was clutching hers so tightly she was losing circulation.

"I'm not goin'."

"I'm going to call Sheriff Richards. He'll take you to a clinic then we'll find you a place to stay. Just for tonight. Tomorrow, if you want, I'll bring you back here."

"I'm not goin'."

She was shaking. He was shaking, too. And she couldn't leave him there.

"There's more to the story, isn't there, Joe?"

His chin to his chest, he rolled forward, and the wail that escaped him was animalistic. Filled with more pain than a human should have to endure.

"You had a baby. A son. And you left him."

The older man's head shot up. He stared at her through tear-filled, bloodshot eyes. "How do you—"

"He's here, Joe. In Shelter Valley. That's how I know about the killer. Your son found him. And he came here to find you."

Where she'd half feared he would collapse, he sat up. Completely straight. "My son is here? In Shelter Valley? Looking for me." His voice was stronger than she'd heard it in five years of visits.

"That's right."

He said nothing for so long Ellen thought she'd lost him to some inner world. Finally, he said, "Call the sheriff. I'll go with you."

JAY WAS AT THE HOUSE packing his things when he heard a car out front. He'd told Ellen they could have sex again tonight.

She'd said she was going to call, too.

Their promises seemed so long ago. More than the eight hours that had passed since they'd seen or talked to each other.

She was wearing the same shorts and cotton top she'd had on that morning. The white ribbed shirt was marked with dust. There were smudges on her shorts. And on her face, too. She'd been crying.

"What happened?"

Surely if there was a God anywhere, Ellen hadn't been attacked again.

She wasn't like his mother. She wasn't going to spend her entire life suffering for the privilege of having been born.

"I... We need to talk."

"Tell me what happened."

"Sit down."

"Not until you tell me what happened. Who did this to you?"

Blinking, she glanced at herself. "No one did anything to me. I've been— I had to help someone who hadn't had a shower in a really, really long time."

Her expression was taut, her hands a little shaky, but her voice was firm.

Jay dropped onto the kitchen chair closest to him. Ellen pulled one over so that she faced him. She took his hand. He'd take it back in a second. As soon as he found out what was going on. One problem at a time.

"I acted on a hunch today, Jay. You're probably going to be pissed as hell, but I hope you'll find compassion in your heart..."

He'd never considered compassion a problem for him. Then a thought struck him.

"Does this have to do with Cole?" She'd said he was going to be pissed. As though she had interfered in his life somehow.

"No. At least...not directly. It has to do with Joe Frasier. That old guy I told you about who lives up on the mountain."

What did a wacky hermit have to do with him?

Ellen played with the fingers of his hand. "When

you told me about the circumstances of your mother's death, I had a thought, a hunch really, but I wasn't sure what to do with it, or even sure if I should do anything at all."

Jay listened, trying to connect her dots. She wasn't making it easy.

"I didn't think it was right to tell you, because I'd been told in confidence and trust was a huge issue." She paused. "Joe's wife was raped and murdered, too. Just like those other women. He was the one who found her. He'd come home from work to find her naked and bleeding all over their living room floor."

"Jesus!" Jay sat back, yet still clung to Ellen's hand.

"Yeah. He was so in love with her, so completely beaten by the sight of what had been done to her, the way she'd been brutalized, that he couldn't handle life. He packed up some things, took money that I now know came from an insurance settlement, shared with another relative of his wife, bought the plot of land by Rabbit Rock, and, other than his walking trips to town when he needed supplies, he never left the place again."

Staring at Ellen, being sucked in by the caring in her gaze, Jay asked, "Did you ask him if something of hers was missing?"

Ellen swallowed. Nodded. And Jay stood so abruptly, the chair crashed to the ground behind him. His wrist hurt, a result of the rough disconnect from her hand. He didn't give a damn.

Her eyes filled with tears.

"Don't say it. Don't even say it," he said, his breath coming in jerky spurts.

He'd been running a marathon his entire life. He couldn't slow down now.

"Your name's not really Jay." The soft voice came from afar. Giving him innocuous information that didn't make sense.

"It's Joe, Jr. They called you Jay Jay for short."

"No!" The shout that echoed through his house was not his. It was violent and filled with pain and...loud. So loud it shook the chandelier.

Ellen didn't flinch. She didn't move.

"He was there, Jay. He found her. You were in your room, crying. He was in shock, crying, too, and afraid to touch you. He called Olivia. She came over immediately. She was the one who called the police. And she took you. A couple of days later, she told him that it was all his fault. That if he hadn't gotten Tammy pregnant, she would still be alive. If he'd had a job decent enough to take care of a wife and child, to move her to a safer neighborhood, she'd still be alive."

"They weren't married." He was cold as ice. And getting colder. Cold enough to rot in hell for the hatred coursing through him.

"I know. Not legally. But they'd had their own ceremony, just the two of them. She wrote their vows. And they wore matching rings around their necks. Their legal marriage was planned for three days after she was murdered."

"He walked away from me."

"Yep. He had no money, no idea how to care for a baby. He was nineteen, Jay. Olivia was thirty-eight. She had a good job. A nice home. She'd spent her twenties taking care of your mother. She adored her and she adored you. She told Joe that letting her have you was the best thing for you."

"She told me he left before my mother was murdered."

"I have no idea why she did that, except that she had to have someone to blame, someone to hate, and she turned on Joe. She told you his name was Billingsley, too. That was his middle name—his mother's maiden name. And it was your middle name. She must have dropped the Walton when she adopted you."

"I wasn't adopted."

"Joe says you were. The birth certificate that exists for you isn't the original. He was named on the original. Joe said your aunt wasn't very fond of men— particularly him. She tried repeatedly to get your mother away from him."

"Their father beat them. Olivia took the brunt of it." He was a robot. On automaton. Back in prison. Surviving.

Until he couldn't.

Ellen still sat where he'd left her. Jay had paced to the living room and back a number of times.

"He wants to meet you, Jay."

"You told him about me."

"Yeah." Her gaze didn't waver. Not even a little bit.

"If he wanted to get to know me, he should have thought of that say, oh, about thirty-two years ago."

"He knows that. But he thought you needed a mother's love more than anything else and that wasn't something he could give you. He loved you enough to give you a good life—a life he wouldn't have been financially or emotionally healthy enough to give you."

Jay swore. Righted the chair he'd knocked over. Paced some more. "That's a cop-out."

"Is it?" Ellen remained calm. Her voice almost

loving. "Are you copping out with Cole? Leaving him with the family that can give him the stability he needs?"

He swung around. "Damn you." The words faded before they were fully out and Jay sank to the chair he'd vacated. He sat, then placed his head in the lap of the woman his mother had led him to help, and let the tears of twenty long years flow.

CHAPTER TWENTY-FIVE

"WHERE IS HE?"

Ellen's fingers, running through Jay's unbound long hair, stilled a second. They were on his couch and his head was on her shoulder. Night had fallen around them.

And she hadn't called her family.

But they hadn't called her, either, which meant that they knew where she was. And that they'd chosen to leave her alone.

Probably thanks to Shelley.

"He's at Big Spirits for the night. They put a bed in the storage room I'm going to paint over this weekend. I called Greg and we took him to the emergency room in Phoenix to be checked over. His vitals are great, and while the E.R. doctor recommended he have a full checkup, they didn't see any reason to keep him overnight. He needs counseling. Probably a lot of it, if he's going to reenter society in any kind of meaningful way."

What she didn't add was that Joe had only agreed to get checked over and cleaned up with the idea of meeting Jay. Without that, the older man was going to hightail it to his cabin and stay there.

Ellen was in no doubt of that.

Other than Jay, the world simply didn't have any-

thing to offer that Joe wanted badly enough to face
the pain for.

She'd learned something vitally important that afternoon watching Joe's struggle. Something she was going
to have face. And soon.

But not tonight.

"I WANT TO HATE HIM."

"I know."

"I've spent my whole life hating him."

"You needed someone to blame. Just like Olivia did.
She handed him to you on a platter."

Thinking over the years of growing up, Jay had new
understanding of so many things. His aunt's reserve.
Her intense love—and distance at the same time. Her
adoration and service to Jay—and her fear of him.

She was a woman who had learned early that men
were evil and she'd carried that belief to her grave.

She'd had to control him so that she wasn't afraid
of him. She'd had to lie to him to keep him where she
could control him.

But she'd loved him. Always. There had never been
any doubt about that.

So, other than the fact that he'd grown up without a
father, other than the time he'd spent in prison because
he hadn't had a parent watching his back the way the
other kids had, had his life really been so horrible?

"I've been alone my whole life."

"So has he, for most of his."

The old man's aloneness had been far more acute
than Jay's. And yet, were they really that different?

"You think he's still up?"

"It only seven o'clock."

"What's he look like?" He had to lift his head soon. To stand up, rejoin his life and move on.

"Smaller than you. He hunches over, like he's got the weight of the world on his shoulders. His skin is leathery, wrinkled from the sun. His hair's gray. Long, but not as long as yours. But his beard might be longer than your ponytail."

They'd tried to get him to shave. He had refused.

"He claims he hasn't shaved since your mother died. She liked to watch him shave. She'd watched him that morning while he was getting ready for work. Joked with him. The next morning, when he got up, he couldn't make himself replace the memory. And he never has."

"Do you believe him?"

"Yeah."

Jay couldn't imagine loving anyone that much.

The fingers in his hair stilled again. And he wished they wouldn't. He wished Ellen wouldn't be only a still shot in the movie of his life.

"Let's go get this over with."

Ellen didn't whoop. Or move excitedly around him. She didn't start talking fast or saying useless things. She didn't even tell him he was doing the right thing. She simply stood, held out her hand and walked with him to the motorcycle.

THE ROOM HAD BEEN PARTIALLY transformed. Instead of shelves, it sported a twin-size bed with oak headboard, a nightstand, dresser and rocking chair to match. The twenty-six-inch television that would be mounted to the wall once Ellen painted was on a temporary table.

But where most of the rooms Ellen visited during the

course of her workday were filled with personal items, pictures and mementoes, Joe's was starkly empty.

Except for the man sitting silently in the rocking chair, staring out the window at the darkness beyond. He was illuminated by the dim track lighting above the bed.

Ellen started into the room, until Jay's hand grabbed her arm, staying her. She waited for Jay to enter with her and close the door.

"You Joe?" he asked, his voice more rough than she was used to.

"Yeah."

"I'm Jay." He stood rigidly, his long hair hanging around shoulders left bare by the muscle shirt he wore with his black jeans and black leather boots, attitude flowing all over him.

Joe rose, one hand on the arm of the rocker, as though to steady himself. He moved slowly, but he came forward until he was standing—straight, Ellen noticed—directly in front of his son.

"And I'm sorry," he said without so much as a blink.

"You didn't think I'd need a father?"

"I didn't think I'd be a good enough one. Your mother had such high hopes for you. You were going to be the man who would carry gentleness to our gender. You were going to change the world."

Joe hadn't told her that. Ellen started to cry and both men turned to look at her. "She was right," she explained.

JAY TRIED TO STAY ANGRY. But he kept thinking about Cole. About how inept he'd felt around the boy.

Jay, Ellen and Joe had been talking for a couple of

hours, sitting in an empty family meeting room that consisted of a couple of couches with a table in between. Mostly Jay had been talking. The old man had more questions than a college entrance exam.

"I have a son." Jay dropped that information into the conversation sometime around nine o'clock.

"Where is he?"

"Living with his mother and stepfather. I found out about him a month ago."

"You didn't know you had a son?"

"I was in prison when he was born." He didn't spare the man any pain. Didn't sugarcoat a damned thing.

Joe apologized over and over again. And continued to ask questions. Most of which Jay answered.

"You ever been in love?"

No way would Jay answer. That was no one's business.

Joe frowned. "All these great things you've done— finding your mother's murderer, that was a great one, son. And saving that girl—you were your mother's son then. And the therapy—helping girls like my Ellen, here—" Joe smiled at her and she smiled back. "But you're a damned fool, too. A chip off the old block. I didn't even raise you and you're still dragging me right along with you."

"What the hell are you talking about?"

Ellen recognized the tone. Not really defensive. Simply Jay pretending he didn't care.

"You might not hole up in a cabin in the woods, but you're as locked up as me."

"Not me. I'm as free as any man can be."

"Depends on what you call free."

"The wind in my hair. My bike between my legs. The sky my only limit. I've got it made."

"You've missed the boat."

Sitting as she was between father and son, Ellen felt like a tennis ball as she looked between the two of them.

"My life is exactly as I want it to be. I answer to no one."

"What about your heart? You ever listen to it?"

"My heart's just fine."

"You're alone, son. Your heart can't be fine. Take it from one who learned that lesson the hardest way possible. Love is the only thing really worth living for, Jay Jay. You aren't living. You're running."

JAY TOOK ELLEN TO HIS place to get her car. They hadn't spoken since walking Joe to his room. They'd agreed to meet again in the morning to figure out where they'd go from there. Joe was pretty fond of his mountain. Jay needed to see the place.

He needed to get out of this place.

"You want to come in?" he asked Ellen as she handed him back her helmet.

"No. I have something to do."

"At ten o'clock at night?"

"I have to go see my mother."

Ellen had grown up with family, the nucleus of a large group of people who loved and needed her.

She belonged here. He didn't.

Joe Billingsley Frasier didn't understand that.

SHELLEY, DAVID, MARTHA and Tim were sitting in the living room, watching *National Lampoon's Christ-*

mas Vacation. In August. Which was so like her family—unconventional, maybe, but together.

"What's wrong?" Martha put aside the bowl of popcorn she'd been holding as soon as Ellen walked in. David paused the video.

"Nothing's wrong. It's been a long day."

"You're a mess, sis," Tim said, lobbing a baseball in her direction.

She caught the ball. And sent it back to him. "I was moving stuff."

"Your stuff?" Shelley asked, giving her a pointed stare.

"No," Ellen said, catching the baseball a second time and tossing it back. "It's nothing to do with me. Listen, guys, can I talk to Mom alone for a minute?"

"How about that ice cream we've been talking about?" David asked.

Shelley dropped the pillow she'd been holding onto the couch as she stood. Tim threw his ball into the air, caught it and followed David out of the room.

"What's up?" Martha asked, her lips pinched.

"We need to talk."

"Okay."

"I have to leave Shelter Valley, Mom."

Martha blanched. But Ellen had to give her credit. She didn't say a word. Yet.

"Not forever. Maybe not even for long," Ellen said, still standing behind the couch, facing the double recliner her mother had been sharing with David. "I love it here, you know that."

Martha nodded. Her eyes wide and filled with fear.

"I'm not planning to sell my house or anything. But I have to know that I'm capable of living elsewhere."

"I never have."

"I know, Mom, but you've probably never doubted that you could, either. You're here because your life is here."

"So is yours."

"What if it isn't? What if Aaron had insisted that I go with him to Colorado, Mom? What if he hadn't given in so easily when I suggested the divorce? We both know I still wouldn't have gone. I'm hiding here. Because everyone here knows what happened. They watch out for me."

"People love you."

"I know. And I love them, too. But somehow during all of this, I've let that love trap me into believing that I don't have the ability to cope outside of Shelter Valley."

Martha sucked in her lower lip.

"I have to go, Mom."

"I know."

Coming around the edge of the couch, Ellen dropped down close to her mother's chair.

"You do?"

Martha nodded. "I've been talking to the girls—and to David—and I know you're right. If you're in Shelter Valley because it's the only place you feel safe, because you're afraid to leave, then you have to go."

"I also love it here."

"Then you'll be back." There were tears in Martha's eyes as she smiled.

WHO IN THE HELL WAS OUT front at eleven o'clock at night? Dropping the hand weight he'd been lifting, Jay went to the door. Tonight was not a good night for the sheriff, or anyone else, to be paying him a visit. He was a little short on patience.

"Ellen?"

"I seem to be making a habit of this, huh?"

"I thought you were at your folks' place."

"I was." She came inside and he shut the door behind her. "And now I'm not."

"I see that."

Had she come to collect her sex, then? He'd told her she could have it.

There was only one problem. He wasn't sure he could give it to her. Not the way she wanted it. Not without—

No. He wasn't going there. Had no room in his life for it.

He was fine. Satisfied. He liked his life. A lot of folks couldn't say the same.

"Are you happy, Jay?"

"What kind of question is that?"

She stood in the middle of his foyer, as though her visit was only fleeting.

"An important one. Joe said you can't possibly be happy while keeping your heart detached from life. I happen to agree with him, but I wonder what you think."

He thought she was nuts. They were all nuts.

And those damned eyes. They were pulling at him again.

"I think…" Silently, he pleaded with her to let him go.

"What?"

"I…" How could one small woman, who'd never lived outside her safe little town, have the strength to overpower him?

And why?

He couldn't spend the rest of his life in Shelter Valley. Or in any one small town.

"Are you happy? That's all I want to know."

"I thought I was." What in the hell was he saying?

"And now?"

"And now I have to get out of this town. It's doing things to me." He left her standing there. Rude or not. He had to figure out what was wrong with him. She'd cast some kind of spell.

Being incarcerated was getting to him. In his room, he pulled out his biggest duffel and started throwing things inside. Randomly. With no plan of where he was going and what he'd need when he got there.

He had to be moved out in another week.

"What things?" She'd followed him.

"Huh?"

"What things is this town doing to you?"

"How the hell do I know?"

"I think you do know, Jay. I think you're scared and fighting it, but I think you know."

"What gives you that idea?" He was still cramming things into his bag.

"Because I recognize the signs. I'm scared, too."

With a wad of underwear in his right hand, he stilled. She was standing right behind him. "Of what?"

"Of all of the things that I can't control. The things that can hurt me no matter what I do to prevent them. The things I don't know and the ones I can't see. But mostly, I'm scared of loving and losing."

There was that word. He'd been avoiding it. Had forbidden himself to say it. Even silently. Hell, he wasn't even allowed to think it.

Love was for...

Ellen?

Her hands slid around him from behind. "I just had a talk with my mother."

Somehow he had a feeling Martha Marks hadn't been pleased with the outcome.

"I told her I have to leave Shelter Valley for a while."

Underwear in hand, he froze in place with her hands crossed at his stomach, holding him.

"I love it here, but I'm hiding, too. I have to know that I'm perfectly capable of leaving Shelter Valley if I want to. I have to know that I can cope...out there."

He couldn't argue there. But he was shocked to hear her say so.

"So I was wondering, do you want to come with me?"

"Where?"

"I was thinking Phoenix to begin with. That way Josh is still close to family, and, I guess, so am I."

"You're planning to move your son out of Shelter Valley."

"For a while at least, yes."

"Cole's in Phoenix."

"I know."

"So what are you suggesting? That we both move to Phoenix, deal with our issues and move on with our lives?"

"I'm suggesting—" her face was buried in his neck, her words directly in his ear "—that we spend the rest of our lives dealing with whatever issues arise, when they arise, but that we do it together. I'm much better at it when you're around."

He was a better man when she was around.

"I love you, Jay."

Oh, God. She'd done it now. There was no way he was getting out of this.

Turning, he thought of his mother. Of her brutal death. And the agony his father had suffered.

He thought of the seedy motel room on the outside of town where Ellen had survived.

And of his father, wasting his life up on a mountain all alone.

He thought of Cole, a boy who was struggling and who might need an example outside of Kelsey's home someday.

He thought of his motorcycle. And the beach.

And he thought of Martha Marks—a woman whose only sin was loving her daughter. Being there for her.

"Then I'm going to ask you to stay in Shelter Valley," he said, meeting Ellen's gaze.

Her eyes closed. Her mouth flattened. She bowed her head and started to pull away.

"And marry me."

Head snapping back up, Ellen gaped at him.

"Shelter Valley is a great place to raise a kid. And for another one to visit," he said. "The rest of the world is a great place to explore during the three gruelingly hot summer months."

Joe wasn't going to leave Arizona. He wouldn't get that far away from Tammy's memory.

And Jay had a feeling he wasn't going to be able to get that far away from his old man, either. They had some catching up to do. A lost boy to raise. A five-year-old he had yet to meet and get to know.

And maybe some new Billingsleys to deal with in the future, too.

"I have one question," Ellen said, her gaze serious.

"What's that?"

"Do you love me?"

"I think that's pretty obvious at this point."

"Maybe. But I need to hear the words, Jay. Do you love me?"

His throat tightened, making air scarce. But Ellen's eyes were right in front of him. Doing that damned thing to him again.

"Yes." He forced the word out. "Yes, dammit, I do, okay? I love you like crazy, Ellen Moore, and if you ever, ever—"

"Shh." With a finger against his lips, she silenced him. "As long as we love each other, the 'if evers' will take care of themselves, Jay. One way or the other. They have to. It's that, or let them lock us up for the rest of our lives."

He knew she was right. If bad stuff happened, they would either survive it or they wouldn't. Either way, it would happen. But the worst thing of all would be to let the fear of the bad stop them from living—and loving—at all.

"I love you," he said, loud and clear, gazing into Ellen's big brown eyes.

"And I love you." Her grin was so bright there wasn't a dark spot left in his heart.

"Your mother's going to love this," he said, grinning back.

"She will. She'll love you and you're going to love her, too. You just wait and see."

The twinkle in her eye invited him to follow her wherever she led. And Jay knew that from that moment on, that twinkle was the beacon that would guide the rest of his life.

Lucky for him that right then, it was leading him to bed.

A little sex therapy, and he'd be a healed man.

* * * * *

COMING NEXT MONTH

Available September 13, 2011

You can find more information on upcoming Harlequin® titles, free excerpts and more at
www.HarlequinInsideRomance.com.

Rafael de Luca had been in bad situations before. A crowded ballroom could never make him sweat.

These people would never know that he had no memory of any of them.

He surveyed the party with grim tolerance, searching for the source of his unease.

At first his gaze flickered past her, but he yanked his attention back to a woman across the room. Her stare bored holes through him. Unflinching and steady, even when his eyes locked with hers.

Petite, even in heels, she had a creamy olive complexion. A wealth of inky-black curls cascaded over her shoulders and her eyes were equally dark.

She looked at him as if she'd already judged him and found him lacking. He'd never seen her before in his life. Or had he?

He cursed the gaping hole in his memory. He'd been diagnosed with selective amnesia after his accident four months ago. Which seemed like complete and utter bull. No one got amnesia except hysterical women in bad soap operas.

With a smile, he disengaged himself from the group

around him and made his way to the mystery woman.

She wasn't coy. She stared straight at him as he approached, her chin thrust upward in defiance.

"Excuse me, but have we met?" he asked in his smoothest voice.

His gaze moved over the generous swell of her breasts pushed up by the empire waist of her black cocktail dress.

When he glanced back up at her face, he saw fury in her eyes.

"Have we *met?*" Her voice was barely a whisper, but he felt each word like the crack of a whip.

Before he could process her response, she nailed him with a right hook. He stumbled back, holding his nose.

One of his guards stepped between Rafe and the woman, accidentally sending her to one knee. Her hand flew to the folds of her dress.

It was then, as she cupped her belly, that the realization hit him. She was pregnant.

Her eyes flashing, she turned and ran down the marble hallway.

Rafael ran after her. He burst from the hotel lobby, and saw two shoes sparkling in the moonlight, twinkling at him.

He blew out his breath in frustration and then shoved the pair of sparkly, ultrafeminine heels at his head of security.

"Find the woman who wore these shoes."

Will Rafael find his mystery woman?
Find out in Maya Banks's passionate new novel
ENTICED BY HIS FORGOTTEN LOVER
Available September 2011 from Harlequin® Desire®!

Harlequin® Romance

Discover small-town warmth and community spirit
in a brand-new trilogy from

PATRICIA THAYER

The Quilt Shop in KERRY SPRINGS

*Where dreams
are stitched...patch
by patch!*

Coming August 9, 2011.

Little Cowgirl Needs a Mom

Warm-spirited quilt shop owner Jenny Collins promises to
help little Gracie finish the quilt her late mother started,
even if it means butting heads with Gracie's father,
grumpy but gorgeous rancher Evan Rafferty....

The Lonesome Rancher
(September 13, 2011)

Tall, Dark, Texas Ranger
(October 11, 2011)

Love Inspired™

Everything Montana Brown *thought* she knew about love and marriage goes awry when her parents split up. Shaken, she heads to Mule Hollow, Texas, to take a chance on an old dream—being a cowgirl…while trying to resist the charms of a too-handsome cowboy. A wife isn't on rancher Luke Holden's wish list. But the Mule Hollow matchmakers are fixin' to lasso Luke and Montana together—with a little faith and love.

Her Rodeo Cowboy
by Debra Clopton

Available September wherever books are sold.

www.LoveInspiredBooks.com

LI87691